The Cooper Kids
Adventure Series®

The Secret of the Desert Stone
The Deadly Curse of Toco-Rey

The Cooper Kids Adventure Series®

(Available from Crossway Books)

The Cooper Kids Adventure Series®

The Secret of the Desert Stone
The Deadly Curse of Toco-Rey

FRANK E. PERETTI

A Division of Thomas Nelson Publishers

NASHVILLE DALLAS MEXICO CITY RIO DE JANEIRO

The Cooper Kids Adventure Series® 2-in-1
© 1996, 2005, 2010 by Frank E. Peretti

Previously published in two separate volumes:
The Secret of the Desert Stone © 1996, 2005
The Deadly Curse of Toco-Rey © 1996, 2005

Published in Nashville, Tennessee, by Tommy Nelson. Tommy Nelson is a registered trademark of Thomas Nelson, Inc.

Scripture is quoted from *The Holy Bible, International Children's Bible*®, © 1986, 1988, 1999 by Thomas Nelson, Inc. All rights reserved.

ISBN: 978-1-4003-1646-5 (2-in-1)

The Library of Congress has cataloged the earlier printing as follows:

Peretti, Frank E.
    The secret of the desert Stone / Frank E. Peretti.
        p. cm. — (The Cooper Kids Adventure Series® ; 5)
    Summary: Fourteen-year-old Jay and his younger sister Lila accompany their father to the tiny African nation of Togwana where they experience a supernatural phenomenon through a
mysterious stone.
        ISBN 978-0-4003-0574-2
    [1. Supernatural—Fiction. 2. Christian life—Fiction. 3. Africa—Religion—Fiction.]
I. Title.   II. Series: Peretti, Frank E. The Cooper Kids Adventure Series® ; 5.
PZ7.P4254Se   1996
[Fic]—dc20   96–1919
                                                                                  CIP

Peretti, Frank E.
    The deadly curse of Toco-Rey / Frank E. Peretti.
        p. cm. — (The Cooper Kids Adventure Series® ; 6)
    Summary: While on a quest to save a piece of history, Jay, Lila, and their father encounter hostile natives and ancient evil forces in the jungles of Central America.
        ISBN 978-1-4003-0575-9
    [1. Supernatural—Fiction. 2. Jungles—Fiction. 3. Adventure and adventurers—Fiction.]
I. Title.   II. Series: Peretti, Frank E. The Cooper Kids Adventure Series® ; 6.
PZ7.P4254De   1996
[Fic]—dc20   96–15641
                                                                                  CIP

Printed in the United States of America
13 14 QVR 0 9 8 7 6 5 4 3 2

The Secret of the Desert Stone

ONE

T he sky was still black, the stars were still out, and dawn was nothing more than a thin, red ribbon along the horizon when the sirens went off, wailing rudely across the vast army camp. As one man, the army of black warriors awoke—there were no dawdlers, no one who dared to slumber beyond reveille. The desert rattled with the slap and clatter of a thousand hands grabbing a thousand rifles. The soldiers leaped to their feet and burst from their tents, dashing across the sand, lining up in long, even rows on the flat desert. They stood at attention, rifles ready, eyes straight ahead, primed for battle.

Field Marshal Idi Nkromo was already awake and strutting about at the front of the camp, watching his army come to life. He was a heavy-set, marble-eyed man with medals and ribbons adorning his chest—most were of his own design, and most he had awarded himself. He scowled; he glared; he growled orders to his lieutenants, his hand always on the gleaming saber that hung at his side.

He nodded approvingly to himself. Yes, this would

3

be the moment, the final engagement, the ultimate display of his power. After this day, his rule over the tiny African nation of Togwana would be complete and absolute. After this campaign across the desert, no one would dare to . . . he became distracted by a muttering, a buzzing among the troops. Nkromo was displeased. Why were they not all standing rigid and silent? Hadn't enough soldiers been beaten or shot to enforce discipline? The light of dawn was just now revealing their faces, and they were staring anxiously toward the desert, exchanging worried glances with each other and whispering through the ranks.

Nkromo drew his saber and bellowed, "Order!"

The soldiers stiffened at attention, but there was still a stirring, and their faces held wide-eyed fear.

"Mobutu!"

"Sir!" Mobutu, a younger, thinner man in a khaki uniform, came on the run.

Nkromo pointed his saber at his army. "Find out who's causing this disturbance and drag them out to be shot!"

Mobutu didn't respond.

Nkromo shot a deadly glare his way, but Mobutu wasn't looking at him. The thin lieutenant and chief secretary was looking toward the desert—the same direction the army was looking. He appeared stunned, his mouth hanging open, his eyes wide with horror.

"Mobutu!"

Mobutu pointed toward the desert. "Sir . . . if you would look . . ."

Nkromo never took advice. "Mobutu, maintain

4

order in the ranks." Then, as if it were his idea, he added, "I think I'd like to survey the desert."

Nkromo turned with a deliberate casualness and looked across the barren expanse rimmed on the north and south by towering, rocky crags, just becoming visible in the light of dawn.

The saber fell from his trembling hand and clattered on the stones and sand.

THUNK! Jay Cooper, fourteen, strong, wiry, and sweating in the sun, swung a sledgehammer and drove the last wooden stake into the ground. Then he wound the end of a heavy rope around it and tightened it down with a few more whacks from the hammer. He had driven several stakes to hold the ropes tied around the base of a huge stone pillar etched with ancient relief carvings, hieroglyphics, and, near the top, the faces of Greek gods. The pillar was massive, at least three feet thick and thirty feet tall. It stood in the center of a vast excavation, the unearthing of what used to be an ancient Greek temple on a high bluff over the Mediterranean.

Dangling like an acrobat by a rope and harness, Dr. Jacob Cooper struggled to tighten a loop of cable around the crown of the pillar, being careful not to mar the chiseled face of the Greek god Zeus. "Okay, Lila," he called, "more slack."

Lila Cooper, thirteen, was perched on the ancient temple wall, her eyes alert and her long blond hair tied back for safety. She was operating a sizable gas-powered winch and feeding more cable to her father.

5

This precarious perch was making her a bit nervous. The excavated floor of the old temple wasn't that far down, only twelve feet or so, but just outside the wall she sat on was a steep cliff dropping several hundred feet to the sea. She could see the barge from the museum floating close to the shore, ready for loading; it was almost eighty feet long, but from up here it was the size of a postage stamp. She tried not to look that direction and pushed the lever to release more cable.

Dr. Cooper edged his way around the face of Zeus like a skilled rock climber, his muscular arms groping for any handhold he could find. When he finally got the cable secure just above Zeus's head, he exhaled a sigh of relief. "Okay, tighten her up."

Lila pulled the lever and the big drum of the winch turned, winding in the cable until it was tight.

Dr. Cooper climbed to the very top of the pillar and sat there like a seagull atop a flagpole. He removed his wide-brimmed hat and brushed back his blond hair, now slick with sweat. Looking thirty feet straight down, he could see his son, Jay, had the bottom of the pillar staked and secured with ropes so it wouldn't kick out when they tipped it over; looking toward the sea he saw his daughter, Lila, on the temple wall, ready to start lowering the pillar with the main winch. On the other side of the temple, Dr. Cooper's two crewmen, Bill and Jeff, were just getting ready to ease a long, flatbed trailer down a dirt ramp to the base of the pillar.

"So far so good," Dr. Cooper said to himself.

The plan was to secure a few more cables to the

pillar, carefully lower it onto the trailer, and then haul it down an access road to the sea. A crew was already waiting there to load the pillar onto a barge and transport it to the Museum of Antiquities in Athens. Barring any disasters, Jacob Cooper and his crew might finish this project today.

Dr. Cooper waved at Bill and Jeff and called, "All right, bring the trailer down."

Bill, a big, mustached man with a southern drawl, climbed into the cab of the old diesel truck while Jeff, limber and usually nervous, stood on the dirt ramp below to give hand signals. The starter growled, then the engine rumbled to life, black smoke bursting from the old stacks above the cab.

Jeff waved and called, "Okay, ease her back . . ."

Bill ground the old beast into reverse and slowly let out the clutch. The truck and trailer started inching down the steep dirt ramp toward the base of the pillar.

Dr. Cooper watched their progress from his lofty perch. The dirt ramp seemed to be working okay although it might be a little steep for that old rig. "Hey . . ." he started to say, "slow up, you're—"

"You're going too fast!" Jeff hollered.

Bill stomped on the brake pedal. Something snapped and the pedal went clear to the floor. The trailer started rolling down the ramp, picking up speed, pulling the truck backward.

"Slow up!" Jeff yelled. He jumped out of the way, rolling in the dirt, as the trailer rumbled and bounced right past him.

Bill tried to pull on the parking brake. It broke

7

off. He killed the ignition. The ramp was too steep, the trailer too heavy. The truck only slid backward down the incline, its rear tires slipping, growling over the dirt.

The flatbed was heading right for the base of the pillar.

Jay ran to get clear and hollered, "Dad!"

Dr. Cooper could see it coming: a big disaster. Maybe they *wouldn't* finish this project today.

CRUNCH! The trailer crashed into the pillar. Dr. Cooper could feel the pillar quiver under him.

Then he could feel it moving. The cable from Lila's winch went slack.

The pillar was falling right toward Lila!

"Look out!" her father yelled, holding on for dear life.

Lila screamed and dashed along the wall to get clear. Jay scrambled to safety as the base of the pillar began to tear loose. *PING! POP!* The heavy ropes plucked the stakes from the ground like rotten teeth.

The pillar picked up speed, falling like a big tree. Wind whistled by Dr. Cooper's head, and his hat went sailing. Then he saw the temple wall pass under him. The top of the pillar was carrying him out over the cliff, over the sheer drop to the sea far below!

THUD! The middle of the pillar hit the temple wall and Dr. Cooper was knocked free by the impact, tumbling headlong toward the ocean.

OOF! The harness he was still wearing came to the end of its rope, and he snapped to an abrupt halt in midair, dangling from the pillar like a puppet on a string.

The base of the pillar began to rise. Bill, Jeff, and Jay grabbed the ropes dangling from it, hoping to hold it down and keep the pillar from flipping over the wall entirely. All three were lifted off their feet, but they hung on anyway, hoping, praying.

Up went their end of the pillar, higher, higher, as Dr. Cooper's end lowered him toward the sea.

Then, with not a man, not a pound, not a single ounce to spare, the pillar came to rest on the temple wall with each end suspended in air, perfectly but precariously balanced: Dr. Cooper dangling from one end, Bill, Jeff, and Jay dangling from the other.

"Oh man," Bill drawled, "now what?"

"Hang on," Lila screamed. "Just hang on!"

There was a low, grating noise. The pillar was beginning to roll along the wall like a big rolling pin, reeling in the ropes from which Jay, Bill, and Jeff were hanging, along with the harness that still held Dr. Cooper.

Dr. Cooper looked below and saw nothing but ocean waves and a tiny, distant barge; he looked above and saw the face of Zeus coming around, then coming around again, much closer, as the pillar kept rotating and reeling him in.

As Lila stepped hurriedly along the wall, approaching the pillar even as it rumbled and rolled slowly toward her, she looked for a stone, a stick, anything large enough to jam under the pillar to wedge it to a stop.

Dr. Cooper ran out of rope. "AWWW!" He was

9

hauled over the top of the pillar as it turned, held fast by the harness around his body and feeling like a roast pig on a spit. If only he had a knife!

Then Bill's rope ran out and the rough surface of the pillar broke his grip. With a cry of pain, he fell to the temple floor.

Out of balance! The base of the pillar began to rise, the top began to sink.

Lila hopped onto the pillar, step-step-stepping as it rotated under her feet, inching her way out from the wall and toward the base where Jay and Jeff were getting tangled in the ropes. No good. She wasn't even half Bill's weight. The pillar was still rolling and tilting toward the sea.

CHUNK! Somebody jammed a stone under the pillar, and it stopped rolling. A man leaped from the wall to the lower end of the pillar, and it sank under his weight.

Back in balance!

"Lila!" Dr. Cooper hollered. "Bring your knife!"

The stranger, a man with blond hair, nodded to her. "Go ahead. I think we can keep it in balance now."

She stepped carefully along the pillar, balancing herself, until she reached the wall. She could see her father, one hand clinging to Zeus's eye and his foot planted in Zeus's mouth, struggling to free himself from the harness. She looked back. The stranger was helping Jay and Jeff untangle themselves.

She stepped out on the pillar, nothing but a sheer drop to the ocean below her, and inched her way out toward her father, the knife in her trembling hand.

The stranger had his own knife and cut away the ropes that had tangled around Jay and Jeff. With his help, they climbed on top of the pillar and sat on it.

"Just like a teeter-totter," said Jay.

But Lila was still edging toward the other end, toward her father.

"Uh . . ." Jay asked the stranger, "how much do you weigh?"

"About one-sixty," the man replied.

Jay looked down at Bill, who was still dusting himself off after his fall. "Bill? How much do you weigh?"

"Two thirty," Bill replied.

The stranger asked Jay, "How much does your sister weigh?"

"Enough," was all Jay answered as their end of the pillar began to rise.

Dr. Cooper took the knife from Lila's hand as he felt the pillar pitch down toward the ocean again. "Lila! Get back! Get off the pillar!"

She spun around and tried to run back. The pillar pitched some more and she slipped. Her fingers dug into hieroglyphics and her foot came to rest on Zeus's beard as the pillar sagged and rocked and the stones in the wall started crumbling.

Jay, Jeff, and the stranger moved as far back as they could, but the pillar was beginning to slide through the wall and there was no stopping it.

"It's gonna go!" Jeff hollered.

Dr. Cooper sliced through the harness rope and got free. "Go, Lila, *go!*"

She crawled, scrambled, and made it to the wall. Now the pillar was sliding past her, bucking and scraping over the stones.

Dr. Cooper grabbed at Zeus's beard, then some hieroglyphics, then some relief carvings, climbing up the downsliding pillar and getting nowhere until he ran out of pillar to climb on. A hand reached out to grab his just as the pillar slid free of the wall and plummeted toward the seashore below. In an instant, Jay, Jeff, and the stranger yanked him to safety atop the wall.

The pillar dropped silently, as if in slow motion, growing smaller and smaller, until it dove into the sandy beach like a spear, making the ground quiver—and making Dr. Cooper wince.

It teetered there a moment then tipped like a big tree toward the ocean . . . directly toward the waiting barge as the barge crew dove for the water.

KAWHUMP! The barge bucked, rolled, and almost capsized from the impact. A mighty wave washed up on the shore.

Lila shut her eyes. They all held their breath. They could hear the last mist from the huge splash hiss down upon the surface of the water.

And then . . . it was quiet.

"Well whaddaya know . . ." Bill muttered.

Lila ventured a peek and saw the barge rocking a little but still afloat. The pillar, with Zeus glaring up at them, was lying in the barge a little crooked and with one end hanging out, but none the worse for wear. The barge crew paddled around in the water, wide-eyed and upset, but safe.

Dr. Cooper started breathing again. His kids, his crewmen, and the stranger could only sit there on the wall, shaken, dusty, thankful to be alive, and totally amazed.

At last Dr. Cooper found his voice and said, "Well . . . we got it on the barge."

Silence. Somber faces.

And then Bill cracked a smile. Jeff snorted a laugh through his nose. Jay burst right out laughing. Dr. Cooper allowed himself a smile, then a grin, then a laugh, shaking his head in amazement. When Lila saw her father laughing, she figured everything was okay and began to laugh too. They all started hugging and shaking hands, happy to be alive, happy with success.

"I don't believe it!" said Lila.

"God works in wondrous ways," said Dr. Cooper.

"Boy, doesn't He!" replied the stranger, shaking Jacob Cooper's hand.

Then, looking at the man directly for the first time, Dr. Cooper recognized him. "Brent! Brent Anderson!"

Brent Anderson smiled broadly. "Hi, Jake. Working?"

"Can't you tell?"

They both laughed and then embraced like old buddies.

"What in the world are you doing here?" Dr. Cooper asked.

"I came to find you."

"Jay! Lila! Meet an old friend of mine, Brent Anderson! He's a missionary to Africa."

"Was," said Brent, shaking hands with Jay and Lila. "And, hopefully, will be again."

Dr. Cooper could hear trouble in Brent's voice. "What's happened?"

Brent's face became grim. "Idi Nkromo and his revolution. He and his military have taken over most of the country of Togwana."

Dr. Cooper nodded with recollection. "He's been in the news lately. A rather dangerous character, I understand."

"Oh, he likes killing anyone who stands in his way, or questions his actions, or doubts his power—and mostly, he hates Christians. He's ordered the churches closed; he's killed and imprisoned believers. Sandy and I barely got out of the country alive."

Bill and Jeff could sense a serious conversation coming. "Uh, Jake, we'll start stowing the gear," said Bill.

"Thanks, guys," Dr. Cooper replied.

The two men made their way back along the wall. Jay and Lila got up and were about to leave them alone, too, but their father said quietly, "Stick around." They sat back down on the wall beside their father.

Dr. Cooper's voice was quiet and compassionate. "You got out all right? You and Sandy and the kids?"

"Yes, we're fine. They're back in the States now. I'm on staff with the mission board until . . ." Brent smiled wistfully.

Jacob Cooper knew his friend. "You're thinking of going back to Togwana?"

Brent nodded. "I'm not finished there, Jake. There's one last tribe of people who live across the desert who have never heard the gospel. Rumor has it they're a deadly bunch, headhunters and cannibals who would just as soon eat strangers as welcome them. But God wants me to take the gospel to those people, and I believe I will, Idi Nkromo or no Idi Nkromo. It'll happen, Jake."

Dr. Cooper admired faith like that. "I'm sure it will."

Now Brent looked his friend in the eye. "Good, because you just might be a part of it."

Jacob Cooper raised one eyebrow and then exchanged a glance with his kids. "Is this going to be dangerous?"

Brent nodded. "It might be."

"Count us in," said Jay, which brought him a corrective look from Lila.

Dr. Cooper wanted to hear more. "How can we help?"

Brent Anderson looked over his shoulder, and they all followed his glance across the excavation. There, looking almost ghostly in long, wraparound garments and intricate, bone jewelry, stood two Africans, apparently men of high office in their country. They were both tall and powerful, with eyes that could bore holes right through you.

"Strange things are happening in Togwana, Jake, things that no one can explain, and that's why I'm here. These men were sent by the Chief Secretary of the Republic of Togwana." Brent gave Dr. Cooper a probing look. "They came to find a spiritual man, a man close to God with wisdom to solve great mysteries. They first came to me in America, but I've brought them to you."

As Jacob Cooper looked into the burning eyes of the two towering visitors, he had a feeling he and his kids would soon be going to Africa.

TWO

When their plane finally landed in Togwana, the Coopers saw military jeeps and trucks parked near the tiny airport terminal. Soldiers were standing about in khaki uniforms and black berets, and even two weather-beaten Russian MIGs were parked under some palm trees. Obviously, a military government was in charge now—in charge of *everything*.

As she looked out the airplane window, Lila couldn't help wondering aloud, "What are we walking into?"

"A brave new world under Togwana's new dictator," answered an attractive African-American woman in her late thirties sitting in the seat directly behind them. She immediately extended her hand. "Dr. Jennifer Henderson, Stanford University."

Dr. Cooper gripped her hand. "Uh . . . Jacob Cooper, and this is my son, Jay, and my daughter, Lila."

"I suppose you were invited by Bernard and Walter back there?"

The Coopers shot a discreet glance toward the

17

rear of the plane where the two somber gentlemen from Togwana were sitting. They'd given their names as Bernard and Walter.

"They wanted somebody who knows rocks," Dr. Henderson explained, "and that's why they invited me. I'm a geologist. How about you?"

"I'm an archaeologist," Dr. Cooper answered. He could have mentioned that he was founder of the Cooper Institute for Biblical Archaeology and specialized in ancient civilizations of the Bible, but he said no more than necessary. The Coopers couldn't be sure who this woman really was; they didn't know if she could be trusted.

"So they want at least two professional opinions regarding their little mystery," said Dr. Henderson.

"I'll be interested to know just what the mystery is," said Dr. Cooper. "The letter from the Chief Secretary was rather vague."

"The Chief Secretary is supposed to be meeting us with a car—and some more information, I hope."

Bernard and Walter helped carry their luggage and led them to a gate that passed through the airport security fence. It was there that they met a quick-stepping, uniformed man with braids on his shoulder and medals on his chest. He smiled broadly and beckoned to them with fluttery little waves from both hands. "Hello! Doctors Henderson and Cooper, yes?" He offered his hand in greeting. "D. M. Mobutu, Chief Secretary of the Republic of Togwana!"

Dr. Cooper shook his hand. "Dr. Jacob Cooper, at your service. These are my children, Jay and Lila."

He shook their hands vigorously, almost comically.

Then he came to Dr. Henderson and had a special greeting for her. "Ahhh, Dr. Henderson, I have looked forward to this moment." With a graceful flourish, he took her hand and kissed it.

She stuck to business. "And I've looked forward to the challenge of the work we're here to do. How soon can we get started?"

Mobutu surveyed the sky. "The weather is improving. You may get your first glimpse of our little problem on the way to the presidential palace."

Dr. Cooper was puzzled. "I'd like that. We're all eager to hear the details of your situation—"

"Come! We have a car waiting!" He called to the two escorts, "Philip! Thomas! Bring their bags!"

"Don't you mean Bernard and Walter?" Dr. Cooper hinted.

"Oh, yes," Mobutu quickly agreed, "Bernard and Walter. Yes!"

Instead of going through the small terminal, they hurried down a narrow walk under a thick canopy of trees and out to a side street. Waiting there was a long, white limousine with tinted windows. Bernard and Walter loaded the luggage into the trunk while Mobutu opened the big passenger door.

"Air conditioned," he said proudly.

The American guests were ready for that and got inside. Bernard and Walter, their mission completed, hurried up a trail into the jungle and were gone.

When the driver hit the accelerator and the limousine lurched away from the curb, it felt like a getaway.

Mobutu sat with them, trying to maintain his cordial smile but looking nervous. He peered out the windows as the limousine raced along the narrow road, first through green jungle then past crude farms and small, mud homesteads.

Dr. Cooper tried to get a conversation going. "So . . . you work for President Nkromo, is that correct?"

Mobutu smiled broadly. "Oh, yes. As chief secretary, I am quite close to the president. I am his special assistant." Then he added with emphasis, "And our new government is working very well. The president is powerful. He has brought order to our country!"

Dr. Cooper simply nodded and smiled. He could sense that Mobutu was having trouble believing his own glowing boasts.

The limousine entered the ragged, unimproved outskirts of Nkromotown, still mostly small homes, barns, and chicken coops made from mud brick, and occasionally, concrete. People and pigs, children and chickens, cattle and oxen wandered freely in the fields, thickets, and side streets.

"You should know," Mobutu suddenly blurted, "that bringing you to Togwana was not the president's idea."

Instantly, all their eyes were upon him.

Mobutu continued, visibly nervous. "I must tell you, the president has little use for outsiders, and even less use for advice, even from those close to him. He does not wish to appear weak or in need of help from anyone."

Dr. Cooper exchanged a glance with the others and then asked, "Is this the reason for the secrecy? Avoiding the airport terminal, racing away in this car, and calling your two men Bernard and Walter?"

Mobutu nodded. "Bernard and Walter do not wish their real names attached to this enterprise in case it should . . ." he had to wrestle the words out of his throat, "in case it should fail."

Dr. Cooper's voice was firm. "Mr. Mobutu, is the president even aware that we're here?"

"Oh, yes," Mobutu replied with an emphatic nod. "Yes, he knows you're here, and he does not disapprove. It's just that . . . " Mobutu's eyes dropped, "he consented grudgingly and warned me that no one should know about it." Then he leaned forward and spoke in a lowered voice, "But you should know, I offered to bring in a geologist and an archaeologist. I did not tell him I would bring in someone with . . . uh . . . *spiritual* credentials as well."

Dr. Cooper began to ask, "Are you referring to the fact that I and my children are—"

"Shh!" Mobutu held up his hand. "Do not speak it. Do not even think it while you are in this country. President Nkromo has already banished thousands who are of your . . . religious persuasion. Those who did not leave were arrested, put into forced labor, and some . . . were executed."

Jacob Cooper's voice had a sharp edge as he

asked, "And yet you brought us here anyway, knowing it could endanger our lives?"

Mobutu bowed a little, acting humble. "Dr. Cooper, this problem we have will take more than a mere scientist to solve."

Jennifer Henderson raised an eyebrow at that remark, but Mobutu continued, "It could require someone with eyes to see *beyond* what is visible."

Dr. Cooper's eyes narrowed as he replied, "Mr. Mobutu, you have much to explain."

But instead of explaining, Mobutu leaned close to the window, looked at the weather, and then rapped on the glass panel that separated them from the driver. The driver looked back, Mobutu shouted some instructions, and almost immediately the driver took a hard left turn off the main road, up a steep, winding road into the hills.

"We're not going into the city?" Dr. Cooper asked.

"No," Mobutu replied, "not yet."

"Where are you taking us?"

"You need to see the Stone first," Mobutu answered, "and then we will talk further."

"The . . . Stone?"

Mobutu added quietly, "We call it a *baloa-kota,* which means an omen, an evil sign. It is why we brought you here. Many, including the president, believe the Stone is magic."

Dr. Henderson was dismayed. "You brought us all the way to Africa just to look at a *rock?*"

Mobutu only smiled at her. "This is your profession, yes?"

A few minutes later, the limousine reached the top of a hill, swerved off the road into some gravel, and lurched to a halt. Then the driver, in his neatly pressed uniform and his cap squarely in place on his head, got out, walked back, and swung the door open with a flourish.

Mobutu stepped out and waited courteously by the door. "Please," he beckoned.

Dr. Cooper, still unsure of the group's safety, ventured a look outside, then stepped out. "It's all right."

The others followed.

They had parked on a lofty bluff overlooking the city and the rolling, jungled hills stretching to the east. The clouds were dissolving away in the afternoon sun and the view was wide, sweeping, and beautiful. Nkromotown was a small city of white stone, gray concrete, and red tile. Dr. Cooper could see a cluster of large stone buildings in the center of the city, most likely the presidential palace and parliament hall now occupied by Nkromo and his military leaders.

"A beautiful city, Mr. Mobutu," he said, turning to look at the Chief Secretary, then turning some more, trying to find him. "A beautiful country, and—"

The sentence died on his lips as he looked toward the west across the vast, rugged drylands. Mobutu was standing on the edge of the bluff with Jennifer Henderson, Jay, and Lila, looking toward the west and then back at him, obviously wanting to see his reaction.

Dr. Cooper didn't know how to react. He didn't

even know what to believe. He blinked, then rubbed his eyes. *I can't be seeing what I think I'm seeing*, he thought.

"Dad . . ." said Jay, his voice a hushed whisper. Apparently he was seeing it too.

"What . . . is that?" Lila asked. "How does it—"

"Is this a mirage?" asked Dr. Henderson.

Mobutu shook his head. "No mirage, Dr. Henderson. What you are seeing is really there."

The clouds continued to thin out, unveiling . . . a wall? A sheer cliff? A towering plateau?

Whatever it was, it totally filled the gap between two mountain cliffs to the north and south, and stretched from the desert floor to a height above the clouds.

"How far away is it?" asked Dr. Cooper, certain his eyes were being deceived.

Mobutu estimated, "From this point, about eighteen kilometers."

"Ten miles!" Dr. Henderson exclaimed.

"Then it's as big as it looks," concluded Dr. Cooper.

"It's a *mountain!*" Lila said, her voice hushed with awe.

The sun was moving toward the west now, so the surface details were in shade and hard to discern. But the shape was stark against the sky, obscured in only a few places by high, fluffy clouds: a rectangle of stone, a huge block, square at the corners, sheer and vertical at either end, and, as far as they could tell, perfectly flat on top. And Lila was right: it was nothing less than a mountain.

"How . . ." Dr. Cooper had trouble finding his breath. "How tall is it?"

"Nearly four kilometers, as close as we can tell."

"That's over ten thousand feet!" Jay exclaimed.

"And we figure it's at least eight kilometers long and two kilometers wide," Mobutu added.

"How long has it been here?" Dr. Cooper asked.

"Just a few weeks, doctor," Mobutu answered. "From here we used to be able to see past those mountain cliffs and cross the flat desert. Now the entire western half of Togwana is hidden from view."

Dr. Henderson actually sank to the ground, overcome by the sight. "Stone? It's of stone?"

"We think it is."

"But how did it get there? What caused it?"

Mobutu frowned. "Dr. Henderson, we hired *you* to answer such questions."

She only shook her head. "But this is . . . this is impossible. Nothing of this size and shape has ever occurred before in nature!"

"And so we call it a *baloa-kota*," Mobutu said somberly. "A dreaded curse, a plague sent upon us! And now you see it with your own eyes: the Stone of Togwana!"

In the presidential palace, a young butler in a green tuxedo swung open the huge, mahogany doors and announced, "Your Excellency, the Chief Secretary with his honored guests!"

They entered the presidential chamber, a room that resembled a cathedral with a high, arched ceiling, stained-glass windows, and pillared, marble walls. At the far end of the room, at the end of a long avenue of red carpet, His Excellency, President and Field Marshal Idi Nkromo, sat behind a desk the size of a battleship. The medals on his chest glittering like a Christmas tree, Nkromo glowered at them, his eyes big and bulging with anger. On the exquisitely paneled wall behind him, a ten-foot high portrait of himself glared with the same angry expression, only twice as big.

"I am Oz, the great and powerful!" Jay whispered, and Lila gave him a corrective poke.

They marched forward, Mobutu at the head, then stood shoulder-to-shoulder in a straight line before His Excellency.

"Your Excellency," Mobutu announced, his spine straight as a rod, "I present to you the scientists from America: Dr. Jennifer Henderson, geologist; and Dr. Jacob Cooper, archaeologist!"

Nkromo gestured toward Jay and Lila, his eyes sending the question to Mobutu. "And . . . ?"

Mobutu blurted, "And Dr. Cooper's two children, Jay and Lila."

Nkromo looked at Dr. Henderson, then Dr. Cooper, then Jay and Lila, his face betraying not the slightest hint of favor at their presence. Then, at long last, he spoke, his voice deep, loud, and intimidating. "I welcome you to the Republic of Togwana! We will do well for each other, yes? You will remove the Stone, and I will pay you well."

"Yes," Dr. Henderson ventured, "we do need to discuss our fee before we—"

"How long will it take?" Nkromo interrupted.

They had no answer; they weren't sure they had even grasped the question.

Dr. Cooper gave a slight bow and said, "Your Excellency, we have only just arrived and know very little about the Stone. If it pleases you, we need to venture into the desert and study it closely to learn what it is and where it came from."

"And how to make it go away, yes?"

Dr. Henderson picked it up from there. "We'll need vehicles and equipment, food and water—"

Nkromo waved her off and declared, "Mr. Mobutu will see to that. Whatever you need, he will supply it."

"Thank you, sir," said Dr. Cooper.

Nkromo rose from his chair; Mobutu took one step backward and the four guests did the same. Then the president patted his big belly and admired the towering portrait of himself. "If I want something done, it will be done, you see? I had ten witch doctors, but they could not make the Stone go away. They could not move it. They could not even make it smaller." He shook his head with regret. "So I ordered their heads smashed in with stones."

Lila gasped. She didn't mean to, it just happened.

His Excellency was pleased at that response. "So, you will not fail, I know. You are scientists from America! You know about rocks! You will please me, I know."

Dr. Cooper tried to keep his voice even as he asked, "Are we to understand, sir, that you expect us to *remove* the Stone?"

"Yes! Take it away!" Nkromo bellowed with an angry wave of his arm. "Remove it far from here, I don't care where! It must not remain in the path of His Excellency!" Then he raised his hands toward them as if to grant a blessing, but the tone of his voice sounded more like a threat. "May you have success!"

THREE

As they hurried across the palace grounds, intent on getting out of there, Dr. Henderson was the first to speak. "Well, I've heard enough. I'm getting on the first plane out of here!"

"If you try to leave Togwana without permission, you will be shot," Mobutu said flatly.

Dr. Henderson's mouth dropped open. "You can't be serious!"

"You're forgetting, this is an African dictatorship," said Dr. Cooper. "Nkromo can do whatever he wants."

"Nkromo is out of his mind!" said Dr. Henderson.

Mobutu cautioned her with frantic little waves of his hand. "No! Never speak ill of the president!" He lowered his voice to share some inside advice. "Even if he is crazy, that doesn't matter! What matters is that he gets what he wants or people die—even you."

"But this is an incredible freak of nature, so huge it's mind-boggling! If Nkromo couldn't move it with all his army, what are *we* supposed to do?"

"But we don't even know what it is yet!" Jay countered.

"And I'm dying to find out," said Lila.

"Well, I don't care to die at all!" Jennifer Henderson snapped.

"Dr. Henderson," said Dr. Cooper softly, touching her shoulder to comfort her, "we could be staring an incredible discovery right in the face, and we'd be untrue to our professions if we ran from it. As for Nkromo, it's obvious he's afraid of it. It's something he doesn't understand and can't control. If we can give him some answers, his attitude might change."

Dr. Henderson finally calmed down a bit and nodded. "Well . . . what other choice do we have anyway?"

Dr. Cooper looked at Lila as he addressed Mobutu. "We have a list for you." Lila pulled several sheets of paper from her pocket and handed them to Mobutu as her father continued, "We'll need vehicles, surveying equipment . . ."

"Seismic equipment," Dr. Henderson added, "and a core drill."

"Oh, and I'll need an airplane, single engine, high wing, with short take-off and landing capability." Dr. Cooper waved at the list. "It's all on there."

Mobutu scanned the long list with widening eyes.

"Oh," said Lila, pulling out another sheet of paper. "And here's a grocery list."

"Come on," said Dr. Cooper. "Let's have a look at that thing."

After a meal and a change into cooler clothes, the Coopers and Dr. Henderson were ready for their first trek into the rugged drylands of western Togwana. They were riding in a Land Rover provided by Mr. Mobutu—it was the first item on the list. Mr. Mobutu came along, not because he wanted to but because Nkromo required it.

The road into the desert was unimproved but apparently well-traveled, at least by Nkromo's armies. It meandered for mile after mile across a dead, forbidding landscape of wind-carved stone pinnacles and deep, eroded gullies, of sun-baked, jagged rocks and blowing sand. With each mile they drove, the Stone grew larger and its top edge higher and more directly overhead, until finally they entered the Stone's afternoon shadow—miles and miles of shadow, as if the sun had disappeared behind a perfectly straight-edged bank of clouds. Jay and Lila had to stick their heads out the windows to see the Stone's top edge thousands of feet above them, black against the flare of the hidden sun.

Dr. Cooper brought the rover to a halt, and they stepped out onto the barren landscape to have a look.

Jay scanned the Stone's top edge with some binoculars, the magnified image quivering from the excitement coursing through him. "I think I see some ice up there. Guess that puts the summit above the freezing level."

"Any features of any kind?" Dr. Cooper asked.

"Nope. That top edge is so straight it looks the same with or without binoculars."

Jacob Cooper shook his head in awe. "Any thoughts, Dr. Henderson?"

Jennifer Henderson seemed transfixed as she stared at the stone.

"Dr. Henderson?" Dr. Cooper asked again, a little concerned.

She looked at him startled, as if awakened from a spell. "What? Oh. No, Dr. Cooper. It reminds me of basaltic columns such as Devil's Tower in Wyoming, . . . but this is nothing like that. I don't see how this can be a natural occurrence." She allowed some of her fear to show as she added, "And I'm not sure we should approach any closer."

Dr. Cooper respected her concerns. "Lila, get out the Geiger counter. We'd better check for radiation." There was no response. "Lila?"

Lila was standing by herself a short distance away, motionless, gazing upon the Stone as if seeing a vision.

Her dad approached her quietly. "Lila? What is it?"

She heard his question and looked his way, but could not think of an answer—at least, nothing that would sound scientific. Scientific observation was done with the eyes, with the ears, with tools and instruments; she was *feeling* something with her heart, something she had no words to describe. Great symphonies made her feel this way. Beautiful sunsets. A Bible verse spoken or read at just the right time.

"I don't know, Dad," she said at last, her voice hushed. "It's just . . . it's just wonderful, that's all."

Dr. Henderson disagreed. "I think it could be dangerous!"

"I'm not afraid," she countered. "I want to get closer. I want to touch it."

"Same here," said Jay, bringing the Geiger counter. He turned it on and twisted the dials. "No radiation. I guess it's safe."

"If it is a *boloa-kota,*" Mobutu said, "it can never be safe!"

"Well . . ." Dr. Cooper stared up at the Stone, scratching his head. "While we're this far away, why don't we take some readings with the transit and get some dimensions?"

They worked as a team, pacing, measuring, peering through an engineer's transit and calculating. By late afternoon, they had some numbers.

"The side facing us runs roughly north and south," Jay said, reviewing his notes. "We don't know about the other sides yet because we can't see them from here, but anyway . . ." He scribbled, then erased, then scribbled again. "If I didn't make any mistakes, the side facing us is right around 20,380 feet long and 9,348 high. That's, uh . . ." he tapped out the figures on his pocket calculator, ". . . 3.86 miles long and 1.77 miles high."

He handed his notes across the hood of the land rover to his father. Dr. Cooper whistled his amazement as Dr. Henderson came alongside to study Jay's scribblings. She could only shake her head as she read them.

"Well done, Jay," said Dr. Cooper. "Now we're ready for the next step."

"Which is?" Dr. Henderson asked.

"We've found out all we can from a distance. Now we're going to have to walk right up and touch it."

"We could be waking a sleeping lion," Mobutu cautioned.

"I don't disagree. But I would find it more un-bearable to remain here, not knowing, not learning. We still have about three hours of daylight."

Dr. Henderson shifted her gaze toward the Stone, its surface flat, smooth, and unblemished, its color a dull, volcanic red. She didn't bother to disguise her dread even as she agreed. "So let's go touch it—but keep the motor running."

The Stone looked like a monstrous wall directly in front of them and continued to loom larger and larger as they approached. After they had driven five kilometers, the south end was fully to their left, the north end was fully to their right, and the top edge was almost straight above them. It made them dizzy to look up at it.

"Perfectly vertical!" Dr. Henderson exclaimed. "Perfectly flat!"

"Hey," said Jay, "I think I see the base!"

They had just come over a small rise. Dr. Cooper eased the rover to a halt. A half mile ahead, they could see the desert road coming to an abrupt end where the Stone now lay across it. But it wasn't just the road that ended here. The whole desert—sand, stones, brush, rock formations, *everything*—ended here as well. Abruptly, cleanly as if cut with a knife, the desert was now divided by a laser-straight wall of reddish stone that seemed limitless as it stretched north and south and soared into the sky.

Dr. Cooper looked north through the binoculars, then south. "The Stone is butting up against sheer cliffs at either end. I don't know if we'll be able to drive around it. It may even be impossible to hike around."

"The Stone is in the path of His Excellency!" Jay quipped, recalling Nkromo's angry words. "Makes me wonder what's on the other side."

"Nooo," Mobutu cautioned with a wag of his head. "You don't want to go over there. It's the land of the Motosas, a desert tribe of cannibals and head-hunters. They are ruthless and bloodthirsty, a real problem we've been trying to eliminate."

Dr. Cooper considered that a moment. "Well, it seems you now have a wall to keep them contained."

Mobutu only scowled and said nothing further.

"Shall we proceed?" Dr. Cooper asked.

"Hard hats, everyone," Dr. Henderson cautioned. "If any debris or ice breaks loose, it'll fall straight down on top of us."

They grabbed their yellow hard hats and put them on. Then Dr. Cooper put the rover in gear and let it tiptoe steadily forward, the idle of the engine and the quiet crunching of its tires over the sand and rock the only sounds. Finally, about fifty feet from the face of the Stone, he braked to a stop and turned off the engine.

Now there was a silence so absolute they could hear the blood rushing through their ears, the *tick*, *tick* of the cooling engine, and the little creaks and groans of the rover anytime somebody moved.

They looked at Dr. Henderson. This was her moment.

She stepped out of the rover and walked carefully,

almost tiptoeing, toward the vast, reddish wall in front of her. The others followed: Jacob Cooper just a few steps behind, Jay and Lila a few steps behind him, and Mobutu a considerable distance back. Dr. Henderson paused several times to look straight up, but kept putting one foot in front of the other until cautiously, furtively, with outstretched hand, she touched the face of the Stone.

Nothing happened. The "sleeping lion" kept sleeping, at least for the moment.

As the others watched, eager to hear her verdict, Dr. Henderson brushed her fingers lightly over the surface, then studied it carefully, scanning back and forth, up and down. They could see she was getting agitated. Reaching into her tool belt, she took out a magnifying glass and studied the Stone's surface very closely, her nose only an inch away.

When she finally turned to look back at them, her face was filled with wonder and fear. "It appears to be *man-made!*"

Man-made? They stood there gawking at the Stone, waiting for belief to set in.

"Oooohh . . ." With a timid, trembling cry, shaking his head in fear and denial, Mobutu backed away.

"All *right!*" Jay blurted, clenching his fist happily. A rock this size was intriguing, of course, but a *man-made* rock this size meant a real mystery!

Dr. Cooper hurried forward and touched the Stone himself.

"You see it?" Dr. Henderson asked him excitedly. "See the tool marks? Someone cut this thing out.

They *carved* it. This isn't a natural occurrence at all!"

Jacob Cooper could see what Dr. Henderson was talking about. Though the marks were very fine and indiscernible from a distance, the surface did betray some kind of highly skilled handwork. He stepped back several paces and looked straight up the immense wall. "That could explain the symmetry, the unnatural, square shape, the straight lines and ninety-degree corners." He returned to touch the Stone's surface again and study it closely. "Ancient stonework . . ." he muttered. "Stonecutting that would have made Solomon proud." He looked straight up the wall, his chin almost resting against it. "This thing was *designed*. But it would have taken years, even centuries to complete! Mr. Mobutu!"

Mobutu answered from a safe distance. "Yes, Dr. Cooper?"

"Tell me again how the stone appeared. You say it's been here a few weeks and no one knows how it came to be here?"

"That's right, doctor. When we all went to bed, the desert was the same as it has been for centuries. When we got up the next morning, this object was here, just as you see it today."

Jacob Cooper slowly wagged his head, at a total loss. "Who could cut out such a huge stone and place it in this desert overnight?"

"And what did they cut it out of?" Dr. Henderson asked. "Imagine the size of the quarry, or the hole that must be left after the stone was removed . . ."

"Maybe it's a meteor," Jay suggested, touching it. "It just fell here from outer space."

"The most gentle meteor in history to touch down so lightly," his dad replied. "No crater, no fire, no signs of an impact."

Lila came close and rested her palms against the smooth surface. *Yes*, she thought. *There's that feeling again. It's like a grand symphony, like a loving embrace, or a warm fire on a cold night.*

Jay was still theorizing. "Maybe some ancient civilization figured out a way to make this thing materialize here from another dimension."

Dr. Cooper built on that idea. "So maybe it's an illusion, a kind of holographic phenomenon . . ."

Lila pressed her ear against the red surface as if listening for sounds. Like finding a familiar face in a crowd, like finding your way again after being lost—that's how the Stone made her feel.

Dr. Henderson became sarcastic. "Or maybe it was planted here by extraterrestrials. Come *on.*"

Dr. Cooper had to laugh, if only to relieve his frustration. "I think we'd better gather some more data before we go any further with theories!"

"Maybe *God* put it here!" said Lila, her face still against the Stone.

Jennifer Henderson only sniffed at that, but Dr. Cooper and Jay paused and looked at her.

"What makes you say that, Lila?" her dad asked.

She hesitated to answer, then finally said, "It just *feels* like God put it here."

"Well," Dr. Henderson laughed, "that's as good an explanation as any I've heard so far!"

Lila broke away from the Stone's surface and glared at her. "Who else do you know who can create something out of nothing, overnight?"

Dr. Henderson was ready to argue. "Young lady, this object was not created out of nothing! It's basalt and silica, the very rock and sand you're standing on! Here, just look." She removed a small pick from her belt and struck the surface to break off a sample.

The steel tool bounced off with a metallic ring but didn't leave a mark. Indignant, Dr. Henderson struck the surface again, but with the same result.

"Basalt?" Dr. Cooper asked with one eyebrow raised.

"We'll wait for that core drill," Dr. Henderson answered, unruffled, putting the pick back in her belt.

Jay was intrigued and touched the Stone, holding his hand against it. "What if God *did* put it here?"

Dr. Henderson lowered her voice, but she was angry. "Well, that would make a nice tale for the Togwanans, wouldn't it? They're superstitious. They resort to religion and spiritualism to explain things they don't understand. Let's just tell them God put it here, and we can all go home a little sooner!"

Dr. Cooper tried to calm her. "Dr. Henderson, belief in God doesn't rule out scientific method and research. No one's saying that."

"But scientific research doesn't rule out God either," Lila added.

Then Mobutu jumped in, and he was angry. "People, you were not hired to discuss religion! You were hired to explain why this stone is here and to find a way to remove it!"

"We have to consider all theories," Dr. Cooper informed him.

"So let's get on with the *scientific* research," said Dr. Henderson, really dwelling on the word *scientific* to rub it in.

"Well, okay." Jay was ready with another possibility. "If this thing really is man-made, then it has to serve some purpose. I'll bet there are rooms and passages inside, maybe burial chambers like in the pyramids. If we can get inside those rooms, that would tell us something."

"The seismic equipment will tell us if there are any cavities inside," said Dr. Cooper.

Dr. Henderson sighed in frustration. "In order to use it, we'll have to get on top."

They all looked at the vertical, featureless, red wall before them. Climbing was out of the question.

"Mr. Mobutu," said Dr. Cooper, "what's the latest on that airplane?"

FOUR

At Nkromo International Airport the next day, Mobutu introduced the Coopers and Dr. Henderson to a single-engine, high-winged Cessna, apparently one of Idi Nkromo's private fleet of aircraft. It was big enough to haul four people and a limited amount of gear. Mr. Mobutu, already afraid of the Stone, was even more afraid of flying, so he kindly offered to stay behind.

Jay and Lila climbed into the backseat and fastened their seat belts. Dr. Cooper took the pilot's seat up front, and Dr. Henderson sat in the seat to his right.

Mobutu came up to the pilot's window and stuck his hand through. "May God grant you a safe journey," he said quietly.

Dr. Cooper smiled, gripping Mobutu's hand. "See you soon."

Within minutes, they were flying over the desert and toward the Stone. From the air it was as big as a mountain, and still higher than they were.

Dr. Cooper was watching the altimeter. "All right, Jay, now we'll find out how close your calculations were. We're climbing through five thousand right now. If you're right, another five or six thousand should put us over the top of that thing."

Soon the Stone filled their vision, rising above the flat desert like an out-of-place, rectangular skyscraper. Dr. Cooper made a slow left turn so they could circle around the south end. The airplane had climbed to nine thousand feet, and they were still below the Stone's summit.

"Take a look at that," said Dr. Cooper, pointing below. "Rugged cliffs at either end of the Stone make it almost impossible to travel around, and the only road through the desert goes right under it! Half of Nkromo's country is on the other side!"

"Beyond his reach," said Dr. Henderson.

"Exactly. If he can't reach that part of the country he can't control the people who live there. No wonder he's so upset!"

The plane continued climbing as it headed south. At nine thousand and eight hundred feet, everyone looked out the right side. Since the desert floor was about 1,500 feet above sea level, they had to be within a thousand feet of the Stone's estimated altitude; soon they would see the top.

Ten thousand feet. The Stone still looked perfectly flat. Then the plane rounded the far southern corner and for the first time they could see another side.

"Incredible!" Dr. Henderson exclaimed.

Jay and Lila were both leaning close to the window on the right, staring in wonder at the Stone's south-facing surface. It too was perfectly flat, perfectly smooth. It met the eastern surface at a precise, ninety-degree angle.

"It's shaped just like a big box!" Jay exclaimed, snapping some pictures.

Ten thousand, nine hundred. They could see the top.

"This is impossible!" said Dr. Henderson. "There is no way in the world!"

"It's not a box," said Lila. "It's a huge block!"

It was all Dr. Cooper could do to keep his mind on flying the plane and his eyes on the instruments. He continued to climb to eleven thousand feet. Below them now, sitting solidly on the desert floor like a brick on a table, was an immense, mountain-sized object that was rectangular in shape: two long sides, two narrow sides, and a flat top, the same color on every side.

They continued circling around to the west side. The western surface looked identical to the eastern, the same smooth, featureless red stone.

"Okay," said Dr. Henderson, looking through binoculars. "I see the desert road coming out the other side."

They all looked, and Jay snapped more pictures. There it was, all right, winding along, crossing more desert, then grassy drylands, and finally disappearing into some rugged, wooded hills in the west.

Lila peered through her binoculars and spotted something. "Hey, I think I see a village down there!"

"Where?" Dr. Henderson asked, training her binoculars downward.

"Uh . . . about a mile off the northwest corner, on

the other side of the grassland, where that forest begins."

"Got it. Oh, it's a big one. At least . . . sixty structures."

"The Motosas," said Dr. Cooper.

"Right."

"They've got some fields planted down there," Lila reported.

"Savages who farm?" Jay wondered.

Dr. Cooper took a long, careful look at the Stone's top. It appeared smooth enough to land on, although lightly frosted with ice. "Well, while we're up this high, I think we should check out that summit."

"All right!" said Jay.

Lila considered how the icy flat top of the stone ended at such a keen, straight edge, and how the vertical sides dropped almost two miles straight down. "Are you sure?"

Dr. Cooper eased the throttle back. The roar of the engine dropped in tone and the plane began to descend. "Everybody check your seat belt. We'll come in a bit high and do a flyover, just to feel how the wind is. If it feels right, we'll land."

He put the plane into a gentle turn, keeping the Stone's flat, rectangular surface in the windshield. So far the air was smooth, just like the top of the Stone.

"Oooh!" Dr. Henderson cried as the plane gave a lurch like an elevator going up.

"Updraft," Dr. Cooper said matter-of-factly. "The Stone's heating up the air around it. The air's rising, and we're in it. This could be a little sporty after all."

He pulled the throttle back to idle as they passed over the straight, sharp edge of the Stone. Suddenly

44

they were no longer ten thousand feet above the ground; the surface of the Stone was only a few hundred feet below them, flat and featureless like the top of a monstrous desk, and lightly dusted with snow that looked like powdered sugar. The plane was bucking a little, tilting and fishtailing in turbulence.

Dr. Henderson cinched up her seat belt as tight as it would go. "I hope you know what you're doing!"

"Aw, this is nothing for Dad," said Jay.

They were less than a hundred feet off the surface. They could see wisps of powdery snow swirling in lacy shapes along the ground, which helped Dr. Cooper determine the direction of the wind.

"Couldn't ask for a wider runway," he said as he added a touch of flaps.

As Jay and Lila looked below, the shadow of the airplane grew larger and larger, coming up to meet them. Then it joined them as the tires chirped on the stone and ice. Dr. Henderson threw her head back and released a held breath.

"Okay," said Dr. Cooper as the plane slowed to a gentle stop, the tires skidding just a little on the powdery ice. "Let's get the work done and get off this thing before the winds kick up."

"We'll set out the sensors for the seismic experiment," said Dr. Henderson. "They're in that wooden crate in the back."

Stepping out onto the smooth, flat surface felt like stepping onto another planet. No desert, no dry lake bed, no other place on earth, could match the perfect, featureless flatness that stretched for miles. Nor was there ever a sight like the lacy wisps of powder-fine ice and snow floating steadily along in ghostly, numberless hordes only inches above the surface. The movement of the powdery ice and snow was so even, so constant, and so vast, that the Coopers and Dr. Henderson couldn't help but feel *they* were the ones moving. It was eerie, unnatural, and spooky. And none of them had forgotten that they were now walking directly on the back of the "sleeping lion."

The sensors were small, hand-sized transmitters designed to sense vibrations in the ground. Jay carried the wooden crate and Lila did the placing as they made a wide circle around the airplane according to Dr. Henderson's instructions. They were wearing oversized jackets borrowed from the Togwanan army, for at just under eleven thousand feet, the atmosphere was much cooler. Thinner, too. Just a short run could make them pant for air.

From where they stood, the airplane looked tiny and singular, like a gnat or a particle of dust resting on a tabletop. Beyond the airplane were almost four miles of laser-straight flat surface. The sight jarred the senses because it simply did not occur anywhere on the planet. Even the ocean on the calmest of days had a horizon because of the curvature of the earth. But the Stone did not curve out of sight in the distance— it just ended at a sheer, straight edge they could see in all directions. Jay was thrilled at the thought of hiking to the edge to look two miles straight down, but he knew there was work to do and little time.

KABOOM! Dr. Henderson's seismic blaster was like a small cannon held in a steel frame and aimed at the ground. When Jay pressed the detonator switch to set off the explosive charge, the device actually leaped a foot off the surface with Jay and Lila standing on it—supposedly to hold it down. Dr. Jennifer Henderson sat calmly in the shade of the airplane's wing, her jacket collar up around her face to block the cold wind, tapping away at her portable computer.

"We should get an image in just a few seconds," she told Dr. Cooper, who was looking over her shoulder. "The blaster sends shock waves through the Stone, and the sensors pick up the echoes. Then the computer interprets the echoes to let us know where the shock waves have been, whether they've passed through rooms or tunnels or different strata of rock. . . ."

The tiny cursor was sweeping back and forth across the computer screen. Line by line, beginning at the top, it was weaving an image like a tapestry. So far the image was one solid field of black. Dr. Henderson started tapping some keys. "Come on, come on . . . don't disappoint me."

"Woo!" Jay hollered as he and Lila hurried back to the plane. "That blaster was some kind of ride!"

Lila was twisting her finger in her ear. "That thing hurt my ears!"

They joined Dr. Cooper and looked over Dr. Henderson's shoulder at the computer image. The black tapestry continued to form on the computer screen as she tapped a few more keys, muttering to herself and scolding the computer, "Come on, don't give me that!"

Finally, the seismic image was complete. Dr. Henderson leaned back, removed her hands from the keyboard, and sighed. "People, unless the equipment isn't working properly, I'm afraid the results are disappointing. The Stone is solid. No rooms, no tunnels, nothing."

"Nothing?" Jay asked, clearly disappointed.

Dr. Henderson shook her head, waving her finger over the image on the screen. "See here? Between the top and bottom surfaces there is virtually no change in density. No cracks. No holes. No gaps or bubbles. Nothing."

"So we haven't progressed much," said Dr. Cooper.

"We may have fallen back a little. We don't even know what the Stone is made of."

"But you said it was basalt," said Lila.

Dr. Henderson shot a glance at the gas-powered core drill lying next to the plane's wheel strut, the drill bit burned and blunted. "While you were setting out the sensors, I tried to drill out a core sample. The drill didn't even make a scratch. If I'm going to be scientific and objective here, I have to admit I don't know what this thing is or what it's made of. I only know it's indestructible."

"Do you still think it's man-made?" Dr. Cooper asked.

Jennifer Henderson sniffed a derisive little laugh. "I'm wondering what the builder used for a chisel. Even though he, or it, or they, left marks, *I* sure can't."

Lila turned her back to a cold breeze that had just kicked up. "His Excellency isn't going to like this."

"Just for my information," said Dr. Henderson, "now that we have the airplane, can't we just fly out of the country from here?"

Dr. Cooper looked across the vast, tabletop surface toward the distant horizon, barely visible beyond the Stone's sharp edge. "Yes, we can. I'm just not sure how far we can go on the fuel we have left."

"Far enough to get out of Togwana would be fine with me."

"But the question is, where can we go? If any of the neighboring countries help us escape, Nkromo would brand them as enemies. I'm not sure they'd want that."

"Well," said Lila, "at least we're safe up here."

As if in response to her words, a disturbing quiver came up through the soles of their shoes.

"I knew it," Dr. Henderson moaned.

The Stone was quaking, all right. Dr. Henderson's computer almost slid off its little stand before she grabbed it. The airplane began to rock, its wings dipping and jiggling. From deep below and all around, there was a deep rumble, like continuous thunder, as a gust of wind whipped across the Stone, kicking up tiny ice pellets that stung their faces.

Dr. Henderson was already throwing her gear into the plane. "Let's go, let's go!"

Dr. Cooper looked to the east and saw a curtain of snow, ice, and boiling clouds coming their way. "Fair weather's over. We'd better get off this thing!"

Lila looked the direction her father was looking and saw the storm approaching. Even so, she insisted, "But we're safe here, really!"

Dr. Cooper just tugged her toward the plane. "Jay, unchock the wheels!"

Dr. Henderson started running away and he grabbed her.

"I've got to get the blaster!" she yelled over the rumble and the wind. "And the drill, and all those sensors—"

"What about the *airplane?*" Dr. Cooper yelled back. "If it gets damaged, we'll never get down!"

The Stone lurched like a bucking horse. The airplane actually skipped backward several feet, and the Coopers tumbled to the ground. The wind began to whip at them angrily.

Dr. Henderson didn't need any more convincing. With a cry of fear, she struggled to her feet, jerked the door open, and clambered inside.

Jay and Lila jumped in the back, Dr. Cooper in the front. The plane was still dancing and side-stepping along the quivering ground as Dr. Cooper rattled off the checklist, his hands flying from lever to button to gauge to switch. "Fuel tanks both, electrical off, breakers in, prop on maximum, carb heat cold . . ."

He twisted the starter switch and the engine came to life, the prop spinning into a blurred disk in front of the windshield.

A blast of wind, snow, and ice hit them broadside from the right. The plane weather-vaned into it, the tail spinning wildly to the left.

"Okay, we're nose into the wind," said Dr. Cooper, jamming the throttle wide open.

The airplane lunged forward, the white swirls of

snow and ice blowing past them like sheets in the wind. The old Cessna bucked, skidded, swerved, and tilted as the wind tossed it about, slapping against it this way, then that way. It gained speed, began to tiptoe, then skip along the surface. Dr. Cooper eased the control yoke back, and it took to the air.

"Are we safe?" Dr. Henderson pleaded.

An angry burst of wind came up under one wing and almost flipped the plane over. "Not yet," said Dr. Cooper, trying to hold the plane steady.

Below them, the sharp edge of the Stone appeared to rotate, tilt, rise, and fall as the airplane was tossed about like a leaf in the wind. The Cessna roared, climbed, struggled, clawed for altitude. Another blast of wind carried it sideways.

"Dad, what is it?" Jay asked. "What's happening?"

"Heat-generated updrafts," he yelled over the roar of the engine. "Convergence, convection, wind shear, I don't know—the Stone's affecting the weather."

The plane lurched sideways, twisting, banking, creaking in every joint. A cloud of snow and ice boiled beneath them like an angry white ocean. Dr. Cooper turned the plane eastward, trying to climb above the storm. Below them, the east edge of the Stone came no closer. The wind was so strong they were standing still!

Then the edge of the Stone began to retreat from them. The wind was blowing them backward!

"Oh, brother," said Dr. Cooper.

"What?" Dr. Henderson cried.

"We're in for a ride. Hang on."

"Can't you do something?"

"If I try to fight against this turbulence, the plane will break apart! We just have to ride it out!"

He eased the throttle back to slow the airplane down, then turned it westward to fly with the wind and get clear of the Stone. The Stone was hidden now beneath an angry mantle of storm clouds, but they could see the clouds breaking over its western edge like water flowing over a waterfall.

"Wind shear," said Dr. Cooper.

"Oh, no," whined Dr. Henderson.

Suddenly, the clouds seemed to suck them down, and they dropped into a nether world of pure white cotton on all sides with no up, no down, no sense of direction.

The altimeter was spinning backward, and they could feel the pressure of the atmosphere building against their ears. Eleven thousand, said the altimeter. Ten thousand. Nine.

They were helpless in a violent downdraft, tossed, twisted, thrown about in the clouds.

Eight thousand. Seven. Six.

And there was nothing they could do, except pray.

FIVE

D r. Cooper had only one course of action available to him, and that was to fly the plane—just keep it under control, keep it flying. The plane was being knocked all over the sky. They braced themselves against the walls of the cabin, the seats, the floor, and each other, and still the plane plummeted earthward. As clouds whipped past the windshield and the plane quivered with every new gust of wind, Jacob Cooper kept an iron hand on the control yoke and the throttle, watching the airspeed and altimeter and making no sudden moves.

They knew that the Stone had to be out there somewhere in all those boiling clouds, but just how close was it? A collision would be no contest.

"Dear Jesus," Lila prayed out loud, "we're in your hands."

Suddenly, light burst through the windows as they dropped out of the clouds into clear air.

"*Yes!*" Jay shouted.

They could see the ground, and it looked awfully close. But the altimeter was no longer winding down. The violent downdraft was contacting the ground and turning sideways, becoming a powerful wind.

But where was the Stone? Every head twisted left and right trying to find it.

"There it is!" Jay shouted. "Nine o'clock!"

They could see the huge wall, dark and ominous in the cloudy gray light, stretching from the earth into the clouds. It appeared to be at least a mile away, and the good news was that the wind had carried them away from the Stone, not toward it.

Just then, they saw grass roofs slipping quickly by below them. Cattle. People.

"The Motosa village!" said Jay. "We're right above it!"

The engine sputtered and coughed. "Well," said Dr. Cooper, fiddling with the knobs and ignition, "what do you know!"

"What?" asked Dr. Henderson.

"We've lost the engine."

"*What?*"

"Carburetor ice, I suppose, or a broken fuel line. Hang on. I'm setting up for a landing."

Dr. Cooper turned the plane into the wind and aimed for a stretch of flat ground. The gusty, unpredictable wind lifted the plane, then dropped it, then knocked it sideways. "Check your seat belts!"

By now, they couldn't get their seat belts any tighter.

The wind dropped suddenly and so did the plane, so abruptly they could feel it in their stomachs. The desert floor rushed up at them, only thirty feet below, then twenty, then ten. Dr. Cooper fought for control as sagebrush, grass, and stones raced by below the wheels.

WHAM! The wind slammed the plane into the ground. The wheels bounced, the plane floated up again, then fell again, the wheels digging into the soft earth, kicking up dust, gouging out ruts. Dr. Cooper pulled back on the control yoke to keep the plane from nosing over as it swerved, bucked, bounced, and rumbled over the ground.

IMPACT! The right wheel hit a large rock. The plane spun in a circle, tilting wildly, the left wingtip clipping the top of a bush. Then the right wheel strut gave way, and the plane collapsed to the ground in a cloud of dust.

And then it was over. The plane sat amid desert stones and scraggly, yellow grass. It was quiet and still now, one strut broken and the right wingtip resting on the ground.

Jay and Lila relaxed, sat up, and looked around, letting out an audible breath of relief.

Dr. Henderson was all folded up with her arms clamped around her head. Only after a long, uninterrupted moment of silence and stillness did she slowly, timidly unwrap herself and come up for a look.

Dr. Cooper still had one hand clamped around the control yoke as he went through his shut-down checklist, flipping switches, turning knobs, shifting levers. In seconds, the aircraft was secure. Then he rested back in his seat, relaxed for the first time in what seemed an eternity of terror, and prayed in a quiet voice, "Ohhh, thank you, Lord, for a safe landing!"

"Thank you, Lord," Lila agreed.

"Thaaaank *you*," said Jay.

"Well, you can sit here and pray if you want," said Dr. Henderson, "but *I'm* getting out of this plane!"

Click, clack, their seat belts came loose and they piled out the doors, Dr. Henderson and Jay having to duck under the drooping wing on the right side.

"OWW!" Dr. Henderson fell to the ground, grimacing in pain, her hand going to her knee.

Jay leaped to her side, followed by Lila and Dr. Cooper. "What is it?"

Jennifer Henderson was hurt and angry at the same time. "I hurt my leg! Dr. Cooper, you broke the plane and me with it!"

Dr. Cooper knelt beside her and helped her roll up her pantleg. Her knee was beginning to swell. "Can you move it at all?"

She lay on her back, her face crinkled in agony, and gave it a try. She could move it, but it hurt terribly.

Dr. Cooper checked the knee as she worked it. "Well, nothing's broken, but your knee is badly bruised."

Dr. Henderson let her head plop on the soft, sandy ground and wagged it in despair. "Why me? Why me?"

"But you're still alive," Lila offered. "And you're safe."

Boom, bubbaboom, buboom, buboom boom. The sound of African drums came floating to them on the wind.

"The Motosas," said Jay. "Their village can't be far from here."

Dr. Henderson gave Lila a despairing look. "I only wish I could run."

"The question is, where?" said Dr. Cooper, surveying the area all around them. The bare desert gave way to a dry, grassy plain with singular trees popping up here and there, but this was still open country and their wrecked airplane had to be visible for miles. "I have little doubt the Motosas know we're here. Those drums could be an alarm."

"Well, I say we try to get back to the other side."

"It would be difficult, if not impossible. The Stone's blocking the road, and those hills at either end would be a tough climb even if you weren't injured."

Dr. Henderson struggled to get up. "Well, I'm not staying here to become somebody's dinner!"

"Can you walk at all?" Dr. Cooper asked, lending his arm.

She put weight on the leg and nearly collapsed again, wincing at the pain. "OWW. . . no."

Dr. Cooper helped her get comfortable on the ground again, then ducked under the airplane's wing and reached inside the cabin.

"I'll try the plane's radio. Maybe we can contact somebody."

Boom boom buboom, the drums kept playing away.

"Do we have any weapons?" Dr. Henderson asked, sitting up.

Jay and Lila looked at each other for an answer.

"A few tools, maybe," said Jay. "A wrench, a screwdriver . . ."

"Rocks," Lila suggested.

Dr. Henderson smiled dryly, looking up at the sky. "I'm the luckiest woman in the world!"

Dr. Cooper tried several times to raise someone on the radio, but he couldn't get an answer. Finally, he set the microphone back in its holder and shut the radio off. "The Stone must be blocking our signal."

The wind had begun to die down as the storm ebbed away. The sun poked holes through the thinning clouds.

Boom boom buboom boom. The drums sounded louder.

Dr. Cooper scanned the countryside. "We've got to find some shelter, some place to hide."

"Dad!" Lila whispered. "I think I saw something!"

They all looked in the direction Lila pointed. To the north was an expansive plain of sagebrush and prairie grass, and beyond that, a thin, scraggly forest. Nothing seemed out of place and nothing moved except the grass in the breeze.

"I don't see anything," Jay said quietly.

"There's somebody out there," Lila insisted.

They noticed for the first time that the drumbeats had ceased. They heard nothing except the gentle hiss of the breeze through the dry grass.

But was the motion in the grass just from the breeze?

Dr. Cooper was the first to see a face emerge, painted with clay and camouflaged with blades of

grass to make it nearly invisible against its surroundings. Slowly, with increasing boldness, the
warrior rose from his hiding place in the tall grass to
his full height, brandishing a spear in one hand,
ready to hurl it at the slightest wrong move.

Lila came alongside her father and held him tightly as another warrior appeared, and then another,
each one painted from head to foot to look just like
the prairie, like he was made of earth and grass. To
the north, and then to the west, and now from the
south, more warriors appeared as if growing out of
the ground, springing up like cornstalks in a time-
lapse movie. It was remarkable how close they'd
gotten without being detected.

"They're very good," said Dr. Cooper.

The warriors came out into the clear, moving
stealthily, catlike, their feet touching lightly, silently
on the ground. With precision and discipline, they
formed a circle, evenly spaced like fenceposts,
around the airplane and its occupants, their spears
ready. Jacob Cooper counted about thirty. They
were not naked, but close to it, dressed for a hunt
and dead serious about it. Their expressions were
grim through all the mud and grass camouflage.

Dr. Cooper raised his hand very slowly, making
sure they could see it was empty, and then gave a
slight wave of greeting. "Hello."

Some of the warriors directly in front of Dr.
Cooper finally spoke, but not to him. They were
looking at the broken airplane, pointing, muttering
to each other, and even getting excited. They called to
some other warriors who hurried over to confer in a

tight huddle. Word began to travel around the circle, and now everyone seemed excited. Two warriors ran back into the grass, apparently to spread the word to the rest of the village, whatever the word was. Those who remained began to stare at Dr. Cooper, pointing at him, discussing him among themselves.

"I'm Dr. Jacob Cooper—"

Twenty-eight arms raised spears. The warriors were fascinated with Jacob Cooper, but still wary of him.

"Dad . . ." Jay whispered and then pointed to the north.

The two messengers were returning, bounding through the grass with the grace and agility of gazelles, and behind them, marching with quick, deliberate steps, were four men and . . . a bush. At least that's what it looked like from a distance— some kind of bizarre plant sticking above the prairie grass with leaves, grass, and even a few small tree branches arranged like a walking flower arrangement. From the way the warriors quieted down and shuffled sideways to make room, this had to be someone important approaching.

The "bush" came closer, and at last they could see a grim, black face in the center of an elaborate headdress of fur and foliage.

Dr. Henderson drew a surprised breath.

Lila gasped right along with Dr. Henderson and then whispered, "Dad, is that Mr. Mobutu?"

Dr. Cooper kept watching as the very important person came closer. At first glance, and from a distance, the man did bear a remarkable resemblance to

Nkromo's chief secretary, but with a second look it was easy to tell, "No, it isn't Mobutu. I believe this is the tribal chief, the man who holds our lives in his hands."

The chief walked briskly into the circle with authority in every step and an ornately carved staff in his hand. He was attended by four men dressed in woven tunics and elaborate belts and sashes of grass and bark—uniforms, obviously, the proper attire for attendants to the tribal chief. As for the chief, besides the towering headdress, he also wore a breastplate of woven bones and bark, a breathtaking sash of crafted leather, leather sandals with bindings that wound up his legs to his knees, and, as the ultimate symbol of power and high office, a genuine pair of jogging shorts with the word *Nike* clearly embossed on the leg.

What might have happened to the former owner of those shorts was something they tried not to think about.

Dr. Cooper gave a slight bow, as did Jay and Lila. Dr. Henderson, still seated on the ground, bowed as best she could.

The chief came forward and eyed Dr. Cooper carefully as some of his warriors whispered counsel to him, pointing at the airplane, gesturing at Dr. Cooper. The chief seemed to agree with whatever they were telling him, and the more they talked, the more alarmed he looked. Finally, he spoke to Dr. Cooper, pointing and giving instructions in the Motosa language.

His words meant nothing, of course, and the

Coopers and Dr. Henderson could only exchange blank looks.

The chief grew impatient, and repeated the order, pointing at Jacob Cooper's head. Dr. Cooper raised his hand and touched his hat. The chief nodded. Dr. Cooper removed his hat and held it in his hand.

There was an audible gasp from the circle of warriors and the chief cocked his head, his face full of wonder.

"Looks like you're in the spotlight," Dr. Henderson said quietly.

"So what do I do to perform?" Dr. Cooper asked.

"English!" the chief exclaimed. "You speak English!"

Dr. Cooper wanted to feel relieved. Was this a good sign? "Uh . . . yes, I do."

"Who are you?"

"Dr. Jacob Cooper, from America. And this is my daughter Lila, and that is my son Jay. And this is Dr. Jennifer Henderson, also from America."

The chief broke into a wide smile, then laughed with joy. Then he bellowed a loud announcement to his warriors. They erupted in cheers, waving their spears in the air, smiling, laughing, hopping up and down.

Dr. Cooper just smiled at them as he quietly told Dr. Henderson and the kids, "Well, we've done *something* to please them."

"Maybe they just heard tonight's menu," Dr. Henderson whispered.

Then Dr. Cooper asked the chief, "Are you the Motosas?"

"Yes, yes!" replied the chief. "Motosas, yes!" He stepped forward, all smiles, all joy. "You come! Come to village! You talk! We hear!"

Before the Coopers understood what was happening, four men locked their arms together to form a chair and lifted Dr. Cooper off the ground like some kind of football hero. Four others did the same for Dr. Henderson, while two pairs of men carried Jay and Lila. With a majestic wave of his staff, the chief led the parade, and, breaking into a song, they headed across the grassy plain.

It was an odd feeling, being carried along by these cheering, mud-painted savages. Jay and Lila tried to smile and act pleased, but they'd heard stories about savage tribes who went to great lengths to win friends just so they could betray and eat them later. Dr. Cooper had heard the same stories and was trying to remember if he'd heard them from Brent Anderson, who had worked in this country.

The parade passed over gently rolling prairie land, through waist-high grass, and past lone, aged trees. At last the Coopers caught sight of the thatched rooftops of the village on the edge of a forest. The trail took them under the sheltering canopy of the trees and then into the center of the village. There chickens and goats scattered out of their path and women and children stopped to stare and wonder at the commotion.

The warriors called to their wives, pointed at the Coopers, and rattled off rapid, excited explanations. The women grew wide-eyed and clapped their hands in awe, chattering among themselves and calling to their children. The main thoroughfare through the village was coming alive with men, women, and children, all gathering and babbling and clapping their hands as they followed the parade.

The Coopers and Dr. Henderson just let themselves be carried along through the village, observing the well-built, multi-roomed, pole and grass structures, watering troughs for the animals carved from whole logs, inventive, hand-woven garments, and intricate jewelry made from stones, bones, and leather.

The thoroughfare opened into a large village square where chickens scratched about and children kicked and chased a furry, fuzzy ball in some kind of team sport. In the center of the square was a well. It was enclosed with a circular wall of stones and topped with a beam from which a bucket could be lowered. At the far end of the square was a large, tent-like structure with a thatched roof but no walls. Beyond that, fields of corn and wheat struggled to survive in the dry climate.

The parade carried the Coopers and Dr. Henderson right up to the big tent-like structure as two musicians started pounding big drums as a clarion call. In response, the rest of the villagers began to gather from the fields, from the huts, and from the dry prairie beyond, chattering with curiosity and excitement.

The men carrying the Coopers set them down gently; the men carrying Dr. Henderson continued to carry her under the big roof. The chief extended his big, powerful arm inside. "Please! Come! We sit! We hear!"

The Coopers followed the chief inside, past rows of log benches arranged in theater-like fashion, to an open area in the front where a large, flat stone served as a one-man platform.

"Wow," Jay whispered to Lila. "If I didn't know we were in a primitive African village, I'd think we were in an old revival tent!"

Lila nodded, smiling at the similarity. "It must be their meeting hall."

Dr. Henderson was already seated comfortably on a log bench in the very front, wincing just a bit as a gray-haired man in a bone necklace and grass skirt examined her knee, nodding and muttering to an assistant or apprentice who nodded and muttered back. This was apparently the village witch doctor.

"It's fine, really," Dr. Henderson protested. "I don't need any spells cast on me, thank you."

The chief motioned for the Coopers to stand beside the stone platform while the people swarmed in from every direction, filling the log benches, chattering, and staring at the Coopers with wonder.

The chief stepped onto the stone and raised his arms to signal for quiet. The place quieted down immediately. He addressed them all in a voice that did not need a microphone or loudspeakers. And he appeared to be introducing the strangers who stood there, still oblivious to what was going on.

Then the chief looked down from his stone platform and grinned at Dr. Cooper. The people grinned, too, snickering with delight. The chief pointed to Dr. Cooper's head, bellowed another few sentences, and then, before Dr. Cooper could resist or react, he reached over and rubbed his fingers furiously through Dr. Cooper's hair. That being done, he stepped back and held out his hands toward Dr. Cooper's tousled head as if to say, "Voilà!"

The people seemed to understand the point. They rose to their feet, laughing, cheering, pointing, nodding, clapping.

"Speech! Speech!" Jay cheered, clapping along, which earned him another corrective poke from Lila.

The chief offered Dr. Cooper his big hand and yanked him up onto the stone. The crowd sat down, and the place got quiet.

"You talk," said the chief. "We hear, yes!"

Then the chief sat down on the front log and waited expectantly with all the others.

Dr. Cooper looked out at all those faces looking back and felt stark naked. What in the world were they expecting him to say? What was he supposed to do? He caught a look from Dr. Henderson. She wasn't saying it out loud, but her eyes sent the message clear enough: "Doctor, you really *are* in the spotlight now!"

The warriors who had brought them here still had their spears in their hands and were eyeing him warily.

Hoo boy, he thought. *If they don't like whatever speech I come up with, we could all be Cooper soup!*

And still the people waited.

SIX

U m ..." Dr. Cooper cleared his throat and gave the people a smile he hoped they would like. "Uh, on behalf of my children and my colleague, Dr. Henderson, I bid you greetings."

Jay and Lila, still standing on the ground in front of the platform, gave a little wave, hoping that would help convey their dad's meaning.

The chief stood up to look for someone and finally caught the eye of the gray-haired witch doctor who had been looking at Dr. Henderson's knee. The chief jerked his head toward Dr. Cooper and the man hurried over and leaped up on the rock, offering his hand. "I am Bengati! Welcome."

Dr. Cooper was relieved to find another English speaker in the group. "Dr. Jacob Cooper. You know English, then?"

"My father was a guide for white hunters. He learned the language, and taught it to me. I have taught the chief and his family, but . . ." He shrugged. "When there is no need to speak it, it is hard for them to remember."

Bengati immediately introduced Dr. Jacob

Cooper to the crowd. Dr. Cooper picked up his cue and introduced his children and Dr. Henderson, and Bengati interpreted again.

The chief spoke several sentences. Bengati interpreted, "Our Chief welcomes you and says the people have gathered to hear whatever it is you have to say."

Dr. Cooper confided in a lowered voice, "I'm not really sure what I'm *supposed* to say. Is there—"

Bengati interpreted Dr. Cooper's confidence to the crowd before he could stop him, and everyone exchanged puzzled looks.

Dr. Cooper hurried to say, "But, uh, we are scientists from America, and we have come here to study this vast, mysterious stone that has appeared in the desert."

The people fell silent and serious when Bengati told them that, nodding their heads, their eyes glued on Dr. Cooper.

The chief asked a question.

"The chief and the people want to know, what does the stone mean?" Bengati interpreted.

"*Mean?*" That question caught Dr. Cooper by surprise. "Uh, well, we're not sure what it means. We've only just arrived and as you know, encountered some trouble with our airplane. We're not even sure where the Stone came from, or how it got here."

When Bengati delivered that answer, Jay and Lila could see it didn't please the crowd at all. In perfect unison, all those awestruck, expectant faces changed to disappointment.

The chief wasn't very happy either. He fired another question, his voice a little more stern.

Bengati interpreted, "You really do not know how it got here?"

"Uh . . . no, not yet."

The chief rose to his feet, exasperated, shaking his head and waving his arms as if trying to erase the whole event. He bellowed an announcement to the crowd, and everyone stood up and started to leave.

"The meeting is over," Bengati told the Coopers. "You did not answer the chief's questions correctly."

"You could have *made up* something," Dr. Henderson muttered.

The chief stepped up to Dr. Cooper, still shaking his head, and made a simple statement.

Bengati interpreted, "Have you no eyes? *God* put it there."

Lila's mouth dropped open. She shot a triumphant glance at Dr. Henderson. The geologist merely sneered.

The chief continued to speak while Bengati interpreted. "We hoped you would teach us, but now *we* must teach *you*."

The chief gave some quick orders to his warriors and stomped from the building, obviously angry and disappointed.

The warriors moved forward and surrounded them again, pushing Bengati to the outside of the circle. The warrior in charge shook his spear and shouted, gesturing toward the village. Bengati called from across the crowd, "You are to go with those men now."

Four warriors got their arms locked under Dr.

Henderson and picked her up, but there were no such seats for the Coopers.

They had to walk, guided by the points of spears.

"Well, it seems our popularity has lagged," said Dr. Cooper.

"Face it, Cooper, you bombed," said Dr. Henderson.

Surrounded tightly on all sides and led by armed warriors, they left the meeting hall and went out into the village square as the crowd continued to disperse. Some returned to their homes, others back into the fields, and several back to the open prairie, disappearing over a low rise. The formidable Stone filled the sky beyond them.

"What do cannibals do?" Lila asked. "I mean . . . do they just throw you into a big soup pot or what?"

Dr. Cooper touched her. "Lila, don't give in to thoughts like that."

Jay sniffed. "Hey. Smells like a barbecue."

"Of course," said Dr. Henderson. "And guess who the main course is going to be!"

Jacob Cooper's voice was firm. "Dr. Henderson, I'll thank you to control such outbursts!"

"Sorry." Her tone said she wasn't.

They seemed to be going toward the smell, marching up a narrow path that wound between the grass huts and beneath the sheltering limbs of ancient trees. When they rounded the last corner, they beheld a sight that made them stare. At the end of the path was a special grass hut, built in and around a massive tree so that the roof timbers were suspended from the tree's lower limbs.

"Now *this* is different," said Jay.

"It's like something out of Peter Pan!" said Lila, captivated. "Where the Lost Boys live!"

The warriors led them up to the front door and halted there in a neat formation. There was a shout and the tribal chief, now without his ornate headdress, emerged from his house and stood before his door, his expression grim, his fists on his hips.

"Ben-ga-ti!" he hollered.

Bengati shouted in acknowledgment as he came running from behind the crowd.

The chief thundered a few sentences as Bengati came alongside to interpret. "The chief wishes to have you as his guests for dinner."

The Coopers and Dr. Henderson exchanged glances. Now just what did he mean by that?

The warriors all bowed slightly and turned away, heading back down the path into the village. The only ones who remained were Bengati and those bearing Jennifer Henderson.

"Come," said the chief, gesturing with his big arms, "You come. Come eat."

Dr. Henderson went first—she had no choice, as the warriors carried her gently through the narrow door. Dr. Cooper, Jay, and Lila followed behind. Their eyes darted everywhere, alert for knives in hands, warriors waiting in ambush, any sign of danger.

Inside the chief's hut, they saw dinner already prepared, laid out in banquet style on a low, rough-hewn table. In the center of the table, surrounded by meticulous arrangements of fruits and vegetables, was a huge roast pig, still hot and crackling, just off the spit.

They were going to *eat* dinner, not *be* dinner.

71

Their relief was so obvious the chief asked through Bengati, "Are you all right? Is something wrong with the food?"

Dr. Cooper waved his hand and shook his head and even chuckled with relief. "No, no, everything's wonderful. The roast pig is . . . it's a wonderful sight to see!"

"Fabulous!" Dr. Henderson agreed, still drawing deep breaths so she could sigh with relief, her hand over her heart.

The chief introduced his family: a beautiful wife with coal black skin and a smooth, sculptured face—"She is Renyata"; a handsome, athletic son just a little older than Jay—"He is my son, Ontolo"; and a beautiful daughter about Lila's age with long, intricate braids—"She is Beset." Then he thumped his chest and announced proudly, "And I am Gotono! I am chief!"

The Coopers and Dr. Henderson bowed in greeting and respect as they shook hands with each of Chief Gotono's family. Jay and Ontolo hit it off immediately and even exchanged a few small gifts. Then, at the chief and Renyata's invitation—and with the four warriors assisting Dr. Henderson— they took their places around the table, sitting on the floor on a comfortable woven mat of straw. The chief extended his hand over the table while he pronounced some kind of blessing, and they started eating. It felt just like family dinner on a Sunday afternoon.

As they ate, the chief spoke and Bengati interpreted. "I apologize for the embarrassment we caused you. You were not who we expected." Before they could figure out what that was supposed to mean, the chief kept right on going. "But now you are guests here with us, and we welcome you."

"Thank you," said Dr. Cooper. "And we apologize that we did not meet your expectations."

Bengati relayed the message in Motosa and the chief laughed. "So you have come to learn of the Stone," he answered through Bengati. "The Stone is a work of our god, but it is a great mystery. We do not know what our god intends by placing it there. We do not yet know its meaning. That is why we asked *you*."

Dr. Henderson got bold. "Well, if you don't know the meaning of the Stone, then how can you be sure your god put it there?"

The Coopers tensed a bit at that question, afraid it would cause offense, but the chief only nodded in approval and gave his answer.

"That is a fair question," Bengati translated.

The chief reached over and took his long, ornately carved staff from its place in the corner. He held it up for all to see, and ran his fingers over the carvings of animals, birds, and trees. Bengati relayed his words, "If you were to happen upon this staff in the middle of the desert, you would think another man left it there. You would not think it suddenly appeared for no reason. And why is that? Because anyone can see it is created. It is carved by a maker's hand. So the Stone is the same way. It is no ordinary stone. It is created by the hand of a craftsman, the hand of our god."

Dr. Cooper could feel Lila's smile before he even looked to see it. He smiled back and threw her a wink.

The chief was continuing. "Our god does nothing without a reason, and soon we will know what the reason is. But this we do know: The Stone will bring us water for our crops, just as it has brought us you. This was all meant to be."

"Water for their crops?" Dr. Henderson wondered out loud.

Dr. Cooper caught her eye, and her meaning. "Sounds geological, doesn't it?"

Dr. Henderson turned to the chief. "You say the Stone will bring you water? How?"

The chief was delighted by the question. "The day is coming to an end. Tomorrow morning, you will see."

After dinner, the Coopers and Dr. Henderson were taken to a large home facing the village square. Like most homes in this village, it was a well-built, sod and grass, post and beam structure that rested on stone footings with a covered porch. The owner was an older woman with a round, jolly face.

"This is Jo-Jota," said Bengati, "a widow of three years and mother of five who are now grown. She has room inside for strangers, and you can all stay here."

"Wow," said Dr. Henderson, "Jo-Jota's boarding house."

"You may stay here in our village while you try to learn the secret of the Stone," the chief said as

Bengati interpreted. Then he looked at Dr. Henderson. "And we will care for you until your leg has healed."

She shook the chief's hand and replied, "Thank you, sir. We are indebted to you."

Dr. Cooper took Jo-Jota's offered hand in greeting. "We deeply appreciate your hospitality."

"Tomorrow," said the chief, "we will see the Stone together, and you will learn how the Stone will bring us water."

When morning came to the Motosa village, there was a strange, overcast dimness about it, as if the sun had come up, but not really. When Lila stepped onto Jo-Jota's porch to stretch and breathe the cool, morning air, she found her brother and father already observing how the Stone had affected the morning light.

"We're still in the Stone's shadow," said Jay.

"The desert, the grasslands, the village," Dr. Cooper observed, looking east, then west, "a lot of the forest, too, is all in the shadow. The sunlight won't break over the top edge of the Stone until mid-morning."

Jo-Jota brought them a breakfast of wheat kernels mixed with raisins, which reminded them of granola, and goat's milk. They had just finished their meal when Chief Gotono, Bengati, and four warriors arrived, all smiles. The chief had appointed himself their official guide and had come to take them on a tour around the village.

The Coopers walked while Jennifer Henderson rode in style in a special chair carried by the four warriors. She griped a little bit, complaining that she was not a cripple, but the Coopers could tell she was actually enjoying herself.

Bengati tried to keep up with the translating as Chief Gotono rattled on and on like a tour guide. The chief pointed out new huts that had been built in a special expansion project for new sons- and daughters-in-law. Next he showed them the recently improved village well. Because of the recent dry years, it was now dug out twice as deep as it had been originally. Then he took them to the sheep and goat corrals, now with dwindling populations due to the loss of grazing land. From there they went to see the spinning and weaving projects that provided clothing, blankets, and household linens. Last, the chief showed them the fields of corn and wheat that were necessary for survival and yet sparse for lack of water.

"But that will change soon," he added.

They passed through the village heading eastward, toward the desert and toward the Stone. As they came from under the wide canopy of the trees and started to cross the open prairie, they could once again see the Stone stretching across the golden horizon and filling the sky like the biggest red barn ever made.

Lila admired the reddish color that seemed so deep on the shaded, western face of the Stone. It seemed to glow around its edges where the hidden sun's rays shot outward like the spokes of a huge wheel. "It's beautiful, isn't it?"

Dr. Cooper studied the Stone's distant outline and quietly asked his children, "Why aren't we afraid of it?"

Jay thought the question a little odd. "Are we supposed to be?"

"Well, come on: It's popped into existence out of nowhere; it's indestructible; it cuts the day in half; it quakes; and we got the scare of our lives in that storm it caused."

Jay considered that. "Well, we're okay now. Nothing really bad happened."

"The people on the other side are afraid of it."

"I've *never* been afraid of it," said Lila.

"And neither have I," said Jay.

"But why not?" their father pressed.

"I don't know," said Lila. "It'd be like being afraid of a sunset, or a beautiful mountain, or a whole forest turning golden in the fall. It's beautiful, and God made it, that's all I know."

"Yeah," Jay agreed. "I think Lila and the chief are right: God put it there."

Dr. Cooper nodded. "Which really makes me curious: What is it about a huge rock that draws such a response from us?"

"Well, what about the Motosas?" Jay asked. "They must be feeling the same thing. I mean, all those people on the other side—Nkromo, Mobutu, the soldiers—they think the Stone's a *boloa-kota*, and they're afraid of it. But the Motosas are glad the thing's here; they think their god sent it."

"Now *that* was interesting, to be sure," said Dr. Cooper. "I'd like to know more about the religious system here. They apparently believe in a creator, in one god."

"And they aren't cannibals, either," said Jay. "I don't know what Mr. Mobutu was talking about."

"Wow!" Lila said suddenly.

They were coming over a rise and could see the vast golden prairie in front of them. Where it faded into the desolate desert basin, the Stone, as solid, immovable, and mysterious as ever, towered above like a pillar holding up the sky. But now they had a new sight to behold.

At least fifty men, women, and children were laboring in a long, straight line, swinging picks and shovels, throwing the stubborn dirt out of a ditch that reached better than a mile across the prairie, into the desert, and to the base of the Stone. It was a marvelous accomplishment considering the primitive tools they were using—no backhoes or bulldozers here, only picks, shovels, muscles, and determination.

The chief was proud of the project, that was easy to see. He traced the path of the ditch in a long, flowing gesture and said with Bengati translating: "For years our life has been hard for lack of water. Our crops have struggled, our well has dropped lower and lower. But now, water will come. It will flow through this ditch from the Stone to our village."

Jennifer Henderson rose awkwardly in her chair and strained to see the farthest limits of the ditch. "But where is the water?"

"It will come," the chief replied.

He continued on, and they followed, hiking along

the ditch through the prairie and into the desert, getting closer and closer to the Stone. Dr. Henderson became visibly nervous again, but the men carrying her actually seemed to be excited for the opportunity to come this close to the Stone.

The Coopers continued to inspect the ditch as they walked along, until it came at last to a sudden stop at the northwest corner of the Stone.

Here, almost as a courtesy, the Stone allowed access to its corner over flat desert ground. Only a few hundred feet away, the Stone was jammed up against the sheer, rocky cliffs, barring any approach to the rest of its north surface as well as denying any passage to the other side. The Coopers and Dr. Henderson had never been to one of the Stone's corners. They'd never touched one or measured its angle, never placed their hands on the keen edge that shot straight up, true as a laser, into the upper reaches of the sky.

Dr. Cooper got there first, and with an excitement that he made no effort to conceal, he touched the corner. He ran his hand up and down it, sighted along the Stone's west face with one eye, then the Stone's north face, then carefully measured the angle formed where the two surfaces met.

"Incredible!" he exclaimed, so excited there was laughter in his voice. "Ninety degrees! Perfectly formed!"

Jennifer Henderson fidgeted in her chair and urged her carriers on. "Come on, get me over there!"

They carried her to the corner where she did the very same things Dr. Cooper had done, her breath quickening with excitement, her face filled with awe.

Jay and Lila took their turn, sighting up the corner, marveling at the dead-straight line and the perfectly square angle.

"*Oh, Lord,*" Dr. Cooper found himself praying, "*what is it? What does it mean?*"

But now Dr. Henderson was carefully surveying the ground and the rocky strata the ditch had cut through. "Dr. Cooper. I don't think I have any good news for us or the Motosas. There's nothing here to indicate any kind of water table or aquifer."

The Motosas standing nearby did not fully understand her words, but they could understand her somber tone. They fell silent, wanting to know what she was saying.

"So you're saying . . . ?" Dr. Cooper asked.

"I'm saying there is no water here," she replied.

The chief seemed to understand what she was saying and touched her arm. Then he spoke, and Bengati translated. "You see with only one set of eyes and see only what is, not what can be."

Dr. Henderson didn't want to argue with their host. "I suppose that's right," she agreed. Then she muttered to Dr. Cooper, "I suppose *he* can predict what the geological forces will do next."

Then Chief Gotono turned to Jay and Lila with a sparkle in his eye. Bengati translated as the chief asked them, "Do *you* see with other eyes? Do you see the water flowing to our village?"

Well, of course they didn't, but they thought they understood his meaning.

Jay ventured, "You're, uh, digging this ditch in faith?"

Bengati wasn't sure how to interpret that.

Lila tried, "It's like a dream, a vision. You don't see any water, but still you believe it will be here."

Bengati interpreted that to the chief, and the chief laughed a deep, thunderous laugh that echoed off the Stone so clearly it sounded like a second man laughing right next to them. "Yes!" He thumped his heart. "In here, I know."

SEVEN

Back on Jo-Jota's porch, the chief and Bengati sat with the Coopers and Dr. Henderson. They were enjoying one of Jo-Jota's fruit juice concoctions as they rested from the day's heat.

The chief spoke, and as always, Bengati translated his words. "I know there is no water in the ditch. I know that no water can be seen. But do you see that well?" The chief pointed to the village well in the middle of the square. "Long ago, when there was no village, our ancestors came to this place. Their chief said, 'This is where we will live.' His people said, 'We cannot live here, there is no water.' But the chief had found a special stone upon the ground, and when he struck it with his staff, water came from beneath it. That water has been there ever since, and that is where our well is today. We are here, and our village is here, because long ago, a chief saw there would be water where once there was none."

Dr. Cooper smiled. The tale reminded him of Moses in the wilderness, striking a rock to bring forth water for the children of Israel. "In our culture, we have a story like that."

"So are you going to strike the Stone as your ancestor did?" Dr. Henderson asked.

The chief looked just a little awkward. "I have already done that, even before we dug the ditch."

Dr. Henderson couldn't hide the fact that she was troubled about all this. "But still you believe there will be water?"

"There is water there," the chief insisted. "Our well is going down. We have dug it deeper, but it is difficult to draw any more water from it. We have tried digging other wells, but cannot dig deep enough through the rock. If the Stone does not bring us water, we will perish. Our god would not let that happen."

Dr. Henderson said nothing and looked toward the square. Dr. Cooper could see she felt sorry for these people. "Dr. Henderson, what about the well these people have now? Doesn't that indicate the presence of water down there, some kind of aquifer?"

She weighed that and finally nodded. "Certainly. There are hills and mountains on all sides of the desert. Cracks and fissures under the ground could carry the rainwater from those hills into a vast reservoir under the desert floor. But even if there was water down there, you heard the chief: It's lying under solid rock and too far down for these people to reach it." She added glumly, her voice quiet and secretive. "And a two-foot-wide ditch across the desert isn't going to make much of a difference."

Dr. Cooper shot a glance over the thatched rooftops of the village and through the trees. He could see the Stone still glistening in the afternoon sun. "Unless something really unusual happened," he offered.

She gazed at the Stone and shook her head fearfully. "You mean something *cataclysmic*. Doctor, any geological event big enough to break open that aquifer would probably wipe out this village in the process. I'd rather not think about that."

Just then, the chief's wife, Renyata, came around the corner with her son, Ontolo, and everyone could see that something was wrong. Renyata looked angry, and Ontolo walked with his head drooping, looking glum.

Renyata spoke quietly to Bengati, who relayed her words to the Coopers. "Renyata would like to know if you're missing a marking stick and some strange skin."

Renyata held up a pencil and some sheets of paper and spoke as Bengati translated. "It is against our ways for anyone to take something that belongs to another. It is the command of our god that we do not steal but work to produce what we desire and then share." She glanced briefly at her son. "I am afraid that my son Ontolo has been bitten by the snake and has done wrong."

Ontolo stood timidly, his eyes awaiting Jay's answer.

Jay was quite dismayed that Ontolo was in trouble. "Ma'am . . ." Jay knew he was about to contradict the chief's wife and tried to do it carefully. "Ontolo did not steal from me." He looked to Lila for her agreement. "I gave that pencil and paper to Ontolo as a gift when we first met yesterday." He reached into his pocket and brought out a crude knife. "And Ontolo gave me this knife. We're friends."

"That's right," said Lila. "It was a trade."

Bengati was only too happy to relay this to Renyata.

When she heard Jay's words, her grim expression melted. She looked embarrassed as she asked a question in halting English, "The pencil is . . . gift . . . to my Ontolo?"

Jay reached into his pocket and brought out another pencil. "Yes. And please, here is one for you as well."

She received the pencil from Jay's hand and looked at it in wonder. Then she put her arm around her son, and it was easy to see she was apologizing. Their faces brightened, they started smiling, and then, in a purposeful gesture, Renyata put both pencils into Ontolo's hand. "Thank you, Jay Cooper. Thank you for pencils." She looked to Bengati who translated the rest of her words. "I will give them both to my son, Ontolo, because he will know what to do with them."

Then the four Motosas laughed together at some private joke as Chief Gotono rose and gave his son a playful hug. "Come. We eat in my house."

Lunch was delightful, but Ontolo could hardly wait to be excused from the table and to pull Jay with him. The big tree Gotono's house was built around also served as a handy staircase to Ontolo's second story loft, and Ontolo led the way, clambering up the trunk while Jay followed.

Jay had to marvel, even chuckle a bit, at the sight of Ontolo's little room. It seemed very much like a primitive version of Jay's room back home. Instead of posters, skates, balls, and sports trophies, it was decorated with Ontolo's trophies: animal skins; brilliant bird feathers; a cane flute; a colorful, feathered spear; and an impressive breastplate made from leather and bones.

But Ontolo had something specific he wanted Jay to see, and he drew his friend's attention to a corner of the room where pieces of flattened tree bark and the stretched hides of small animals were stacked like schoolbooks on a small table. Ontolo picked up a piece of the bark, a flat, smooth surface about eight inches across, and put it in Jay's hand.

Jay looked at the piece of bark, not knowing what to expect. When he saw the bark was covered with tiny, orderly shapes and squiggles in neat rows, he took more than a second look. These were not just picture symbols or crude depictions of animals and adventures. The small, delicate scratches made with a sharp stick and the dark juice of berries had an unmistakable purpose.

Writing!

Jay pointed at the piece of bark in his hand and asked, "Did Ontolo do this?"

Ontolo nodded happily and immediately showed him a piece of skin stretched over a vine hoop. More writing. Ontolo pointed at the first character and indicated the sound it represented: "Oh." Then the next character and its sound: "Nnnn." Then the next: "Tuh." Then came "Oh," followed by "Llll," and finally, "Oh" again.

Jay pointed at the characters and sounded out the word himself. It was easy. "On-to-lo."

Ontolo got so excited that Jay feared he would fall out of the loft and onto the dinner guests below. "Ontolo!" he shouted, pointing at the word on the skin and then at himself. "Ontolo!"

"Yes," Jay nodded, realizing what he was seeing. "Ontolo. Your name."

"Ontolo is . . ." Ontolo looked around the room until his eyes lighted on the trunk of the big tree that held up the house. He tapped it with his fingers.

Jay tried to figure out what Ontolo was saying. "Ontolo is a tree?"

Ontolo shook his head, laughing at Jay's slowness in catching on. He tapped his chest with both hands. "Ontolo: My name is man . . ." But he couldn't think of the next word in English and tapped the trunk again.

"Man of tree?" Jay guessed.

Ontolo half-nodded and crinkled his face.

"Man of the tree?"

Ontolo only shrugged, not quite satisfied. "Man of the tree. Yes."

Ontolo took the skin from Jay and then, with one of the pencils Jay had given him, wrote two more characters and gave it back. "You see?" He pointed at the first character and made the sound it represented, "Juh."

87

Jay guessed the sound of the second character. "Ay."

Ontolo nodded, pleased with his pupil's progress.

Jay read the whole word. "Jay."

Ontolo laughed, totally pleased with how well this was working.

Jay pointed at the other skins and pieces of bark, all covered with Ontolo's strange marks. "Ontolo, you made all this?"

Ontolo was jubilant. "Yes. Ontolo make, in here!" He tapped his head, indicating it was all his own idea.

Jay was stunned. "Ontolo," he said, putting the skin back in Ontolo's hand, "write what I say."

Ontolo didn't fully understand, so Jay made motions toward his own mouth and then tapped on the skin and pointed at Ontolo's pencil. "Write: *i*." The *i* sound Jay made was like the *i* in *big*. Jay tapped the skin again. "Write it."

"*Eee?*" Ontolo asked.

Jay nodded. "Close enough."

Ontolo shrugged and made a small mark.

"Now write *Nnn*."

Ontolo formed another character, greatly enjoying the feel of the new pencil.

Jay made the sound of *Th,* and Ontolo made a face. He had no mark to represent that sound.

"Well how about *Tuh?*" Jay asked.

Ontolo nodded and scribbled. That would work.

Back in the main room, where the grown-ups visited and Beset was teaching Lila how to weave a beautiful headdress, Dr. Cooper looked up toward the loft where the two boys had been hiding out for quite some time. "It's awfully quiet up there."

Chief Gotono and Bengati laughed together at a private joke, and then the chief explained through Bengati, "I think Ontolo is playing with the pencils. He likes to draw and make funny marks."

"Jay?" Dr. Cooper called.

"Dad!" came Jay's answer as he swung from the loft to the trunk of the tree and started climbing down. "Dad, you've got to see this!"

"See what?"

Both boys came climbing, almost sliding, down the tree, full of excitement. Dr. Cooper had to wonder what was brewing, but the chief didn't seem too alarmed or curious; apparently his kids were always excited about something.

Jay landed on the floor and waited for Ontolo to drop down behind him. "Dad, you won't believe this! It's history, happening right here!"

Chief Gotono looked puzzled and Bengati tried to explain what was going on, though no one in the room really knew.

Jay took the skin from Ontolo and showed it to his father. "Look at this! It's a written alphabet!"

Dr. Cooper's eyes narrowed as he studied the weird little marks. Dr. Henderson hobbled over for a closer look. "An alphabet," he said. "You mean, this is Ontolo's invention?"

Bengati was still translating to the chief. The chief got Dr. Cooper's question and answered it through Bengati. "Like I said, Ontolo likes to make funny marks. He thinks he can make a piece of skin or bark speak words."

"He can!" Jay exclaimed.

"He is pretending," said the chief. "It is a game."

Jay received the skin back from his father and handed it to Ontolo. Then he bowed slightly and addressed the chief with proper respect. "If it please you, sir: Your son Ontolo has put *my* words on this skin, words he does not know but has still captured for all time." He turned to Ontolo. "Ontolo, go ahead: Read."

Ontolo was grinning, excited, and a little nervous as he began to speak the sounds his marks represented. "Een tah bee geening goad kree ate ted ta hay vons ond ta ert."

He looked up. His father seemed puzzled. Obviously the sounds were meaningless to him.

Dr. Cooper was more than pleased. He was awestruck. So was Dr. Henderson, and Lila.

"Is there more?" Dr. Cooper asked.

Jay nodded to Ontolo and Ontolo read some more. "Ond goad sayd late tare bee lite ond tare was lite."

Jacob Cooper chuckled, slowly shaking his head with wonder. "I see your point, Jay. This *is* history."

The chief noticed the response his son was getting from his visitors and asked Bengati about it.

Bengati was a bit awestruck himself and tried to explain.

Lila understood every word Ontolo had read, and repeated them all. "In the beginning, God created the heavens and the earth. And God said, let there be light, and there was light."

"Does Ontolo understand what he has read?" Dr. Cooper asked.

Bengati inquired of the boy, and then answered, "No. Ontolo doesn't know what he has read. He only knows the sounds your son Jay gave him to write down."

"This young man has invented a phonetic alphabet!" Dr. Henderson exclaimed.

"Bengati," said Dr. Cooper, "did *you* understand the words Ontolo just read?"

Bengati's eyes were wide with wonder as he answered, "At first, I did not. But then, when I heard more, I could tell: Ontolo was reading *your* words. English words."

"Tell Chief Gotono that his son has created a way to capture words—anyone's words—and place them on bark or stone or paper." Bengati started to explain this to the chief even as Dr. Cooper continued. "Because of this, your words, the words of your children, the stories of your ancestors . . . anything spoken, can be kept safe, for all time, for all generations."

The chief thought that over, then shrugged a little. He responded through Bengati, "The words of our mouths are kept safely in our heads. We remember the stories; we remember our ancestors and their names and what they did. We tell our children, and they tell their children."

Dr. Cooper respectfully countered, "But now you can receive and understand the words of other men as well. The pages of books can carry their words to you from far away." As Dr. Cooper said this, he opened his hands in front of him, pantomiming opening a book.

All motion in the room ceased abruptly. Chief

Gotono and Bengati stared at Dr. Cooper with widened eyes, then looked at each other. The sudden silence scared Jay and Lila. Had they caused a terrible offense somehow?

Bengati was the first to move again as he pressed his palms together in front of him. He opened them up as if opening a book, his eyes upon the chief, his lips quietly speaking words in Motosa.

The chief looked at Bengati's open hands, then at his creative son, and his lip began to quiver.

Bengati made the book opening gesture again, his eyes wide with wonder as he looked from his hands to Dr. Cooper and back again.

Finally, the chief opened his hands like a book, raised them toward heaven, and then, with deep, quaking sobs, he began to weep.

EIGHT

B ack at Jo-Jota's, Dr. Henderson took a nap while the Coopers visited quietly on the porch, trying to figure out why the chief had suddenly dismissed everyone from his house. Chief Gotono had seemed so troubled, like he needed to be alone with his thoughts. The unveiling of Ontolo's phonetic alphabet had been a special moment, of course. But it seemed to have been the opening-a-book hand gesture that had made the chief weep, and he certainly had not attempted to explain why.

Their little meeting didn't last long. The village drummers, three men and an apprentice no older than ten, took their places outside the big meeting hall and began beating out an intricate, rhythmic song on deep, bass drums, a hollow log, and what appeared to be the steel wheel of an old car.

"It is time!" came a call from across the square. It was Bengati, coming on the run. "Come! We gather for our meeting!"

Lila wasn't ready for socializing. "Right *now?*"

Bengati beckoned. "Come. The chief will speak."

The Coopers scrambled to prepare. Jay didn't

have his shoes on, Dr. Cooper had to put on his shirt, and Lila needed to brush out her hair before she put on the headdress she'd made. As for Dr. Henderson, she didn't feel like going anywhere and started griping about it—whining, actually. But then her four loyal carriers showed up with her chair, and that settled that.

They hurried with the other villagers to the meeting hall and got there just in time. Bengati showed them to a log bench off to the side where he could quietly interpret the proceedings for them.

All the people, young and old alike, had gathered once again, sitting row upon row, dressed in colorful woven garments and dangling, clinking jewelry of leather, bone, and stone. There was a dull murmur in the crowd as people visited quietly; one or two babies cried.

Suddenly, without introduction or explanation, a man stepped onto the large, flat speaker's stone and started singing—or was it chanting? His voice was a powerful tenor, and the melody soared like the flight of a barn swallow. He sang a line of the song, and the people, as one voice, echoed it back with great power and hauntingly beautiful harmony. It gave Jay and Lila goosebumps.

The chanter delivered the next line of the song. The people echoed it back once again. Then came another line and another echo, and so it went. As the song progressed, it built in emotion and volume. As it ended, many in the group closed their eyes as if in prayer, closing themselves in with their own thoughts and feelings, their bodies swaying with the music.

More songs followed, and it was easy to see that these people weren't just having a singalong around a campfire. They meant deep, spiritual business.

Dr. Cooper was totally fascinated, leaning forward in his seat, watching and listening. Finally, he turned to Jay and Lila and said, "I think we're in church."

Jay and Lila nodded. That's what it looked, sounded, and felt like, all right. They stole a look at Dr. Henderson, and were startled to find that she was quite captivated, unconsciously swaying to the music, a rare smile on her face.

When the singing ended, it left a very sweet and peaceful mood about the place.

"Now the chief will speak," Bengati whispered.

With his full headdress in place and his arms outstretched, Chief Gotono got the immediate, respectful attention of his people. He began his speech—or was it a sermon?—in his characteristic, booming voice.

Bengati leaned close to the Coopers and Dr. Henderson and began to explain in a hushed voice what the chief was talking about. "The chief is telling the story of his father's father, Chief Landzi, who first brought our people here from across the desert and found water when he struck the rock."

When Bengati leaned away to listen some more, Dr. Cooper exchanged a quizzical, puzzled look with his kids.

"Dad," said Jay, "doesn't this sound like the story of Moses?"

Dr. Cooper had no time to answer. Bengati was

leaning toward them again, quietly recounting the chief's message out of the corner of his mouth. "Now the water is gone, but the chief says that if we turn from evil and seek after God, God will answer us and bring us water from the mighty Stone in the desert."

The chief raised his voice even louder and pointed west toward the mountain-sized Stone. Bengati explained, "The chief says that God has sent His holy mountain to speak to the tribe. Just as He sent Ontolo to save Mobutu, He has sent this Stone."

"Ontolo? Are you talking about—" Jay started to ask, but the sermon ended and another song began. This time the people stood to sing, clapping and waving their hands.

When the meeting ended, Dr. Cooper suggested, "Let's get back to Jo-Jota's and compare notes. The whole idea of the Motosas being savages and cannibals just doesn't hold up."

They sat on the big front porch and watched the village kids play while Jo-Jota brought them slices of bread and melon to snack on.

Dr. Henderson took a refreshing bite of melon and commented, "Sure, I found their rituals fascinating and their music enjoyable, but I see nothing unusual about their religious beliefs. They believe they've offended their god and so their god has taken away their water. It seems an appropriate myth for a primitive, agricultural society."

"That's not what's unusual," said Dr. Cooper, "What's unusual is that their religious system has no trappings of paganism: no magic rituals, no appeasing of evil spirits, no nature worship . . ."

"No idols," Lila added.

"That's right," said Jay. "And they only have one god, not several."

"That's the first thing that caught my attention," said Dr. Cooper, leaning forward in his chair. "They don't have a rain god, or a sun god, or a god of fertility, or a god of the crops or seasons or whatever. Their god is bigger than all that. Consider that Stone out there. Any other pagan culture would have fallen into worshiping that thing, sacrificing to it, chanting and using magic to appease it. But these people have a god big enough to have created it and put it there. Their god is bigger than nature, bigger than creation."

Dr. Henderson finished chewing her piece of melon. "Dr. Cooper, I suppose you want to believe that these people are Christians or something?"

Jay, Lila, and Dr. Cooper all checked each other's eyes and knew immediately that they shared the same suspicion. Dr. Cooper put it into words. "They may not be Christians in the way we would think— not Baptists, or Methodists, or Pentecostals. But considering that no modern-day missionary has ever come to these people to preach Christianity, I can't help wondering about the similarities."

"What similarities, if I may ask?" said Dr. Henderson.

"One god, bigger than all creation, who created all things, who tells these people what is right and wrong."

Jay piped in, "He teaches them that stealing is wrong, that they should work hard and share."

"And it's obvious that these people have a personal relationship with their god. They love him."

Jay asked, "So who's the Ontolo the chief talked about? I mean, I don't think he meant his son when he spoke about how God sent Ontolo to save Mobutu."

"And who is Mobutu," Dr. Cooper asked, "other than our somewhat shady host on the other side?"

Jay had already decided, "I'm going to ask Ontolo. I want to hear that story."

Dr. Cooper nodded. "And I'm going to have a heart-to-heart talk with the chief to find out where their religion really came from, where they got their stories and traditions."

"Like the one about the snake," said Lila.

They looked at her curiously.

"Don't you remember? When Renyata thought Ontolo had stolen Jay's pencil, she said that Ontolo was bitten by the snake, and that's why he did wrong."

Jay's and Dr. Cooper's faces brightened with recollection.

And then, like a bolt of electricity, the possible meaning of that expression hit them all.

"Ooohhhh boy . . ." said Lila.

"Where's Bengati?" Dr. Cooper asked, jumping to his feet.

The chief agreed to meet with Jacob Cooper the next morning. When Dr. Cooper arrived, the chief was sitting outside behind his home, carefully carving another staff, this one for his son.

"The staff of my father tells the story of our family in pictures," he said through Bengati. "But now I think Ontolo will want a staff on which he can make his own marks."

Dr. Cooper and Bengati sat with Chief Gotono under the shade of the big tree his house was built around. It was just the three of them, and the chief seemed quite relaxed. Dr. Cooper hoped this would be a good time to ask some big questions. Through Bengati, they began to converse.

"Chief Gotono, I hope all is well."

"All is very well, Dr. Cooper. I have had much to think about in a short time. You are right. Ontolo's strange marks can capture words that will remain for all time and can bring us the words of other men. Our God has chosen many ways to speak to us, but I never thought He would speak through the little marks created by my own son."

"Chief Gotono, can you tell me how you came to know your god?"

The chief looked thoughtfully at the staff he was carving as he spoke and Bengati translated. "There was once a young man who had many gods. His gods were in the sun, and in the moon, and in the trees, and in the crops. Some gods helped his people bear children, and some gods took the children away through death. But there were too many gods, and they were too small, and they would not speak. They would not tell the people what is right and what is wrong.

"So, this young man knew in his heart that there

had to be one God who made all things and supplies all things and can teach the people how they should live."

The chief looked toward the rugged mountains that rose above the grassy plain, his thoughts going back into history. "I journeyed into the desert and knelt in the sand, asking this great God to reveal Himself. And God spoke to me and said, 'Because you seek me with all your heart, you will learn of me, for I will reveal myself in everyday things.' And so it has been." The chief smiled, but his eyes were still sad. "We have heard from our God, but we still wait to hear His name, to know who He really is."

Dr. Cooper's heart went out to this man. "Chief Gotono, there is a wonderful book you must see." He pressed his palms together, then opened them as if opening a book. He could tell the chief recognized the gesture immediately. "It will tell you the name of your God."

The chief held up his hand. "First, I must tell you a dream I had. But you must tell no one else."

Dr. Cooper agreed and listened to the dream.

Lila and Beset sat together in the grass in front of the chief's house, working on a headdress even more lovely than the first.

"Beset . . ."

"Yes, Lila?"

"Do you remember when your mother thought Ontolo had stolen the pencil from Jay?"

Beset cocked her head and focused on Lila with

her huge, dark brown eyes. "Yes. What is in your thinking?"

"Your mother said Ontolo was bitten by the snake. What does that mean?"

Beset smiled, removed the headdress from Lila's head, and then spoke as she adjusted its size. "It means, Ontolo has done a bad thing. Ontolo did not steal pencil, but my mother did not know, so she say Ontolo bitten by the snake." She looked at Lila directly. "You are good. Your father, your brother, they good. But many people are bad. They do bad things, they are not kind. We say they are bitten by the snake. It is a story we tell."

Beset put the headdress on Lila's head again to check the size. "Long ago, we all had the same mother. You, me, my mother and father, all had the same mother. One day, a snake say to her, 'Come to my tree, and I give you something to eat,' but she say, 'I cannot eat your food, it will kill me.' But the snake say, 'No, you eat my food, you be very wise, and you never die.' So she come to the tree to get food, but then the snake bit her. He poison her. He put in her bad things: hate, and stealing, and bad thoughts and anger. And then she die."

She removed the headdress, satisfied with its fit, and picked up more yarn to weave around the headband. "Now all her children have the same poison. They do bad things, think bad things, and they die. So when someone do something bad, we say, 'They are bitten by the snake.'"

Lila could feel her heart pounding and her hands shaking. She tried to relax, not wanting Beset to be concerned, but her voice still quivered just a bit when she asked, "Beset, where did that story come from?"

Beset shrugged. "It is a story we tell. And now Ontolo has made the story on skins with his little marks."

"We have a story like that. It's—"

"Dad!" came a cry from the forest beyond the village. It was Jay's voice, and he sounded absolutely beside himself. "Dad! Lila!"

Lila and Beset leaped to their feet, expecting something terrible, and ran to the edge of the forest. Dr. Cooper and Chief Gotono had heard Jay's cry and also came on the run.

"Dad!" came Jay's voice again.

"Jay!" Dr. Cooper responded. "Where are you?"

They heard the thrashing of brush and the pounding of footsteps and finally saw Jay and Ontolo racing out of the forest like two wild men.

Jay spotted his father and dashed over, grabbing him. "Dad! You won't believe it!"

Dr. Cooper suddenly had his hands full of wildly excited son. "Are you all right?"

"You won't believe it!" Jay hollered again. "Back there, in the forest!"

"What!? Jay, calm down!"

"Ontolo showed me, he told me about it, and you'll never believe it!"

The chief was grilling Ontolo, trying to find out what all the hubbub was about. Ontolo wasn't nearly as excited, but he was getting a real kick out of watching Jay have a fit. He started to give his father an explanation.

"You gotta see it, Dad!" Jay insisted, tugging at his father. "You won't believe it!"

Dr. Cooper had to get firm. "Won't believe *what?*"

Jay finally got it out. "The Man in the Tree!"

Dr. Cooper immediately looked at the chief, hoping for some explanation.

By now the chief had been brought up to date by his son, and he answered, "Ontolo!"

Dr. Cooper didn't know what to think of that and just stood there, waiting to hear more.

Jay was giddy with excitement. "Ontolo! The name Ontolo means Man in the Tree! I thought it meant Man of the Woods or something, but it means Man in the Tree!" He tugged his father's arm again. "Come on! You won't believe it."

Lila was one big bundle of curiosity. "Let's go!"

"Where are we going?" Dr. Cooper asked as he followed his son.

"Ontolo!" the chief said again with a laugh. "Man in the Tree!"

Dr. Cooper looked around for Bengati and found him, following right behind. "I am here, Dr. Cooper. Don't worry."

They entered the forest, walking down a well-beaten path among the giant, gnarled trees that had stood here for centuries through rain, drought, wind, and sun.

Dr. Cooper asked Bengati, "What is it we're going to see?"

Bengati looked at the chief, who began to relate a story as Bengati translated. "There once was a young man who stole a pig from a neighboring tribe. When warriors from that tribe tried to chase him, he came to this forest and hid in a tree. They would have found him, except a bolt of lightning struck a tree nearby, breaking off a large branch and leaving a scar on the tree that was shaped like a man. The warriors saw that shape, and shot their arrows at it. They thought they had killed the thief, and so they left."

This sounded like the chief's other story about the young man, Dr. Cooper thought. "And you were that young man, Chief Gotono?"

The chief smiled and came to a stop by a huge tree with deeply furrowed bark and thick limbs. With a wide sweep of his hand, he indicated the trail that still wound through the forest toward the mountains. "I was the young man who fled with a stolen pig. I ran up this very trail," he pointed to the huge tree beside him, "and climbed this very tree. There is the branch on which I sat while my pursuers came looking for me."

Now the chief grew very solemn, his hard gaze commanding everyone's attention. "But do you understand, Dr. Cooper, that our God saved me from my pursuers when I deserved to die? God sent lightning from the sky and put another man in a tree to take my punishment."

The chief turned onto a side trail that led through the brush toward another tree as large and gnarled as the first. The others followed. He stopped on the far side of the tree and looked up, pointing. "Ever since that night, our people have remembered the Man in the Tree who took away my punishment, and I have given his name to my son as a remembrance."

Jay and Lila got to the front of the tree before their father. Dr. Cooper could see Jay pointing and Lila looking, and then he saw Lila's face go pale as her eyes widened with awe—or was it fear?

He came around the tree and looked up to see where the chief was pointing.

And then he froze as well. Words failed him. All he could do was look and try to believe what he was seeing.

About twenty feet up the big, gnarled trunk, a large limb had been blasted off by lightning, leaving a gaping scar where wood and bark had been torn away. The shape of the scar looked like a man: Bark had been peeled to form a body and two legs, and where two upper limbs had broken off, the scars looked like the man's outstretched arms. Just above the arms, a burl formed the shape of a drooping head.

The Man in the Tree appeared to be impaled there, hanging by his arms. A few broken arrows could still be seen embedded in the bare wood, shot there by the chief's pursuers so long ago, and part of a spear was still embedded in the man's side.

NINE

"The Man in the Tree . . ." Jay said in a hushed voice. "On-To-Lo."

Dr. Cooper quoted the chief's words as a question, "'God sent Ontolo to save Mobutu'?"

Bengati asked the chief about it, and the chief nodded and answered through Bengati, "Mobutu was my name when I was young, before I became Gotono, the chief. That night, God showed me my guilt and the price that guilt can bring, but He paid the price Himself and let me live to do what is right. He spoke to me and revealed Himself, just as He said He would. I returned the pig to its owners and also gave them two of my goats to pay for my wrong. I have never stolen again, and my people have learned never to steal. Through Ontolo, the Man in the Tree, our God has spoken."

"Just like the Lady and the Snake," said Lila, tugging on her father's arm.

"What's that?" Dr. Cooper asked.

"Beset just told me another story. Listen to this." She quickly recounted it to her father and brother.

They were awestruck, overwhelmed.

"Man, oh man, oh man," Jay muttered.

"Your God *has* spoken," Dr. Cooper told the chief in a hushed voice. "I must tell you, we have stories just like yours of a lady and a snake and especially of a man nailed to a tree—" Suddenly his legs felt weak and shaky.

Lila's legs seemed to be trembling as well, and she almost lost her balance.

Jay looked down to see if he'd stepped on uneven ground.

Then a low, ominous, rumbling sound reached their ears. The branches of the big trees began to quiver overhead; the leaves began to tremble.

The chief shouted a phrase as he toppled to his knees, his eyes skyward. Bengati toppled as well as he translated, "He speaks again! Our God speaks again!"

"The Stone!" Dr. Cooper exclaimed.

They started to run back up the trail, staggering, weaving to and fro, bracing themselves against one tree and then another as the ground constantly shifted under their feet. They could not see the Stone from these woods, but they could still hear the deep, rumbling sound, like a mighty avalanche, echoing all around them.

When they finally emerged from the trees, they met Dr. Henderson, hopping and hobbling toward them, using a long stick for a crutch and fighting every second to remain on her feet. "Dr. Cooper, where have you been? The Stone's waking up!"

The earth reeled again. Jacob Cooper ran to Dr. Henderson and caught her just before she fell. "Hang onto my arm."

She grabbed on, dropping the stick. Together they

hurried up the path as the ground continued to rumble under their feet. Motosas ran from their homes, down the paths, and through their village.

But wait. The villagers were not running in panic or fear. They were hurrying—men, women, and children—out of the village and onto the open grasslands where they gathered like excited spectators to gawk at the Stone, pointing, chattering, even praying. To see the looks on their faces, this wasn't a dangerous natural event—it was a spiritual visitation!

"We've got to get out there," Dr. Henderson gasped, trying to walk. "We've got to observe what it's doing."

The rumbling began to subside; the shaking settled down to a small quiver. By the time they reached the village square, the earth was quiet again. The village was empty, but nothing appeared to be damaged, and apparently no one was hurt.

"We need the binoculars and the surveying equipment," said Dr. Henderson. "We have to note *any* changes in size, shape, position—*anything.*"

"I'll get my knapsack!" said Lila, running back toward Jo-Jota's.

"We'll have to bring the transit from the airplane," said Dr. Cooper.

"Let's get out there!" said Dr. Henderson.

The Motosas were starting to trickle back into the village. For now the show was over.

"Good thing the villagers are coming back," said Dr. Henderson. "That thing's unstable. It could erupt; it could topple; pieces of it could break off. . . . We don't know *what* it could do."

"We're going out to study it," Dr. Cooper told the chief. "But please, tell your people to remain here. It may not be safe to get too close."

The chief nodded and gave the order. The Motosas called to their stragglers, who began to return. Then Chief Gotono said to Dr. Cooper in English, "But I will come. I will see Stone, hear Stone speak."

Lila returned with her knapsack. "Here's the equipment. Did I miss anything?"

"Not yet," said her father, taking the knapsack. "But I think I see a problem developing." He noticed the look on Ontolo's and Beset's faces when they saw Jay and Lila all set for a trek into the desert.

Ontolo started to argue with his father, pointing at Jay and Lila, and it was easy to guess what the topic was.

"Uh, Jay and Lila," said Dr. Cooper, "I have a difficult favor to ask of you, and I hope you'll understand. You know I'd take you along without hesitation, but you see the situation developing here? If you go with us, then Ontolo and Beset will want to go, and if they can go, then the rest of the villagers will feel they should be able to go as well, and we'll end up creating a huge safety risk."

Both Jay and Lila slouched with disappointment. They couldn't help it.

"Guess you're right," Lila moaned.

Jay needed a moment to think it over but then called to Ontolo, "Ontolo! Let's go! Show me your game!"

That sounded good to Ontolo. With Jay and Lila in the lead, the four kids ran back into the village.

Dr. Henderson was impressed. "Those are good kids you have."

Dr. Cooper nodded as he watched them go. "The best." He started picking up the equipment. "Shall we?"

Ontolo ran home and returned to the village square with a weird, fuzzy ball fashioned from goathide and stuffed with nutshells instead of being inflated with air. All he had to do was walk through the square with that thing and all the other children came running, ready to break into teams and get the game going. Lila was assigned to Ontolo's team; Jay was assigned to the other team, captained by a friend of Ontolo named Suti.

Beset, knowing the most English, explained the rules to Jay and Lila, pacing off the boundaries of the playing field in the village square. "Jay kick ball this way . . . Lila kick ball *this* way . . ." The game looked like a combination of soccer and basketball: the ball was moved with the feet, but tossed by hand through a squarish goal once the player was close enough.

Ontolo's team threw the ball into play from the sidelines and the game began. Jay and Lila had both played soccer as well as basketball, so they were able to dive right into the game and keep the ball moving. The Motosa kids didn't know English, but they knew a good game when they saw it. Before long, Jay and Lila were fully accepted as valuable teammates, and when Jay scored his first point, his teammates were ready to make him an honorary Motosa.

At the edge of the grasslands, on the brink of the desert, Dr. Henderson and Dr. Cooper could see things were stirring around the Stone. A thin cloud of dust still lingered above the desert floor from the quaking, and high above the Stone's crest, ice particles that had been shaken loose were being carried away in wispy clouds by the wind.

Dr. Henderson scanned the upper edge through binoculars. "I don't want to believe this, but we might have some expansion happening along the top edge."

She handed Dr. Cooper the binoculars, and he checked it out. Almost two miles above them, the sharp edge of the Stone had a white, frosty edge. Large cracks had appeared in the ice as if the edge had stretched. "I see what you mean." Then he gave the binoculars back and directed her attention to the Stone's northwest corner. "And unless my eyes deceive me, there's a new ridge of dirt piled against the Stone."

She could see freshly disturbed earth all along the Stone's length, just like dirt pushed in front of a bulldozer's blade. "My *word!* It's growing. And yet . . . there are no growth cracks in the Stone itself, only in the ice and in the earth at the base."

She handed the binoculars to Chief Gotono and Bengati, who called them the Big Eyes. Having heard Dr. Cooper and Dr. Henderson's conversation,

Bengati was able to explain to the chief what was happening, and the chief nodded as he saw it for himself.

"We'll get the transit from the airplane to do some sightings," said Dr. Cooper. "Let's pace things off and triangulate and see if what we think has happened has really happened." With help from the chief and Bengati, Dr Cooper and Dr. Henderson began to measure the Stone's new dimensions.

At that very moment, high atop the rocky cliffs that pressed against the Stone's north end, three figures stole carefully over the rocks until they found a hiding place in a deep crack. They were tough, battle-hardened scouts from Idi Nkromo's army, dressed in camouflage fatigues and armed with rifles, pistols, and knives. They had hiked, climbed, and explored these hills for a day and a night, trying to find a route over them and around the Stone. Their efforts were finally rewarded. From this vantage point, they could view the entire desert on the Stone's west side, and through binoculars they spotted Dr. Cooper and Dr. Henderson, along with two men from the Motosa village—just four tiny figures on the barren landscape. They muttered words of victory to each other and started to lay plans.

Dr. Cooper scribbled some calculations on his writing pad, gazed through the transit one more time to doublecheck, and then ran the numbers again. "Well, the figures confirm what we've seen: The Stone has grown roughly 240 feet in both height and width."

"And yet it hasn't changed shape at all," Dr. Henderson mused. Dr. Cooper looked long and hard at the Stone, coming to a conclusion he found difficult. "The Stone isn't real, is it—not in the normal, material sense?"

Dr. Henderson thought the question over, then shook her head. "It's there, it's observable, and by all appearances it's physical. It's as hard as a diamond, maybe harder. It's shaking and gouging the earth. And yet, you're absolutely right: There *is* something unreal about it." She looked at him, and he could see fear in her eyes. "I guess I'm trying to say it's not of this world."

The village square had never seen such a hubbub. The two white-skinned foreigners turned out to be fierce competitors, very good with their feet, and their skill and determination only made the others play harder, loving every minute of it. The grown-ups, fascinated and amused by the sight, began gathering on the porches and along the edges of the playing area to cheer their teams on. Beset had scored a goal for Suti's team, but Lila came right back by catching a rebound off a teammate's head and hurling the ball through the goal. The score was even, three to three.

Suti took the ball out of bounds for his team as

arms went up everywhere trying to block his throw. Jay scurried into the clear along the side boundary line, and Suti shot the ball to him.

Blocked! A tall, stringbean of a kid diverted the ball with his hand, and it went sailing toward one of the houses. Lila was closest and went racing after it, hoping to take possession before it went out of bounds.

Too late. The ball rolled over the line, bounced through a flock of chickens that went scurrying and flapping, then rolled under a house. Lila dropped to her hands and knees, brushed the grass aside, and peered into the dark recesses under the thatched structure. She thought she saw the ball resting near a large corner post that held the house up, so she hurried closer on her hands and knees. Yes, there was the ball, almost hidden behind the large square stone that served as a footing for the post.

She reached for the ball. It was just beyond the reach of her fingertips. She stretched further—then stopped.

The kids were eager to continue the game. She could hear them shuffling and waiting.

But for the moment, her mind and eyes were pulled away from the lost ball. She turned her head and took a second look.

A large, square, reddish stone . . .

Now the kids were hollering at her. She could hear Beset calling, "Hurry up! Hurry up!"

She brushed aside some grass with her hand. The stone was cut, chipped, chiseled into a square shape. It was—

114

So suddenly it startled her, a ray of sunlight broke through the grass and shadows and lit up the side of the footing stone, making it sparkle. She spun her head and looked toward the east.

Just over the tops of the houses, through the leafy treetops, she saw the sun peeking over the top of the Stone in the desert like a fiery sunrise. One thin beam of light pierced through the trees, seeking out that one little stone right next to her.

"Jay," she called, her voice choked with fear, excitement, awe, shock, amazement. She called again, "Jay!" and then she nearly screamed, "JAY!"

He came on the run, afraid she'd hurt herself, been bitten by a snake or spider, broken a leg, gotten pinned under the house. "What! Are you all right?"

"Jay . . ." By now she was panting with excitement, rising to her knees, pointing at the foundation stone. "Jay, look!"

Jay looked and saw the foundation stone. He didn't get her point.

And then he did. He cocked his head to one side and looked again, his eyes tracing the beam of light from the little foundation stone to the sun now rising over the Stone in the desert. Pieces, thoughts, ideas were coming together in his mind.

Lila had already put several things together. "It's a foundation stone, Jay! It holds the house up!"

By now, Ontolo and Beset had come over to see what all the fuss was about. "Lila is hurt?" Beset asked.

Lila didn't answer that question but quickly

asked them a question of her own. "Do *all* the houses have stones like this?"

Ontolo looked at Beset who translated the question as best she could, but neither of them seemed sure they'd understood Lila correctly.

Lila scrambled to see for herself. She ran around to the rear corner of the house, swished the grass aside, and found another reddish, square stone just like the first. Jay went with her, and soon they discovered that not only this house, but also just about every house, was sitting on the same, reddish, square stones.

"Ontolo," said Jay, his voice broken with excitement. "Ontolo, why?"

Ontolo's face said, *Why what?*

"Beset." Jay beckoned to her urgently. "Beset, why are the houses built on these stones?"

She understood the question, but shrugged as if it held no importance. "Houses . . . stay strong. Houses not sink."

Lila and Jay exchanged excited looks.

"I think I'd better go and get Dad," Lila said with a trembling voice.

Jay concurred. "I think you're right."

Lila took off running through the village square, out of the village and out over the grasslands.

But no sooner had she left when there was a rustling and babbling in the crowd and Jay looked up to see the chief and Bengati returning from another direction, along with Dr. Cooper and Dr. Henderson.

"Dad!" he called.

Dr. Cooper and the other three could tell something was brewing. The chief asked immediately, "What happen here?"

Jay beckoned to them and then pointed to the foundation stone Lila had uncovered. "Bengati, why are all the houses built on these stones?"

Both the chief and Bengati chuckled as if they'd heard a silly question. Bengati answered, "To keep the houses from sinking into the ground. Long ago, it rained much, and then the ground would become soft and the houses would sink and the posts would rot. So we learned to build upon these stones."

"But . . ." Jay wasn't getting the answer he wanted. "But every house is built this way. Is this, you know, another tradition?"

Bengati was translating for the chief, who explained as Bengati interpreted, "Yes. It is something taught us by our forefathers. The rocks are like our God, you see? Our God is like a solid stone under our feet to keep us from sinking. When I stand on a large stone in our meeting hall, and when we build our houses this way, it shows us how we must build our lives upon our God."

Jay pointed at the foundation stone. "Why are they cut square?"

Bengati and the chief exchanged puzzled looks as if they'd heard another silly question, and then Bengati ventured an answer. "So they will not roll. So they will stand there and not move."

Dr. Cooper was already looking to the east as Jay said, "Look, Dad! Look at the Stone! It's cut out, carved, just like the foundation stones. It's square, and flat, and solid, and doesn't roll away."

Jacob Cooper was also figuring it out. "The wise man . . ." he murmured as he looked at the huge Stone in the desert and then at the small foundation stone. "Matthew chapter seven: 'Everyone who hears these things I say and obeys them is like a wise man. The wise man built his house on rock. It rained hard and the water rose. The winds blew and hit that house. But the house did not fall, because the house was built on rock.'"

Bengati translated the words to the chief, and he nodded. "Yes," he said through Bengati, "this is our tradition."

Dr. Cooper's voice was hushed with awe. "In a way, the Stone *is* speaking!"

TEN

The chief and Bengati drew near as Dr. Cooper removed his hat, nervously ran his fingers through his blond hair, and bored holes in the ground with his eyes. Jacob Cooper was thinking, formulating, riddle-solving, overwhelmed by the thoughts now streaming into his head.

"The Stone," he muttered, "a stone of stumbling, a rock of offense . . . signs in the wilderness . . ." Then he stiffened as if hit with a bullet—it was actually another thought that came to him with the *force* of a bullet. "Water from the rock! Water from the rock, *of course!*"

Dr. Cooper dug out his notebook and pen and started scribbling down his thoughts even as he spoke them, mostly to himself, but also to Dr. Henderson and Jay. "God spoke in special ways in the Bible; He used object lessons like . . ." Scribble scribble. "The tabernacle in the wilderness . . . the brass serpent Moses raised on the pole . . . the sacrificial lamb, and Abraham almost sacrificing his son Isaac . . . the Passover feast before the Hebrews left Egypt . . . Jonah in the belly of the fish for three days and three nights . . . the stone that brought forth water when Moses struck it!"

"I don't get it," said Dr. Henderson.

Dr. Cooper was getting excited. "These people have been seeking after God. Their chief went into the desert and asked God to reveal Himself, and now I'm convinced that God has answered that prayer. He's been showing Himself to these people."

"Exactly," said Jay.

"He's been speaking in symbols, stories, object lessons: the story about the Lady and the snake, the account of the tribal chief who brought his people here and struck a rock that brought forth water, the Man in the Tree, the stones they build their houses on, and now . . ." Dr. Cooper took several steps across the square and extended his hand toward the mountainous Stone that towered like a sentinel over the village. "The Stone in the Desert! The greatest, mightiest Stone of all! A stone of stumbling, a rock of offense . . ."

"What?" Dr. Henderson exclaimed. "Would you mind decoding all this for me?"

Jacob Cooper was becoming jubilant as more scriptures came to mind. "Remember Jesus quoting the Old Testament scripture about the stone the builders rejected becoming the cornerstone? Jesus was referring to Himself. He was calling Himself the cornerstone, the stone upon which we build our faith, our very lives!"

"But for those who don't believe," Jay recalled, "he'd be a stone of stumbling and a rock of offense. He'd only get people upset."

"Like His Excellency Nkromo and his bunch on the other side," Dr. Cooper said with a wink.

Bengati translated all of Jacob Cooper's words, and as the people all around the square heard them, they were spellbound. The kickball game was forgotten. The children and fathers and mothers and warriors and workers began to draw closer, wanting to hear more.

Now Dr. Cooper turned to the Motosas and said, "People, I believe you are right about the Stone. I believe your God sent it."

Dr. Henderson sniffed a little chuckle. "Well, that's what you should have told them all along."

"For *your* God is also *my* God."

That turned her head. "But hey, take it easy!"

Dr. Cooper continued to speak as Bengati translated. "Your God has spoken to you through stories and traditions," he said, "and through the Man in the Tree. Now He speaks through this mighty Stone that He has sent!" Dr. Cooper thought of another scripture. "In the Bible . . ." He thought he'd better explain what the Bible was. "Uh, God's words, written for all to see—"

The chief broke into a glowing smile and made the opening-a-book hand gesture. "My dream, Dr. Cooper. Remember my dream!"

That got Dr. Cooper all the more excited, to the point of preaching. "The words of God say that the stone is precious to those who believe, but will be hated and rejected by those who do not believe. Well, we were always wondering why you were never afraid of the Stone when the people who live in the east are terrified. Now we understand. No one has to be afraid of the Stone if they know the Savior it represents. Chief Gotono, we know this Savior! We know His name! He is—"

Just then, everyone heard a distant scream coming from the desert.

"What was that?" Dr. Henderson asked, alarmed.

Dr. Cooper knew his daughter's voice. "Lila!" He looked around immediately, verifying she was not present.

Jay suddenly came to awareness. "Oh man, in all the excitement I forgot! She went into the desert to look for you!"

"What?"

"She saw that stone under the house and made the connection and ran to get you to tell you and . . ."

"And she's still out there?"

Chief Gotono had heard the scream as well. "Lila, your girl?"

"Yes!"

The chief bellowed the information to his people, and there was an immediate babble of concern. Some of the kids were ready to run right out and find Lila but were held back by protective parents. Several warriors, better skilled for the task, ran for their spears.

"We go," said the chief. "We find the girl Lila!"

Dr. Henderson grabbed the stick she'd been using as a cane. "And I'm going too."

Dr. Cooper and Jay, Dr. Henderson, Chief Gotono, Bengati, and six warriors hurried out of the village and across the grasslands, calling Lila's name, fanning out, heading for the desert.

Chief Ontolo sent his warriors in several different directions, some south and north across the grasslands and some straight into the desert. Then he, Bengati, Dr. Cooper, and Jay ran straight ahead, toward the Stone, calling Lila's name. Dr. Henderson followed as quickly as she could.

They came to the place where Dr. Cooper and the others had set up the transit and done the surveying and calculations. It was the most likely spot where Lila would have come in her search for them, but she was nowhere to be found.

The chief shouted in a voice with the power of a ship's horn, "LILA!"

The Stone echoed back with incredible clarity, "LILA!"

They crossed the grasslands while warriors continued to search to the north and south of them, then pressed on into the desert where rocks the size of houses and cars cluttered the sandy landscape as if they'd fallen from the sky. The afternoon sun was growing hot, and the desert was becoming like an oven. They wouldn't last long out here without shelter—but neither would Lila.

They spread out, the chief to the right, Bengati to the left, the Coopers and Dr. Henderson straight ahead. The terrain was getting rougher, rockier. Dr. Cooper, Jay, and Dr. Henderson had to start climbing over and working their way around massive rock formations.

When they reached the bottom of a rocky hollow, Dr. Cooper stopped. "She wouldn't have come this way looking for us. She knew we were surveying, and you can't do that from here."

They started to turn back.

Three soldiers, rifles ready, leaped from behind the rocks and stood in their path. It happened so quickly it startled them, and Dr. Henderson almost lost her balance.

They heard a clattering on either side and saw more soldiers, at least twenty, popping up from behind the rocks, aiming rifles at them. They were surrounded, with no way to escape.

They raised their hands in surrender. The soldiers rushed in, shouting orders they couldn't understand, grabbing them, checking them for weapons, handling them roughly.

Dr. Cooper tried to explain their situation. "I'm Dr. Jacob Cooper and—"

An officer hauled back his arm as if to strike him.

Dr. Cooper shut his mouth and said no more.

Jabbing with their rifles, the soldiers forced them to walk, and they began the hazardous journey to the forbidding and treacherous hills that pressed against the Stone's north side.

The forced hike around the Stone and down into the desert to the east took several long, grueling hours. Prodded along by their captors, Dr. Cooper, Jay, and Dr. Henderson followed a twisting, winding, barely discernible path through the rock formations and boulders, up steep rock faces, over featureless, rocky shelves as hot as a griddle, and along narrow ledges with hardly enough room to walk. When Dr. Henderson lagged behind, the soldiers half-carried, half-dragged her to make her keep up.

Steadily, painfully, they made it out of the hills

and down to the flat desert on the Stone's east side, their feet and ankles aching, their bodies exhausted, their throats dry and crying out for water.

Then came a sight all three had expected. Up ahead, among the large, scattered rocks, the armies of Idi Nkromo had pitched camp in the shadow of the Stone. His Excellency must have developed new boldness to venture this close.

They entered the army camp past the camouflaged, desert-colored tents where soldiers nervously cleaned their guns, sharpened their knives, and watched them pass with steely, cold expressions. All of Nkromo's trucks, tanks, and cannons were there, lined up in a row, facing west, as maintenance personnel swarmed over them quickly, frantically, like ants in a disturbed anthill. There was tension in the air, as tight as an overwound clock. And fear. The Coopers noticed how often the soldiers looked to the west to see what the Stone might be doing.

They reached the center of the camp and stood before an especially large tent. By all the colorful banners draped across its front, the rope fence stretched all around it, and the armed guards watching over it, they easily guessed that it was the field barracks of His Excellency, Field Marshal Idi Nkromo.

"Dad!" came a welcome voice.

Dr. Cooper's heart leaped as he saw Lila, safe, but in the custody of another band of soldiers. The soldiers released her to run to her father and brother, and she embraced them with tears in her eyes. "I went out to find you, and they grabbed me. I thought I'd never see you again!"

"It's okay, sis," said Jay. "We're together now, no matter what else happens!"

There was a shout and the beating of a huge drum. Any soldier not occupied with the prisoners snapped to attention and all eyes went toward the field marshal's tent. The tent door flapped open. Some guards stepped out to take their places on either side. Then, with as big and impressive an entrance as he could muster, His Excellency stepped out of his tent wearing battle fatigues, a kettle-sized helmet, a saber in a scabbard, and several pounds of medals. He was most unhappy and glared at the prisoners with big round eyes as he stomped toward them.

"Well . . ." said Jacob Cooper, spotting Chief Secretary D. M. Mobutu following right behind Nkromo, also decked out in fatigues, gold braids, and medals.

Nkromo stopped abruptly just a few yards in front of them, planting both feet in the sand with a precisely timed military stomp. D. M. Mobutu marched up smartly and stopped alongside his boss. Mobutu was looking a little shaky and seemed to be avoiding Dr. Cooper's eyes.

"So we meet again, Dr. Cooper!" Nkromo growled. "You and your band of thieves and traitors and spies! How dare you try to flee the country with my airplane!"

"What?" Dr. Henderson squawked. "That's the biggest pile of baloney I ever heard! We got caught in a storm and crashed! We almost got killed!"

Nkromo cocked an eyebrow. "You look fine to me."

Jennifer Henderson stuck out her injured leg. "Yeah, like I always walk around with a crutch!"

Dr. Cooper locked eyes with Mobutu. "Mr. Mobutu, you did tell him you provided us with that airplane, didn't you?"

Mr. Mobutu maintained a straight, military posture as he said, "If His Excellency says you stole the airplane, then you stole it."

Dr. Henderson had some choice words she wanted to share with Mobutu, but the president thundered, "You are traitors!" before anyone could say anything. "You were brought to this country to remove the Stone, and what do you do? You flee in a stolen government airplane and consort with the enemy!"

"The *enemy?*" Dr. Cooper reacted.

D. M. Mobutu stepped forward, looked to His Excellency to be sure he could speak, and then said, "You have consorted with His Excellency's enemies, the Motosas."

Jacob Cooper was horrified. "You can't be serious! The Motosas, your enemies? They mean no harm to anyone! You should be proud to have such good people as citizens of your nation!"

The two guards on cither side of Nkromo raised their rifles threateningly. Mobutu held up his hand to call them off and then cautioned, "Dr. Cooper, please, remember whom you are addressing and guard your tone of voice."

Dr. Cooper calmed himself with great effort and spoke in a quiet, almost secretive tone. "Mr. Mobutu, just what is going on here?"

Mobutu shook his head with regret. "I warned you not to go into the land of the Motosas."

Jay retorted, "Yeah. You said they were cannibals and headhunters!"

Mobutu held up his hand to beg their patience. "I was hoping that would be enough to keep you away from them. I knew it would be certain death for you to be seen with those people."

Dr. Cooper guarded his tone as he explained, "Mr. Mobutu, really, we had no choice! We were caught in a storm and had to land!"

"That is not the way His Excellency sees it," said Mobutu. "His army scouts saw you consulting with Chief Gotono, and they saw your children playing a game with the Motosa children."

Dr. Cooper sighed. "We didn't know the Motosas were His Excellency's enemies. We saw no reason in the world why they should be." Then he added forcefully, "And we still don't!"

Mobutu kept trying to play the role of Chief Secretary of the Republic of Togwana, standing straight and sounding official. Even so, his hands were shaking, and when he spoke, the emotions he tried to hide gave his voice a little quiver. "His Excellency has done much to purge our nation of undesirables and rebel groups so that we may be one nation under Nkromo. The Motosas . . ." He had to swallow. "The Motosas have been declared undesirable and must be eliminated."

Lila gasped, incredulous. "No, you can't do that!"

Mobutu tried to explain. "The Motosas have a

special kind of faith which the, uh, Republic of Togwana cannot tolerate."

"Which *Nkromo* can't tolerate," Jay whispered to Lila.

Mobutu drew closer and lowered his voice as if speaking in confidence. "Only weeks ago, His Excellency was about to launch a war of extermination against them. He and his armies were prepared to slaughter them all, burn their village, and wipe their memory from the face of the earth."

"Until the Stone appeared," said Dr. Cooper.

Mobutu nodded. "It blocked his way, planted fear in his troops, thwarted his plans. He could not reach the Motosas. His cannons could not remove the Stone, and neither could his witch doctors. So we sent for you."

Dr. Cooper was insulted by the idea. "You wanted us to remove the Stone just so you could attack and kill a peaceful, virtuous people? You must be insane! Even if I could move the Stone, I would never—"

Mobutu shot up his hand in warning. "Do not say it, doctor. Your life hangs in the balance."

"You are spies!" Nkromo bellowed, pointing his big, fat finger at them. "You are siding with the enemy!"

Dr. Cooper took a fleeting moment to observe the tension in Nkromo's face, the nervous trembling in his hands. The tyrant was not as brave as he tried to appear. Dr. Cooper spoke clearly and carefully, choosing his words for their effect. "We have learned much about the Stone, if His Excellency is interested."

Nkromo gazed up at the Stone, trying not to look too interested. But he was very interested. "What have you learned?"

"We discovered it to be chiseled out, but not by human hands. The Stone is not of this world, Your Excellency." Dr. Cooper paused, considered, and then delivered the punch line. "We have concluded that the Stone can only be removed by the *God* who put it there."

"The God who—" Nkromo's eyes looked like they would pop, and he clenched his fists in rage. "You dare to speak to me of God? *Idi Nkromo* is god in Togwana!"

Dr. Henderson muttered to Dr. Cooper, "Your gift for diplomacy boggles the mind."

Nkromo took several steps toward Dr. Cooper and locked eyes with him. "God cannot stop Idi Nkromo! Idi Nkromo is not afraid!"

Dr. Cooper stood his ground, not flinching, not breaking his gaze with the ruthless tyrant, and finished his thought. "It is our conclusion, Your Excellency, that whoever challenges the Stone challenges *God!*" Dr. Cooper could see Mr. Mobutu out of the corner of his eye, and could tell his words were not being wasted on the Chief Secretary. Good.

As for Nkromo, he looked stunned for only a brief moment but then spoke defiantly, "We can go *around* the Stone! We will go *around* God!" Nkromo's eyes darted about, looking at all the soldiers watching him. "I sent soldiers to search, and they found a way, so we will go. The trucks and tanks and cannons cannot go, but my men can go."

He paused and looked around the parade ground. Dr. Cooper could tell Field Marshal Nkromo was performing for his troops, giving them a show of courage. "So it is the Motosas your God has hurt, not Idi Nkromo! Without the tanks and cannons, the Motosas will not die quickly." Nkromo was so amused by that thought his anger even subsided. He shouted more to his troops than to Dr. Cooper, "The Motosas will suffer before they die!"

The soldiers raised their rifles and cheered.

Mr. Mobutu cringed.

Dr. Cooper shot a glance at the Stone, now a towering silhouette in the afternoon sun, cold and silent—for now. "Mr. Nkromo, given the research data we have, I'm not sure God placed the Stone there just to block your path and protect the Motosas. He may have put it there to teach them— and you—a lesson."

"Your God will teach *me* nothing!" Nkromo snapped his fingers and the soldiers guarding them started shoving and yanking them along, moving them toward a large rock at the far end of the camp. "*I* will teach *you!* You are spies, and spies we shoot!" Nkromo waved his hand, and ten of his special guards came forward, rifles ready.

Lila, Jay, Dr. Cooper, and Dr. Henderson were shoved up against the big rock at gunpoint. The squad of ten soldiers lined up in a neat, straight line just thirty feet away, at attention, rifles at their sides, ready to hear the order to fire.

Nkromo came forward, ready to deliver that order, but first he drew a deep breath and pasted on

131

a phony, gracious smile. "Dr. Cooper, I am merciful. I want you to live. Do you want to live?"

Jacob Cooper could hear some kind of deal coming and hesitated to answer.

Dr. Henderson spoke right up, even raising her hand. "Count me in!"

Nkromo extended his hands, palms up. "Then make the Stone go away, and I will know you are my friend! I will let you live." He shrugged. "Don't make it go away, and you will die."

Dr. Henderson sighed, her shoulders drooping.

Dr. Cooper remained resolute. "Your Excellency, I strongly advise you to listen to me. The power that lies behind the Stone is greater than any of us can begin to understand—"

"Ready . . ." Nkromo shouted. The ten riflemen raised their rifles, ready to shoot.

ELEVEN

Here's a fine mess you've gotten us into!" Dr. Henderson moaned.

Lila touched her brother's hand. "I love you, bro."

He looked back and smiled. "I love you, too, sis."

But then, a thought, a feeling, came to her. "Wait a minute." She crinkled her face as she considered it. "Something's going to happen!"

"Aim . . ." Nkromo yelled.

Dr. Cooper could see straight down the barrels of the ten rifles when he shouted, "Your Excellency! You hired us to study the Stone, and I have not finished giving you my report!"

The word *fire* was just on Nkromo's lips, but he didn't say it. He looked Dr. Cooper in the eyes, then raised his hand to hold back the riflemen. They relaxed, holding their rifles across their chests. Nkromo stepped forward impatiently. "What now?"

Dr. Cooper looked at the Stone, then back at Nkromo, with carefully timed, occasional glances at Mr. Mobutu. "You should know, the God who placed the Stone there is not just the God of the Motosas. He is the God of all men, to whom all men—even you, Mr. Nkromo—must bow, now or later. The Stone is a sign, a message from Him, and according to our written data . . ." Dr. Cooper drew a Bible passage from memory, "'The person who falls on this stone will be broken. But if the stone falls on him, he will be crushed.'" Nkromo started to smile in mockery, but Dr. Cooper wouldn't let him get away with that. "We took careful measurements, Mr. Nkromo! The Stone is growing, even as I speak! Based on the, uh, written data, there is a strong probability that the Stone will grow until it overruns you. It will strike you down, you and all your armies, and you will be swept away without a trace unless you humble yourself and honor the God who speaks through the Stone!"

Nkromo took that in and thought about it, his eyes glaring at Dr. Cooper and then at the Stone. His breathing was labored, his hands trembling. He was trying to look strong and unshaken, but Dr. Cooper could read the fear in his eyes. Finally, Nkromo spoke, his teeth clenched. "Dr. Cooper, I see nothing happening!"

"Well," Dr. Henderson tried to soothe him, "there *are* different interpretations of the data—"

"You will!" Dr. Cooper insisted.

Nkromo forced a smile. "When?"

Dr. Cooper looked heavenward for just a moment and then answered boldly, "Now!"

Nkromo backed away a step as if expecting something. All the soldiers were looking toward the

Stone with wide, frightened eyes. The ten men in the firing squad fell into disarray, muttering to each other, their rifles drooping toward the ground. Mr. Mobutu had his back against a big army truck, looking like *he* was about to be shot.

Dr. Henderson muttered, "Jacob Cooper, I almost hope you're right."

A long, suspenseful moment passed.

But nothing happened.

Nkromo broke into a smile, and then he laughed. Stepping quickly backward, he gave the order, "Ready!"

"Well, nice try," said Dr. Henderson.

"I still think something's going to happen!" said Lila.

The guards raised their rifles once again, though some of them seemed a little hesitant.

"Mr. Mobutu!" Dr. Cooper called. "You have known the God of the Motosas! You know the Stone is of God or you would not have sent for a godly man!" Mobutu was too timid to answer. "If you side with Nkromo now, you will perish with him!"

Mobutu just stood there, stiff with fright.

"Aim!" Nkromo shouted, his hand raised as a signal, and once again, the Coopers and Dr. Henderson were looking right down the long barrels. Nkromo was feeling cocky now. He kept his hand up, prolonging the moment. "Perhaps you would like to pray, Dr. Cooper—if you think God will hear you!"

Dr. Cooper sighed, then reached for Jay's hand as

Jay reached for Lila's. Then, surprisingly, Dr. Cooper felt Dr. Henderson grab his other hand. He looked her way, and she said simply, "Count me in."

He smiled and lifted his eyes toward heaven. A verse of Scripture came to mind, and he recited it. "'During danger he will keep me safe in his shelter. He will hide me in his Holy Tent . . . he will keep me safe on a high mountain.'"

Nkromo dropped his hand. *"FIRE!"*

Jay and Lila didn't remember hitting the ground. They only realized, suddenly, that they were lying in the sand, smarting a bit from the fall and wondering where the bullets had hit them. They could see their father, rolling in the sand and reaching for Dr. Henderson who was crying out, curled up in pain. The rifles had gone off; their ears were still ringing from all the shots.

But then they noticed something really odd: The soldiers in the firing squad were all on the ground too. Even Nkromo was rolling and wriggling in the sand, trying to get his feet under him again, having a fit, screaming at his soldiers.

And it wasn't just Nkromo and his firing squad; the whole army camp was on the ground, hollering, screaming, wriggling, and struggling to get up again.

Jay looked at Lila. "Something happened!"

She nodded back, starting to grin.

They struggled to their knees and checked themselves for wounds, but found none. The firing squad had missed. Everyone had been knocked down.

They were knocked down again as the earth gave another mighty lurch. Nkromo's men also toppled to the ground with a clattering of rifles and anguished cries of terror. The earth had come alive. It was shaking and rumbling, and the sound of thunder seemed to come from everywhere, pounding upward through the ground, throbbing in their ears, rattling the trucks and tanks and cannons and making the small rocks dance. The whole army camp was falling into chaos.

"Mr. Mobutu!" they heard their father shout. They could see him on his knees and one hand, pointing at Mobutu with the other hand. "Whom will you serve? Decide now!"

Mr. Mobutu was lying on his side, trying to prop himself up on one elbow, his eyes darting about as if witnessing the end of the world. His mouth was wide open as if to scream, but terror had stolen his voice.

Nkromo struggled to his feet and staggered about like a drunken man as the earth rolled and shifted under him, his long, silver saber in his hand. He waved his saber at the Coopers and Dr. Henderson and started screaming *"FIRE! FIRE!"* at his firing squad. The ten men regathered, grabbing onto each other for support as they struggled to their feet and got their rifles back in position to carry out his order.

"Mobutu!" Dr. Cooper yelled. "Choose!"

Mobutu finally got to his feet, his knees bent and his arms outstretched for balance as he beheld in horror the chaos around him.

"FIRE!" Nkromo screamed again, and once again the soldiers tried to aim their rifles toward the

Coopers and Dr. Henderson. In all the shaking and rumbling, the rifle barrels wavered and wiggled. The soldiers could hardly stand up.

"Mobutu!" Jacob Cooper yelled one more time.

From the west came a sound like an avalanche, like thunder, like a volcano erupting. It grew in intensity and shook the quaking ground even more.

Mobutu looked to the west, toward the Stone.

And then he decided.

He shouted something to the firing squad. Two of the soldiers looked his way. He gave them an order, and they immediately stepped out and trained their rifles on their fellow soldiers! The remaining eight looked at the two, then looked toward the Stone, and quickly reached a decision. They dropped their rifles and fled. The two soldiers closed in to protect the Coopers and Dr. Henderson, their rifles raised, preventing anyone from approaching them.

Jay and Lila got to their feet and staggered toward their father who was also standing and helping Dr. Henderson off the ground.

"Dad! Those two soldiers!" Lila shouted.

Dr. Cooper was smiling even as he held tightly to Dr. Henderson to help her balance. "I know. Bernard and Walter, Mobutu's two accomplices! I thought I recognized them."

Mobutu ran in a jerky, zigzag course and finally came near. "The God of the Motosas!" he yelled, pointing to the west. "You are right! He is bringing His destruction upon us!"

They all looked west and saw a sight their minds could not understand. The Stone looked higher than it ever had before, and now they could tell the top edge was slowly rocking like a monstrous ship on the ocean, heaving left, then right, growing, reaching, filling the sky with acres and acres of dark, stony expanse. All along the base of the Stone, a tidal wave of rock, dust, and sand was building higher and higher, rolling and tumbling toward them, dug up and pushed along by the sheer, flat face of the Stone.

"It's growing!" Dr. Henderson cried, shaking her head in utter astonishment. "Growing at a phenomenal rate!"

"Growing *and* moving," said Dr. Cooper. "It's headed this way."

Mobutu hollered to Bernard and Walter, who immediately ran away on an assignment. "They will bring a vehicle! We must flee for our lives!"

Nkromo's army had already decided on that course of action. Even though Nkromo was waving his saber and screaming for order and discipline, a thousand soldiers were looking to the west and seeing something bigger and far more frightening than Idi Nkromo.

They dropped their rifles—some even yanked off their boots so they could run faster—and started abandoning the camp, fleeing across the desert. Those closest to the trucks and tanks jumped inside and started them up as scores of soldiers swarmed onto the vehicles like flies on raw meat. With engines roaring and wheels and tracks spinning, the huge, green vehicles thundered through the camp, running over and through tents, smashing through tables and equipment, trampling anything that got in the way as they made their escape.

"Well let's not just *stand* here!" Dr. Henderson cried, pointing toward the Stone.

The Stone was picking up speed, closing on them faster and faster, moving over the desert like the very hand of God, scraping up a mountain of earth before it and rumbling like a million freight trains.

Bernard and Walter came running and staggering back with a bad report. Mobutu passed the news to the others: "There are no vehicles left! We'll have to flee on foot!"

Dr. Henderson yanked at Dr. Cooper's arm, trying to pull him east. "So come on, let's go!"

"No," said Dr. Cooper, looking at the advancing wall and the rolling, crashing wave of earth in front of it. "Not that way."

"*What!?*"

He pulled Jay and Lila close. "We'll run toward it. We'll run *toward* the Stone!"

"*Toward* the Stone?" Mobutu gasped.

Dr. Henderson could see the Stone still advancing, moving far faster than a human could run; she could also see the army fleeing, leaving clouds of dust behind their wheels, tracks, and feet and getting a very nice head start. "Cooper, you're crazy! You're out of your mind!"

"No, he's *right*," Jay countered. "Everything he's said about the Stone is coming true! The Stone *is* sent from God!"

"How can you believe that?" Dr. Henderson squawked.

"Just take a look," said Dr. Cooper.

She was already looking, of course. The desert floor was being ripped up and rolled up like a huge carpet before the Stone as it continued to advance. Large rock formations—some hundreds of feet high—were being smashed and disintegrated like glass bottles, the pulverized pieces flying hundreds of feet through the air, the sound of their destruction like exploding bombs.

"Even without that bad knee you couldn't outrun it," Dr. Cooper argued. "None of us could, and we certainly can't move fast enough to get around it."

"So we're dead . . ." she moaned.

"Not if . . ." Mobutu was still terrified, but beginning to see Dr. Cooper's point. "Not if God is merciful."

"He's merciful," said Dr. Cooper.

"Oh yeah, *right!*" said Dr. Henderson, watching the Stone demolish the desert.

Lila reached over and grabbed her arm. "Dr. Henderson, the Stone represents Jesus! If you really want to live, you don't run *from* Him; you run *to* Him!"

Dr. Henderson looked at Lila, then at the Stone, then at the retreating army still running, then at Dr. Cooper, and then she stood there, wrestling with the decision.

BOOM! Another rock formation the size of a skyscraper exploded into particles.

Dr. Henderson wilted, swayed her head, then finally spouted, "All right, all right!"

"That's the stuff!" said Dr. Cooper.

Bernard and Walter didn't even need an order from Mobutu. They just came up to Dr. Henderson, made a chair of their arms, and picked her up. Then the Coopers, Mr. Mobutu, Dr. Henderson, and Bernard and Walter set out across the desert, hiking directly toward the Stone without veering to the right or to the left.

It was tough going. The earth was still quivering and quaking under their feet, throwing them off balance, rocking them from side to side. All they could do was hold onto each other in a desperate effort to stay on their feet and keep taking one perilous, chancy step after another.

The desert terrain was no help. With the shaking, the sand often seemed to liquefy as it closed over the tops of their feet. They had to keep dodging around loose stones that rolled, danced, and tumbled over the ground like living things. The air was turning brown with dust that stung their faces and clogged their nostrils. They could feel the grit between their teeth.

OOF! A violent, sideways lurch knocked them all down and Dr. Henderson screamed in fear and pain. Bernard and Walter bore her up again, and they all kept going.

KARROOOM! A tall, teetering pillar of rock gave way and toppled like a big tree right in front of them. They leaped back, covering their heads as sand and pebbles rained down. Then, picking their way through the rubble, they kept going.

The top edge of the Stone blotted out half the sky and seemed to be splitting the whole world in half.

The rolling, tumbling mass of earth in front of the Stone had grown to the size of a small mountain range, and the roar of the cascading earth, sand, and stone was so loud it was the only sound anyone could hear.

Faith, Lila thought as she watched the mountain-sized pile of tumbling earth coming right toward them. *This has to be faith.*

"Lord," Dr. Cooper prayed, the thunder of the Stone's approach drowning out his voice, "receive us. Shelter us, I pray!"

"God," said Dr. Henderson, anticipating what it would feel like to have a cubic mile of earth come crashing down on top of her, "get us through this or take a gun and shoot me!"

All they could see was the Stone, the tumbling earth, the flying debris, the sky now brown with dust. They could feel the rush of dirty, dusty air being forced along ahead of the Stone's immense, flat surface.

The earth lurched again, and they toppled to the sandy ground. Looking up, they saw the Stone's top edge move across the sky directly overhead. They were being pummeled by small rocks and sand, the first particles of debris flying out from the mountain of earth the Stone was bulldozing before it.

This is it! Dr. Cooper thought. In only seconds they would be buried under a rolling mountain of debris.

They felt the ground stop shaking.

They looked all around. As far as they could see, the desert was quaking, shifting, shaking under a boiling shroud of dust.

But under their fallen bodies, the ground seemed perfectly solid, perfectly still. They looked at each other. *What's happening?* their eyes said.

Jay was the first to think his eyes were playing tricks on him. He blinked, looked several directions, then blinked again, trying to be sure he was really seeing the desert drop away all around them. "Hey . . ."

"Hang on," said Dr. Cooper. "Don't move!"

They all felt a sensation like going up in an elevator, and then their eyes confirmed that the brown, dusty mantle over the desert floor was dropping away. They were rising above it, just like an airplane flying up through the clouds into clear blue sky.

Lila's hand felt empty space. She looked, then screamed in horror and surprise and clutched at the earth that remained under her. Right next to where she lay was a sheer drop. Dirt and sand were still shifting and sliding over the edge. Dr. Cooper grabbed hold of her, and then they all grabbed each other as they realized the abrupt edge extended all around them.

They were resting on a platform, a weird-shaped chunk of desert floor that was rising higher and higher, and just in time. With a thunderous roar and a billowing cloud of dust, the massive pile of earth and torn up desert rolling in front of the Stone cascaded directly beneath them, tumbling and falling like a Niagara Falls made of earth. Strangely, they felt no quiver, no shaking, no danger. It was like standing on a safe look-out platform, high above it all.

Finally, they could see what had happened. A large arm of rock, an extension from the Stone, had risen up beneath them, lifting them and the desert floor they were lying on. Now it was drawing them in, shrinking in close to the sheer face of the Stone to form a wide, safe ledge. They could feel the wind rushing around them. The Stone was carrying them like passengers, cradling them on a safe ledge above the destruction as it continued to grow, slide, and tear up the desert.

Dr. Cooper was awestruck as he peered over the edge and watched the incredible cataclysm. "He will keep me safe in his shelter . . ." he said in wonder. "He will keep me safe on a high mountain."

Lila was squealing with delight. "I knew it! I knew God would take care of us!"

Jay was really enjoying the ride of his life. "Is this what you call the Rock of Ages?"

Dr. Henderson shook her head, totally bedazzled, shocked, awestruck. "You guys are too much!"

"Now do you believe?" Lila called over the noise.

Dr. Henderson peered over the sheer edge at the tumult below. They were riding—it seemed like flying—over the desert several hundred feet in the air, the wind rushing around them, the earth boiling, shaking, tumbling, and rumbling beneath them. It was like having a comfortable box seat from which to observe the end of the world—or its creation. "This is . . . this is unbelievable!" Then she added, "But I believe it!"

To the west of the Stone, across the wide grasslands, Chief Gotono and all the Motosas braced themselves against the old trees that sheltered their village and watched in holy amazement as the mountain from God moved. It was sliding, rumbling, digging its way away from them, moving toward the cities and people of the east. Beneath them, the ground quivered and rumbled, but it was nothing dangerous. Every Motosa, young and old, was accounted for and every home was solidly built on stone footings. The people would be all right; their houses would stand.

In awe, several Motosas fell to their knees and cried out to God for understanding. Many came to the chief and asked him the meaning of it all, but he only told them to keep watching, and to pray. Understanding would come later, he said. God was speaking again, and soon they would know His message.

But what was that new sound? A trickling, a babbling, and then a rushing . . . like a river.

The chief looked down at his feet just as water swirled around his toes. It was cool and brown from the silt it had picked up on its way across the grasslands, but it was water! He cried out, not in fear, but in boundless joy. Then he started shouting to the others, waving at them to come look.

They came on the run and watched the long, meandering ditch they had dug fill with rushing water!

They left the shelter of the trees and started running across the grasslands to see more of this miracle. When they came over a rise, they shouted, they screamed, they danced for joy and amazement.

Where the Stone had once stood there was now a deep, square depression in the earth, and in the center of that depression was a foaming, spouting, gushing fountain of water hundreds of feet high! The Stone had broken open a deep well, and now a mighty lake was forming, its waters not just filling the ditch, but overflowing it, filling the dips and low spots, flowing around the high spots, carrying water through the grasslands to the village and the crops.

The Motosas fell to their knees, raised their hands toward heaven, and sang to God.

"Look!" said Dr. Cooper, pointing below. "Nkromo's army!"

From their platform high on the smooth, flat face of the Stone, they could see hundreds of little dust clouds rising from the desert, kicked up by the feet, wheels, and tank tracks of the fleeing army—and the Stone was catching up.

"They're not going to make it!" Dr. Henderson cried, shaking her head.

"Look!" said Mobutu. "I see His Excellency!"

They searched in the direction Mobutu was pointing and finally spotted one tiny figure standing defiantly in the path of the Stone, one hand outstretched to point a silver saber, the other hand a shaking fist.

Mobutu shook his head in sorrow and wonder. "He still defies the Stone! He defies the God of the Motosas!"

The rolling, building mound of earth was tumbling toward the tiny little dictator with great speed, but he would not budge; he only stood there, a lonely little speck in the desert, shaking his fist in hate.

When the huge, mountainous wave of earth, stone, and sand rolled over Idi Nkromo, it only took an instant. First he was there, and then he was gone.

TWELVE

T hey sat on a mound of soft rubble: sand, dirt, small stones, bigger boulders. It was suddenly quiet—so suddenly that the Coopers, Dr. Henderson, Mr. Mobutu, and his two loyal sidekicks were the only things still shaking. The air started to clear up as the dust drifted away on a steady north breeze. The first question on everyone's mind was, *Where are we?*

They knew they were on solid, steady ground—at least, it wasn't rolling or tumbling. But they were up high, on a long range of hills they'd never seen before. To the east they could easily see the beginnings of green jungle and the white buildings of what had been called Nkromotown. But now that it was the capital of a small, free country no longer under the iron hand of a dictator, another name could be found.

To the west, they could see the largest, longest, deepest skid mark in the world, if not the known universe. The Stone had carved a deep, flat rut across the desert, and now, at the far end, an expansive lake was forming. The nation of Togwana would have to redraw its maps because it now had an entirely new geography: a vast lake where once there had been a desert and the hills upon which they sat that the Stone had scraped up.

Nkromo's army was gone. Some had perished with their boss under the moving mountain of earth. The rest had scattered into the jungles and small settlements to the east, no longer a powerful force now that their wicked leader was dead.

As the afternoon sun washed over the Coopers and their friends, they began to grasp the fact that the Stone was gone too. They could all remember the platform they were sitting on descending again, just like a plane coming in for a landing. They could remember the desert coming up to meet them, and they could even remember rolling gently off that platform onto this long, bulldozed pile of earth the Stone had created. But no one saw the moment the Stone vanished, and none could say just where it went. All they knew was it had done its work, left them here, and then disappeared as quickly as it had come.

Dr. Henderson was the first to speak. "Now that, my friends, was some kind of ride!"

Dr. Cooper was already on his knees. To pray his prayer of thanksgiving, all he had to do was remove his hat. "Lord, You have shown us that You are mighty indeed! But Your mercy is also as great as Your might, and for that, we thank You!"

"Do we ever," said Jay.

"Amen," said Lila.

"You're real, God," said Dr. Henderson. "You've gotten through to me. I believe."

Then they all sat there quietly, thoughtfully, pondering what had happened.

"Togwana will never be the same," said Mobutu, looking east and west. "We have a whole new country now."

"In more ways than one," said Dr. Cooper. "The geography is different, but you're also rid of Idi Nkromo. Now you and the rest of the people can rebuild Togwana the right way."

Mobutu nodded with understanding. "As God leads us. I have much to repent of. I have much to set right."

Dr. Cooper smiled at that. "No better time to start than right now, Mr. Mobutu."

"By the way," said Lila. "Thank you, Mr. Mobutu, for saving our lives."

"Yeah, thanks," Jay said, and then they all extended their thanks to Mr. Mobutu, Bernard, and Walter.

"Don't thank me," said Mobutu. "Thank your father. He knew."

Jay and Lila looked at their father. "Knew what?"

Dr. Cooper smiled at Mobutu. "Go ahead and tell them."

Mr. Mobutu sighed and then confessed, "I am a Motosa. Chief Gotono and I are from the same family, the Mobutus. We are cousins."

Lila's eyes got big, and then she slapped the ground with the realization. "So that's why you look so much alike!"

Mobutu nodded with a smile. "I grew up in the Motosa village. I knew of the Motosas' God."

"Remember the story of the Man in the Tree?" Dr. Cooper asked his kids and Dr. Henderson. "'God sent Ontolo to save Mobutu.' Mobutu was the chief's name before he became chief. I had a hunch there was a connection."

"And you guessed that I would fear God?" Mobutu asked.

Dr. Cooper eyed Mobutu knowingly. "I knew you did, somewhere deep in your heart."

Mobutu nodded. "My days among the Motosas were long ago, and I journeyed far from home to follow a man who was really a devil." He shook his head sorrowfully. "How thankful I am that God intervened and saved my people from Nkromo. How thankful I am that He saved *me!* Ontolo has saved Mobutu again—even when *this* Mobutu does not deserve it."

"Ontolo," Jay considered. "The Man in the Tree."

Mobutu smiled, nodding his head. "And a Stone the size of a mountain!"

"The same God, the same Savior," said Dr. Cooper.

But Dr. Henderson was still perplexed. "Well fine, Dr. Cooper, but that doesn't explain how you knew the rest."

He gave her a puzzled look. "What do you mean?"

She knew he was teasing her a bit. "Don't give me that! How did you know the Stone was going to, you know, grow, and move, and take out Idi Nkromo?"

152

Dr. Cooper raised an eyebrow, a twinkle in his eye. "Dare I refer to the Bible again?"

Dr. Henderson threw up her arms in surrender. "Go ahead, go ahead."

"All through the Bible you can find scriptures that compare Jesus to a stone or a rock: The rock in the wilderness that produced water when Moses struck it . . ." They all shot a glance at the lake still growing as water gushed out of the earth. "'And they all drank the same spiritual drink. They drank from that spiritual rock that was with them. That rock was Christ.' Oh, and then there's the rock upon which the wise man built his house . . ."

"And we saw how the Motosas used that idea," said Lila.

"Just like the stone the builders rejected that became the cornerstone. And then there's that scripture in Daniel . . ."

"Oh, yeah!" said Jay, recalling it.

Dr. Cooper explained. "When Daniel interprets a dream King Nebuchadnezzar had, he tells about a huge stone that was cut out without hands that smashed and destroyed all the evil kingdoms of the world, then grew into a mountain that filled the whole earth. It's a very exciting picture of Christ, and how He would eventually do away with the world's evil powers and fill it with His glory instead."

"I love it!" said Lila.

"So . . . since the Stone seemed to be God's way of showing the Motosas—and us—the power and majesty of Jesus Christ, I figured the Stone might act out that picture in the Book of Daniel."

Dr. Henderson cocked her head and raised an eyebrow. "Wasn't that kind of a long shot for a man about to *be* shot?"

"Well . . ." Dr. Cooper thought it over. "Considering everything else God has done to reveal Himself to the Motosas, it had to happen, and I knew Idi Nkromo couldn't last, not if the Motosas were to survive and Chief Gotono's dream was to come true."

That got their interest. "What dream?"

Weeks later, a small, single-engine airplane soared over Togwana's new lake and landed gently on the lake's western shore, only a quarter of a mile or so from the Motosa village. Green fields of wheat and corn flourished and sheep and goats drank their fill at the water's edge. The grasslands were greening up, and new homes were being built. Things had changed in Togwana.

As the plane taxied to a stop not far from the village, Brent Anderson, the once-exiled missionary, gazed out the window, drinking in the scene. "This is it, Jake! This is the village I wanted to reach! I know the Lord has called me here!"

Jacob Cooper shut down the engine and smiled at his friend. "I think they know it too. They've been expecting you for a long time."

Dr. Cooper, Brent Anderson, Jay, and Lila all stepped out of the plane while throngs of Motosas came running from the village, cheering and waving. It was a day the Motosas had been promised for years, and now it had finally arrived. Just as they had done for Dr. Henderson weeks ago, the warriors made chairs of their arms and bore all four of the visitors aloft, carrying them through the newly thriving grasslands, into the village, and into the big meeting hall where the rest of the villagers had already assembled.

The chief was standing on the large, square stone in front, ready to welcome them. Brent Anderson was brought right to the front, introduced to the chief, and then embraced by the powerful, jovial man dressed like a big bush. The Coopers took a bench over to the side where Bengati was waiting to interpret the proceedings for them.

The chief raised his big arms, and the crowd fell silent. Then he began to speak.

Bengati leaned close and interpreted for the Coopers. "You all know the dream our God gave me: That someday a man with blond hair would come down out of the sky and open the leaves he held in his hand," the chief made the gesture with his hands that symbolized the opening of a book, "and that the leaves would speak and tell us the name of our God. I never understood how leaves could speak, until my son . . ." The chief had to stop a moment to choke back tears as he looked down at Ontolo, who sat in the front row with paper and pencils he'd received from the Coopers, ready to write. "Until my son found a way with his little marks. Now, the leaves can speak. Now, the man from the sky with light hair has come!"

The crowd cheered. The Coopers cheered.

The chief continued, "You know that Jacob Cooper came to us from the sky with light hair and much wisdom, but he was not the man in my dream." Then the chief added with a twinkle in his eye, "But we were not wrong about Jacob Cooper and his children—they were just early!"

The people laughed.

The chief guided Brent Anderson onto the large speaking rock and said to the crowd, "Here is the man our God has promised!"

Brent Anderson, moved to the point of tears, took his big, black Bible, opened it, and began to read to them from the Gospel of John, interpreting the Scriptures directly into Motosan, a language he had already learned.

All over the building, people's faces glowed as they listened, looked at one another, and then made the opening book gesture with their hands. The leaves, they agreed, were now speaking.

"For years your God has spoken to you of Himself and His Son who came to earth to save you," Brent said in Motosan as Bengati interpreted for the Coopers. "He showed you through your stories how sin can bite like a snake and destroy you. He showed you through the Man in the Tree how He would provide someone who would take away the bite of the snake by taking sin's punishment upon Himself. According to your own story, He sent Ontolo to save Mobutu."

Dr. Cooper smiled quietly as he looked across the room and saw D. M. Mobutu, the new president-elect of Togwana, sitting next to Chief Gotono, his cousin. The new government and the Motosas had already established a friendly, working relationship.

Brent continued, "Finally, He showed you how this Man in the Tree would not remain a man in a tree, dying from the arrows and spears of sin, but would someday come to earth as a mighty mountain that would sweep evil from the earth, give us rest from our enemies, and water our lands."

Lila folded her arms as if she were cold. "Wow, this is giving me goosebumps!"

Jay pointed across the room. "Look at Ontolo."

Lila looked to see the chief's son writing down what Brent Anderson was saying, using his own alphabet.

"He wants to start writing out the Bible in Motosan," said Jay. "Looks like God thought of everything."

Brent turned a page in his Bible. The leaves continued to speak. "Because God so loved all people, He sent His Son to save not only Motosas, but all people. If we believe in His Son, we will not die, but will live forever with Him."

That got a cheer from the crowd. It was what they'd been waiting to hear for years.

"Even now, even today, the Man in the Tree, the one you call Ontolo, will save us and take us back into His arms. I have come to tell you about Him and to tell you His name."

There was a gasp from the crowd and even from the chief.

"The name of our God!" said Bengati in a hushed, excited voice. "We have waited so long. . . ."

"His name is Jesus," said Brent, "the Man in the Tree, who takes away the sins of the whole world."

Dr. Cooper wiped a tear from his eye. Jesus. The Man in the Tree. The Savior. The Stone the builders rejected. The Chief Cornerstone. The Stone that would someday destroy all wicked kings and fill the whole earth with His glory.

He had come at last to the Motosas.

The Deadly Curse
of Toco-Rey

ONE

Chico Valles, machete in hand, hacked his way along the narrow trail, oblivious to the constant chatter of cicadas and the raucous screams of tropical birds. Sweat trickled down his stubbled face. The thick, encroaching jungle pressed in on him from every direction. It reached with limbs, slapped with leaves, grabbed with vine tendrils. He forced it back with his machete and pressed on as he did every day, running errands for Basehart the American.

Finally he reached the clearing where the Corys had set up their camp. He stopped.

The camp looked deserted. The large tent sagged a bit as if a pole had broken. Cookware, clothing, and food were strewn about under the blue tarpaulin lean-to. The wooden camp chairs and portable table were overturned by the fire pit. A portable camp stove lay on its side, bent and broken, and orchids now lay scattered on the ground, spilled from a vase. Except for the noises of the jungle, Chico heard no sound. Except for the slow crawl of an iguana on a limb overhead, he saw no movement.

Chico tightened his grip on the machete.

"Kachakas," he muttered, his eyes darting about. Then he called, "Hello! Señor Cory!"

No answer.

Steeling his nerves, Chico took a few cautious steps forward, emerging from the jungle with the machete outstretched. He watched every direction for hidden dangers, lurking enemies. He could detect no sign of another human being—at least none still alive.

Then he heard a low, garbled hissing from the tent. A snake? He instinctively drew the machete back, ready to strike. Then he inched forward, trying to get a view through the tent's open flap.

The inside of the tent appeared to have been raided by wild animals. Blankets, sleeping bags, books, charts, and tools were scattered everywhere. The tent fabric had been torn, and one of the support poles was indeed broken.

"Señor Cory!"

Again, no answer. Chico walked closer and stuck his head into the tent.

He found the source of that strange hissing sound. A handheld two-way radio lay on the floor, the case broken and splintered, its dial still glowing. Had someone tried to call for help? Where were they now?

Chico ducked into the shadowy interior, his feet shuffling through scattered clothing and trodden papers.

"Señor—"

His eyes caught a sparkling, golden glow in one corner, and he stared, spellbound. "*El tesoro,*" he whispered. The treasure.

On a steel footlocker stood a tall, ornately

engraved vase of gold, several golden cups, a gold jeweled necklace, and small, golden statues of ancient gods and warriors. They all glistened as if newly polished in the faint light that came through the doorway.

Chico took a furtive look outside, then reached down to grab the vase.

The glistening, golden surface felt slick and gooey.

And then it felt like fire. He yanked his hand away with a cry of pain and was horrified to find thin yellow slime on his palm and fingers. It began to penetrate his skin, bubbling and fizzing, burning like millions of red-hot needles.

He frantically wiped his hand on a blanket, then tried to find some water, anything to remove the slime. Searing pain flashed up his arm and he began to scream.

So great was his terror and agony that he didn't see the shadowy figure appear in the doorway, crouching like a lion. When it leaped upon him, the impact jarred him senseless.

The birds cried out, thundering from the treetops. The cicadas cut their song short. The iguana disappeared around the trunk of the big tree.

The tent came alive, lurching and bulging this way and that. Chico's screams mingled with the eerie, cougarlike snarls of his attacker.

At the Langley Memorial Art Museum in New York City, Dr. Jacob Cooper, hat in hand, strolled quietly through the Hall of Kings. Statues, busts, masks, and relief carvings of ancient kings glowered at him from their pedestals along both sides of the vast marble hall.

"Dr. Cooper?" A small man in a dark suit came close and looked up at him.

Jacob Cooper looked down with curiosity. "Mr. Stern?"

The little man smiled. "Mr. Wendell. I work for Mr. Stern. Please come with me."

Dr. Cooper followed him to the end of the hall and through an unmarked door into a large workroom and archive. Shelves lined the walls from floor to ceiling, all loaded down with books, documents, and historical artifacts. In the center of the room stood a large worktable where artifacts were restored and prepared for display.

A gray-haired, well-dressed man sat at the table. He rose when Jacob Cooper entered the room. "Dr. Jacob Cooper?"

Dr. Cooper reached across the table and shook his hand. "Mr. Stern?"

"Thank you for coming." Mr. Stern looked at his associate, who took his cue and left the room. Then Mr. Stern asked, "You *are* alone?"

"Yes, and no one knows of our meeting, just as you requested."

Mr. Stern smiled. "I apologize for the secrecy, but your fame goes before you. And I have reason to believe certain interests would not be happy to see you involved in our little project. Please, have a seat."

Dr. Cooper sat at the big table and Mr. Stern returned to his seat opposite. He rested his hand on an old leather carrying case. "Dr. Cooper, the matters we are about to discuss are of a delicate nature. Human lives are at stake . . . and I'm afraid some have already perished. Have you heard of the lost city of Toco-Rey?"

Jacob Cooper probed his memory. "A legendary city full of treasure somewhere in Central America?"

Mr. Stern brightened, nodding his head. "Toco-Rey is believed to have been built by the Oltecas, who thrived during the decline of the Mayan empire and vanished into history almost 600 years before Columbus."

Dr. Cooper wrinkled his brow. "I've heard a little about it from a treasure hunter who seemed rather obsessed with the place."

"Ben Cory?"

Dr. Cooper smiled. "So you've met him?"

Stern's face grew solemn as he announced, "I'm afraid he is one who has died, Dr. Cooper."

Jacob Cooper was saddened by the news but not entirely surprised. "What happened?"

"He was working for us, searching out the lost city, and—" Mr. Stern's eyes grew wide with excitement, "we believe he found it! He and his crew brought artifacts out of the jungle: gold, jewelry, jade, sculpture. Cory was elated, and so were we. But soon after, he and his party were ambushed in their camp and killed. Every last artifact was stolen. We think the local natives, the Kachakas, are responsible. They claim to be descendants of the Oltecas, charged with guarding the city from outsiders."

"Foreign treasure hunters, in other words."

"Not in this case!" Mr. Stern countered. "Ben Cory was hired by the Langley Museum, and his quest was not just for treasure but also for knowledge, for history itself. Here. Let me show you." Mr. Stern flipped the leather case open and carefully drew out some old parchments and a worn, cracked leatherbound logbook. "The museum acquired these recently: the journal and maps of José de Carlon, an early Spanish explorer who went to Mexico shortly after Hernán Cortés had finished his conquests. José de Carlon wasn't much of a soldier or conqueror; he was too preoccupied with treasure hunting. Rumors of a lost city, the final stronghold of Kachi-Tochetin, king of the Oltecas, lured him south."

Mr. Stern carefully unrolled one of the brittle, aging maps as Dr. Cooper leaned over the table for a careful look.

"See here? The map shows his route through the jungles to the lost city, and he even marked out where the ruins are. According to his journal, he and his men found Toco-Rey in 1536, six centuries after the city was deserted. Ben Cory and his men used this map to find the treasure, but they were killed before we could find out how, or where."

Dr. Cooper could see where this was going. He fidgeted a little and sighed. "Mr. Stern . . . I'm an archaeologist. Perhaps another treasure hunter . . ."

Mr. Stern leaned forward, intense. "Dr. Cooper, treasure hunting is exactly what we are trying to *prevent!* For years, the ruins of the Mayas have been ravaged and looted by souvenir seekers, and now that Toco-Rey has been found, the same thing could happen there. We could lose a priceless store of Oltecan history and culture to looters—unless we find the treasure first and rescue the artifacts. I know you are a man who cares about such things. I know you would want to preserve history."

Jacob Cooper took a moment to consider. As founder of the Cooper Institute for Biblical Archaeology, he had devoted his life to preserving the past. It had vital lessons it could teach about the present and the future. Saving another piece of history from treasure hunters, black marketeers, and greedy collectors would certainly be in keeping with his and the Institute's goals. "So," he said at length, "you want me to pick up the trail where Ben Cory left off?"

Mr. Stern nodded. "You can follow the maps and notes of José de Carlon, just like Ben Cory did. With your skill and expertise, it should be no problem at all to retrace Cory's route to the treasure."

"No problem at all?" Dr. Cooper leaned back, his fingers lightly drumming his chin. "There's just one thing I'd like to understand. . . ."

"Yes?"

"If José de Carlon found this treasure, why is it still there? Why didn't he carry it off?"

Mr. Stern hesitated, as if unprepared for the question, then sighed. "You may as well know. In his journal, José de Carlon comes across as a very superstitious man. He was afraid of booby traps, magical curses, ancient evil forces. He and his men actually dug their own tunnel into the tomb of Kachi-Tochetin in the hope that they could sneak in secretly and evade any curses or traps." Then he added, "Apparently they didn't succeed."

Dr. Cooper had to prod him to continue. "Go on."

Mr. Stern gave an awkward chuckle and tried to shrug off his words even as he spoke. "He says his men found the treasure, but they all went mad, became like raving animals, and killed each other. He barely got away alive and left the treasure behind, convinced there was a curse on it." Mr. Stern chuckled and shrugged again. "So the treasure is still there, untouched for centuries."

"And guarded by a bizarre curse?"

Mr. Stern leaned over the table, lowering his voice. "Dr. Cooper, we both know this will be no picnic. Of course there are dangers: thick jungle, poisonous snakes, hostile natives. The area is remote, and we can expect little or no government assistance or protection. And . . . well, who knows? Kachi-Tochetin was a fierce, marauding warrior. He conquered peoples and cities all over ancient Mexico and Central America, sacrificing and slaughtering thousands. His treasure is undoubtedly the loot he stole from those he conquered. So maybe the tomb *is* booby trapped somehow. As for a curse . . . well, I understand you are a man of prayer, so I assume you aren't bothered by such things."

Jacob Cooper smiled. "I've run into more than my share of curses and hexes and magic spells, and my God has been greater than all of them."

Mr. Stern drew a deep breath. "Dr. Cooper, you are our last hope. Can we count you in?"

"Welcome to Basehart City," said the handsome, white-haired man in the white shirt and broad straw hat. He could have been a wealthy plantation owner or an English gentleman, so refined was his manner. "This is without a doubt the finest vacation resort in the entire jungle—excluding all the others, that is. I'm the founder, Dr. Armond Basehart."

Dr. Cooper climbed out of the jeep and shook Basehart's hand. "Dr. Jacob Cooper, and this is my daughter, Lila. That's my son, Jay."

Lila Cooper, thirteen, got out of the jeep and stretched. Removing her straw hat, she wiped a slick mixture of sweat and mosquito repellent from her brow. Like her father and brother, she was wearing light clothing. She'd braided her long blond hair to keep it off her neck. Even so, the tropical jungle felt hot, sticky, and uncomfortable.

And Basehart City was nothing to admire. Within a small, tight clearing surrounded by a solid wall of jungle were three travel trailers parked in a U shape. A large blue tarpaulin stretched between them. Two native huts with stick walls and thatched roofs and two mud-spattered trucks completed the encampment. It had taken the Coopers a full day's journey to get here, riding over miles and miles of bumpy, muddy road through jungle so thick they could only see a few feet into it. They were a day's journey from the nearest flushing toilet.

Lila smiled a tired smile. *This is going to be better than I thought.*

Jay Cooper, fourteen, was still working on being tall like his father, but he was already strong. And he had his father's sandy blond hair and piercing blue eyes. He took a moment to study the surroundings, feeling the curious stares of the native workers. One was butchering what looked like a pig, another was building a lean-to, and the third was burning trash in a small fire. Directly above, the treetops formed a tight, dark frame around a circular patch of blue sky. Brightly colored birds perched in the branches, screaming at one another in voices continually alarmed about something.

Adventure, he thought. *I can just feel it!*

Armond Basehart took them to the dismal-looking trailer that faced his own across the small, makeshift courtyard. "This is our special guest suite. You'll have running water from the trailer's supply tank—Juan and Carlos will keep it filled for you—and a limited supply of electricity from the trailer's batteries. Please try to conserve it. There's an outhouse behind this trailer, but check it for snakes before you use it. As you can see, we provide only the best accommodations for our guests."

Dr. Cooper looked around the inside of the trailer. It was a twenty footer, with a small kitchenette, dinette table and benches, a closet-sized shower, and beds for at least four. Everything looked old and well traveled. But in this rugged country, these *were* luxurious accommodations. He set down his duffel bag. "We'll take it."

They got settled, and then Dr. Basehart filled them in. "Ben Cory, his brother, John, and their associate, Brad Frederick, had a camp set up about a half mile farther into the jungle, closer to the ruins. I chose to stay here in the main camp with the supplies, the workers, the vehicles, and my lab, of course. Besides serving as the team doctor, I am also doing a little private research, collecting and categorizing some of the local fungi."

Dr. Cooper spotted a narrow, new trail leading into the jungle. "Is that the trail to the Corys' camp?"

"It is. I can have Tomás take you there now if you like."

Jacob Cooper reached into the trailer and pulled out his gunbelt. "Jay! Lila! Let's go!"

Dr. Basehart touched him on the shoulder. "Uh, Dr. Cooper . . . you may not want your children to go. As you probably know, the Corys died violently."

Dr. Cooper considered that as he checked his .357 and slid it into the holster at his side. "Where are the bodies now?"

"We buried them not far from their camp."

Jay and Lila emerged from the trailer, ready to get started.

Dr. Cooper reassured his host, "My kids haven't seen everything, but they've seen enough in our travels. They'll be all right."

Dr. Basehart accepted that, then he called to one of the workers. "Tomás!"

"Sí, señor." Tomás came running.

Dr. Basehart introduced them. "Dr. Cooper, Jay,

Lila, this is Tomás Lopez, my assistant." Tomás shook their hands, grinning a toothy grin, happy to be of service. "He'll take you to see the Corys' camp and answer any questions you have."

Tomás's smile vanished, and he looked wide-eyed at his boss. "Señor Basehart . . . is that such a good idea?"

Basehart became quite impatient. "Tomás, I will not have this discussion again with you! There is nothing to be afraid of!"

"But—" Tomás got a cold glare from his boss and cut short his protest. "Muy bien."

Dr. Basehart told the Coopers, "When you return, I'll show you the video tape the Corys made of their findings. It will give you an idea of what they were doing and possibly give you some clues to follow."

Dr. Cooper nodded. "I'll definitely want to see that."

Tomás eyed the holster on Dr. Cooper's hip. "Ah, you have a gun. That is good. Come with me."

Tomás stopped by his hut to grab a rifle and a machete, then he led the Coopers down the trail into the jungle. The thick vegetation closed in around them, making them stoop and push branches aside. The thick canopy overhead choked out the daylight.

Tomás was upset. For several minutes he muttered to himself in Spanish, and then he shared his thoughts with the Coopers in English. "This is not a safe place! It is magic, you know. *Bad* magic. We should not even be here!"

They journeyed farther into the deep jungle, surrounded by noisy birds and cicadas, until finally they saw a bluish glint ahead. Tomás slowed his pace and crouched as if sneaking up on something. The Coopers instinctively crouched as well and followed.

"There," Tomás whispered, gesturing toward a small clearing with his machete. From the edge of the clearing, they could see the ragged tent and blue tarpaulin lean-to, the camp where the Corys had been ambushed. "Before we go farther, I will warn you: You will see blood inside, and terror, and signs of Kachaka magic. The Corys came this far, and now they are dead." He looked directly at them. "There is a curse on this place. If you go farther, you may end up dead too. So decide!"

TWO

The Coopers were cautious but not afraid. With firm resolve, they stepped into the clearing, moving carefully, observing every detail. Tomás followed behind, sticking close, eyes wary, the rifle and machete ready.

The camp was a disaster area with camp chairs knocked over, the tent half collapsed, the camp stove overturned on the ground, food and supplies torn, scattered, and spilled everywhere. It had been a mess to begin with, and now scavenging animals had made it even worse.

Jay found a small, thin reed stuck in a tree trunk near the tent. "Dad."

Jacob Cooper went over and examined it without touching it. "Poison dart."

Tomás nodded warily. "The Kachakas. They use poison darts and blowguns. The poison kills in seconds."

Lila noticed the overturned vase and scattered orchids. "I bet these orchids were beautiful before they wilted."

Tomás smiled crookedly. "Americans. They

would pay lots of money for such flowers in their own country. Here, we see them everywhere."

"All the tools are still in place," Dr. Cooper observed, checking the collection of shovels, picks, brush hooks, and metal detectors near a tree. He found a large wooden chest, eased the lid open, and whistled his amazement at the contents.

Jay came to look. "What is it?"

"Explosives," said his father. "That always was Ben Cory's style: Just blast away and get the treasure out, never mind the historical value of the site." He closed the lid gently, with great respect for what the chest held. "Let's have a look in that tent."

The tent had half-fallen. Dr. Cooper found a long stick near the firepit and stuck it into the tent to prop up the roof.

"We'll have to gather up all these notes," he said, indicating the papers scattered on the floor. "We need to know everything the Corys knew."

"Careful!" Jay cautioned, pointing to another poison dart that poked through the tent.

Lila picked up one of the sheets of note paper. It was heavy, sticky, and stained red. "Euuughh."

"I told you there would be blood," said Tomás from outside where he nervously stood guard. "The Corys were slaughtered in this tent."

There was blood, all right, spattered on the floor of the tent, on the clothes, work boots, and gear. The Corys *had* died violently.

Jacob Cooper kept his tone calm and even. "Lila, I think we need one more set of eyes and ears outside. We don't need any surprises."

Lila welcomed the idea. Her face pale, she quickly ducked outside.

Dr. Cooper drew a deep breath and spoke to Jay. "Let's do it."

He and Jay began gathering up the notes, drawings, charts, and maps from the tent floor, separating them from the shirts, socks, bottles, and boxes lying everywhere.

Jay spotted a small notebook partially hidden under some wadded up rags. He reached for it then jerked his hand away, his heart racing. "Dad!"

Dr. Cooper's hand went to his gun. "What is it?"

Lila poked her head in. "What is it?"

Jay backed away from the pile. "There's something under those rags."

The rags were wiggling and heaving.

Lila stifled a cry of fear, pressing her hand over her mouth as Tomás stuck his head into the tent. "Qué pasa?"

"I think we've got a snake in here," said Dr. Cooper. "Stand back." He found a piece of broken tent rod and extended it toward the rags, prodding them slightly. The motion stopped. He slowly lifted the rags.

They saw a fluttering, a flash of dull yellow and heard a tiny, shrill scream!

Lila screamed as well, and Jay and Dr. Cooper ducked. A strange, fluttering, flapping shape shot from the rags and began banging and slapping against the walls of the tent like a trapped bird.

Tomás hollered, "Get back! Get back!" and plunged into the tent, swinging his machete. The thing continued to fly, land, leap, bump against the tent, and flutter over their heads. Lila jumped away from the tent; Jay and his father dropped to the floor. Tomás kept swinging.

SPLAT! The machete finally made contact and the animal landed on the tent floor, fluttering like a wounded bird, flopping about like a fish.

Jay and Dr. Cooper got to their feet. Tomás stood over the thing, machete only inches from it, venting his supercharged emotions in rapid, coarse Spanish. They started to approach.

Tomás shot his hand out toward them. "Stay back! Wait!"

The thing finally stopped flopping and Tomás relaxed, breathing in deep breaths of relief. He beckoned to them, and they approached as Lila stuck her head back into the tent, eyes wide with curiosity.

Tomás pointed at the thing. "*Caracol volante.* We call them carvies. A flying slug."

"A *what?*" Jay exclaimed, still trembling a bit.

"Amazing!" added Dr. Cooper, bending for a closer look. "I've heard such tall tales about them! I never thought they were real!"

"They are not seen very often," said Tomás. "They are rare and only come out at night."

There at Tomás's feet, a loathsome little creature lay dead. It looked like a big garden slug, about six inches long, with a yellowish, slimy hide. But instead of feelers, it had tiny, black ratlike eyes. On either side of its soft, gooey body, glistening skin extended outward to form winglike fins, much like those of a stingray. Tomás used the tip of his machete to snag a fin and extend it to show the Coopers.

Lila came in and peered over everyone's shoulder. "Wow . . ."

"Not a slug, actually," Dr. Cooper explained to his kids. "But it *is* a member of the mollusk family— and one of the strangest."

"Don't touch it!" Tomás warned. "The slime is deadly poison, the same the Kachakas use to tip their darts." He glanced quickly around the tent. "See? There is slime on the tent fabric and on some of the clothes. Be very careful. It will burn through your skin and kill you."

Without having to be told, they all backed carefully out of the tent and then checked their clothes for any traces of slime.

"Most of it has dried up, which is good," said Tomás. "It has to be fresh to burn through your skin."

"What was that thing doing in there?" Dr. Cooper wondered.

"It was probably attracted by the blood. Carvies are flesh eaters: They feed on dead animals, blood, meat of any kind. There were probably others in the tent last night. This one decided to sleep under the rags."

Jay shook his head. "So that's one more thing to worry about—besides the biting insects, the poisonous snakes, and the hostile natives."

"How far away is the Kachaka village?" asked Dr. Cooper.

Tomás shrugged. "I have never been there. It's

somewhere beyond the ruins, I think. But the Kachakas claim all this land, and they aren't happy that we're here." Tomás cocked his head toward the woods just beyond the camp. "The Corys have already learned that. Come this way."

They followed him into a small clearing. There, marked with crude wooden crosses, were three graves. "Ben Cory, John Cory, Brad Frederick," said Tomás, pointing out each one. "Gone in one night, their treasure stolen."

Jacob Cooper had seen enough. "All right, let's get these materials back to the compound and see if we can sort them out. And then we'll watch a movie."

After hiking back to the compound, they ate a hurried dinner—roast pig cooked over the fire by Tomás's coworkers—and then settled into their trailer to examine the notes left behind by the Corys. In the light of a gas lantern, Jay and Lila carefully cleaned, sorted, and stacked the materials, and Dr. Cooper laid them out in orderly fashion on the dinette table to study them.

"Hmm . . . ," he said, using a small flashlight to illuminate some hard-to-read areas. "I'm impressed. The Corys put a lot of time into mapping out the ruins. Look here: Toco-Rey was built on top of the ruins of a previous city, which was built on top of the ruins of a previous city, and so it goes. It's only about a mile square and used to be walled like a fortress. It would have been easy for Kachi-Tochetin to hole up there for years and defend his loot from his enemies."

Lila spotted a dark, square shape someone had drawn near the map's eastern edge. "I'll bet that's the burial temple Ben Cory wrote about." She leafed through a pile of freshly scrubbed materials and pulled out a ragged-edged notebook. "Yeah, take a look at this."

Dr. Cooper quickly flipped through the notebook, then compared the scribblings and sketches with the map on the table. "Lila, you're right on the money. It *is* the burial temple. Ben Cory guessed they'd find the treasure there. He figured since Kachi-Tochetin was such a gold-hound, the old king probably had himself buried with it."

Jay produced some smaller maps, roughly drawn with pencil and now faintly bloodstained. "I think these maps lay out the route they followed to get to the burial temple."

Dr. Cooper laid the maps out on the table and traced the route with his finger. "Looks like the same route José de Carlon took centuries ago: up the slope past the waterfall . . . across the swamp . . . through the main gates of the city . . . around the Pyramid of the Moon and due north up the Avenue of the Dead . . ."

"Avenue of the *Dead?*" said Lila.

"Sounds inviting," quipped Jay.

A knock on the screen door startled them. "Hello. How goes the battle?" It was Armond Basehart.

"I'm encouraged," replied Dr. Cooper. "The

Corys kept a thorough record. We should be able to retrace their route first thing tomorrow morning."

Basehart was visibly pleased. "Good enough! Well, I have the Corys' video ready. Come on over and have a look."

Outside Basehart's trailer, Tomás yanked the starter rope on a portable gas generator. Inside the trailer, the electric lights came on and so did a computer monitor perched in Basehart's tight little living room. Basehart had the Corys' video camera, and after fumbling a little with various buttons, finally got a picture on the screen.

The Coopers leaned forward as one person, gazing intently, and immediately recognized the Corys' camp in the jungle. The camera jiggled, panning the camp, showing the tent, the campfire, the table and chairs. Even the vase of orchids was standing upright on the table, the orchids in much fresher condition. "And this is our tent, and over here we have the fire, and here's our nice outdoor dining room . . ." went the cameraman's prattle.

Then a young man appeared from behind the tent, carrying some firewood. He was tall and thin, with a smile so wide and teeth so white it caught your eye. "And here's Brad, doing the chores . . . ," continued the narrator.

Brad shot back, "Did you get a shot of the treasure?"

"No," the cameraman answered, "I'm doing establishing shots here."

Then came a voice from off-camera, "Well, get the camera over here, Ben. You're wasting Mr. Stern's time."

"Ehh, everybody's gotta be a director." The camera did a quick, blurry pan to the table near the firepit, and then it picked up the glimmer of gold— a lot of gold.

"Will you look at that!" Jay exclaimed in a near whisper.

"Here's just a preview of what we found," said Ben the cameraman, zooming in for a close-up of incredible gold artifacts: an ornately engraved vase of gold at least two feet tall, several golden plates and cups, a necklace of gold and jewels, and at least a dozen golden figurines only a few inches tall.

Hands entered the picture, holding another vase and wiping it down with a rag. "We found these in the tomb and carried them out through the tunnel. Everything is pretty dusty down there. We wore dust masks, but still came out of that place all dirty. No problem though. See here? It just takes a rag to clean the artifacts and they polish right up."

The camera zoomed back to show John Cory, a long-haired, bare-chested man. John set the vase down and picked up some of the small figures to show to the camera, wiping them some more with his rag. "We have here tiny figurines of a bird-god, possibly another form of Quetzalcoatl, the feathered serpent god."

Ben, from behind the camera, explained, "These were stationed all around the walls of the room like sentries, probably to guard the treasure from spirits of the dead, maybe even from living enemies—"

John butted in, "There were other guards there too, but they weren't much help."

Ben laughed. "No, they sure weren't. We're going to take the camera and some lights with us tomorrow. We should get some great shots of the treasure room and the tunnel—"

"If we can get past the slugs," Brad quipped, coming into the picture and turning some of the artifacts for better viewing.

John agreed, "Yeah, the carvies can be a bit of a problem. They like the tunnels and underground areas just like bats like caves, but we're dealing with it."

"We'll retrace our route for you," came Ben's voice from off-camera, "which closely matches the route taken by José de Carlon more than four hundred years ago."

"The old guy was right about the treasure," said Brad.

"But wrong about the curse," said John, indicating the treasure on the table. "I mean, here's the treasure, and here we are, safe and sound."

"Okay," said Ben, "let's get this stuff into the tent." Then, in a louder, announcer's voice, "Stay tuned, folks, for tomorrow's exciting venture into the burial temple of King Kachi-Tochetin!"

The computer monitor went black.

Dr. Basehart turned off the video camera. "That's it. They were ambushed and killed that very night. They never went back."

Dr. Cooper looked at his kids for their reaction.

Lila was troubled. "Is the treasure worth it?"

Her father reflected on the question. "Some people are greedy enough to take the risk. For others, . . ." He sighed. "Well, we should be willing to ask that question more than once on this trip."

"A tunnel," said Jay. "We're definitely looking for a tunnel."

"Perhaps the original tunnel dug by José de Carlon and his men," Dr. Cooper said. "And apparently inhabited by more *caracoles volantes*."

"Oh *great!*" Lila moaned.

Dr. Basehart was quick to say, "But the Corys got around the carvies somehow. They got into the treasure room!"

Dr. Cooper rose to his feet. "And so will we. Let's call it a day and get some shut-eye. We'll confront those poisonous slugs—"

"And snakes," added Lila.

"And hostile natives with poison darts," added Jay.

"Tomorrow," finished Dr. Cooper.

THREE

The night passed slowly, as any night filled with fear and foreboding will. Lila lay in a bed toward the back of the trailer, staring up at the ceiling, listening, thinking. Again and again she replayed the memory of the Corys' blood-spattered tent and the poison darts they had found. Jay, lying very still in the bed across the trailer from her, listened carefully for the sound of footsteps stealing close to the trailer. As he peered out the narrow window, he hoped he wouldn't see the glint of a killer's eyes lingering in the bush. Dr. Cooper wasn't lying down at all. He sat on his bed—the dinette folded down to make one—listening and watching.

Draping a thin blanket around her shoulders, Lila got up and went to her father's side. "Dad, you okay?"

"So far," he said softly. He put his arm around her, giving her a loving squeeze as he looked out the windows again. "It's very quiet out there."

"I can't sleep."

"Neither can I."

"Me neither," came Jay's voice from his bed.

185

"Which makes me wonder why everyone else can."

Lila bent down and peered out the window as well, seeing no activity, no lights, and hearing no sounds beyond the constant night chatter of the jungle. "Are they all asleep?"

"I think so," said Dr. Cooper. "I just did a little patrolling around the camp without encountering anyone on watch—no sentry, no safeguards at all. If I could do it, then a whole tribe of Kachakas could sneak into this camp and never be noticed. Either Basehart and his men are too dense to get a clue from what happened to the Corys, or . . ."

"Or what?" asked Jay, coming up front to join them.

Jacob Cooper thought a moment, but then he shook his head. "I don't know. It doesn't make sense." He turned from the window to face his kids. "But we have to get some sleep. Let's take turns keeping watch. I'll take the first shift for two hours."

"I'll take the next," said Jay.

"Then me," Lila said with a shrug.

"I'll leave my gun by the door. Each of you keep it beside you on your watch."

And that's how they spent the rest of the night.

The morning air was warm, wet, and full of earthy smells when the Coopers emerged from their trailer. Armond Basehart was already up and active, barking orders to his three men. Tomás and his two friends, Juan and Carlos, appeared moody and somber. They kept their eyes on the jungle as they gathered equipment and crammed provisions and tools into large backpacks.

"Well, good morning," Dr. Basehart greeted them. "Did you sleep well?"

Dr. Cooper couldn't help noticing his host's well-rested, almost chipper demeanor. "Well enough. How about yourself?"

"Just fine, thank you. Well, grab some breakfast and get yourselves ready. The day wears on!"

Jacob Cooper, Jay, and Lila had their backpacks ready. They ate a quick breakfast of fruit juice and granola and then geared up.

Dr. Cooper slipped into his "map vest," which had many deep pockets where he could carry maps and charts close at hand. He neatly tucked the Corys' maps and photocopies of the original de Carlon maps into the pockets, strapped on his revolver and backpack, put on his hat, and was ready to go.

They headed out, Dr. Cooper leading, making their way back along the trail that led to the Corys' campsite. Jay and Lila followed directly behind their father; Dr. Basehart and his three workers followed behind them. As the jungle closed in around them, the mood of the group darkened, and there was little talking. Even Armond Basehart's hurried, commanding manner had fallen away and he, like the others, stole along the trail quietly, eyes wide open and attentive. Tomás's face clearly indicated what was on his mind: Kachakas. Magic. The curse. His two friends, Juan and Carlos, each carried rifles and pointed them every direction they looked as if expecting an enemy behind every tree.

They pressed on through the thick growth like fleas on a dog's back, stepping over, ducking under, and sidestepping the branches and leaves that brushed and raked against them. The sounds of birds and insects made a constant rattle in their ears.

When they reached the camp, they found it further deteriorated, torn, and scattered by another night's visitations of scavenging animals. Tomás, Juan, and Carlos began muttering to each other in Spanish, and Dr. Basehart had to shush them.

Dr. Cooper pulled out Ben Cory's map sketched in pencil, then carefully walked around the camp perimeter until he found the crude trail the Corys had hacked through the jungle. Without a word, he beckoned to the others, and they continued, the jungle closing around them more than ever.

They hiked and crept for another half-mile or so, and then they began to climb a shallow rise. Dr. Cooper consulted his map. So far, everything checked out. Another half-mile should bring them to—

They froze in their tracks. Tomás aimed his rifle up the rise, the barrel quivering in his trembling hand. Dr. Cooper's hand went to the .357 on his hip.

Somewhere out there, deep within the tangle of jungle, something was screaming. It was not the cry of a bird or the howl of a wild dog, but something far more eerie and strange. It rose in pitch, then fell, then rose again, in long, anguished notes of terror, or maniacal rage, or pain . . . they couldn't tell.

It faded, and then it was gone. They stood silently for a long, tense moment, listening. But they heard nothing more.

Dr. Cooper looked to Dr. Basehart for an explanation.

Armond Basehart gave him a blank stare, then he turned to his men. "What was that?" he hissed.

They looked at each other, jabbering in Spanish, then shrugged at him, shaking their heads. "We do not know, señor," said Tomás. "We have never heard that sound before."

Jay and Lila could feel their hearts pounding and took some deep breaths to steady themselves. They watched their father, who remained still, listening, thinking.

Dr. Cooper looked back at his children, then at the rest of the party. "We're going to stay close together, right?"

They all nodded in full agreement. No problem there.

Dr. Cooper turned and continued up the trail without a word. The others followed, climbing the rise, all the more attentive to every sound, every movement around them.

A tree limb moved! Juan swung his rifle around as everyone froze.

A green tree snake, slithering down the limb in a slow, lazy spiral, flicked its long, red tongue at the air. Juan relaxed and exhaled.

The sound of rushing water reached their ears. Jacob Cooper checked his map. "This should be the waterfall."

The waterfall was like a silken veil, dropping about ten feet into a deep pool edged with moss.

"Beautiful!" Lila exclaimed.

"Let's go swimming," Jay wished out loud.

"Let's get out of here," Dr. Basehart urged. "We can't hear if something's sneaking up on us!"

They kept climbing and reached the top of the rise. Like a moat to block their path, swampy land lay before them, stinking with rot, buzzing with black insects. It rippled with the twitches of larvae and the slithering of water snakes. Dry ground was scarce; the crooked, moss-laden trees and clumps of spear grass rose out of the black water as if growing from a mirror.

Dr. Cooper pulled another map from his vest pocket and snapped it open. "We're close. This swamp was probably used as a moat at one time. The city gates are just on the other side." He looked around, searching for something. "The Corys found a way across and are supposed to have marked it."

Jay pointed. "Dad, I think I see a red ribbon over there."

He saw a ribbon tied around a crooked tree branch, and beyond that, another. "Watch your step, everybody."

The ground was soft and spongy beneath their feet. Sometimes they had to walk ankle-deep in the murky water as they moved carefully from a tiny mound of spear grass to a flat stone to a fallen log to a gooshy, muddy island. They zigzagged across the swamp from each red ribbon to the next.

Another scream, this time closer! Lila flinched,

pulling her hands near her face. Tomás spun left, then right, rifle ready, eyes wide with fear.

From within a tall clump of spear grass, a jawless, mossy-green skull stared back at Tomás and he screamed.

Then Juan screamed.

Then Carlos screamed.

"Quiet, you fools!" Dr. Basehart shouted, looking pretty shaken himself.

Dr. Cooper doubled back to have a look and used his machete to brush the spear grass aside. This skull was not alone. Beyond it, in a long, straight row, were several others, all impaled on the ends of poles, and all green with moss. They'd been here a long while.

"Kachaka magic!" Tomás hissed, his voice squeaking with fear.

"What do you make of it, Dr. Cooper?" Dr. Basehart asked.

"Yes, probably Kachakas," Jacob Cooper replied. "This sort of thing is used as a charm to ward off unwelcome spirits—or people. It's a warning, a scare tactic." He shot a glance at the three terrified workers. "Works pretty well."

"Dad," Lila called. "I think I see the ruins."

He hurried to the front of the line again and bent to peer through the jungle growth. Lila was right. Some distance away, a fierce-looking, toothy face of stone, splotchy with moss and lichens, glared back at them through the trees. Just a few more careful moves between red ribbons should get them there.

No one wanted to remain in the swamp with the

skulls, so they made those few careful moves quickly. They stood before the imposing gateposts of Toco-Rey: two basalt pillars carved in the shape of warriors with feathered headdresses, standing at least twenty feet tall. Judging from their snarling expressions, the warriors weren't designed to make visitors feel welcome.

Tomás, Juan, and Carlos got the message. They were ready to turn back right then and there.

Jacob Cooper, however, was fascinated. "Notice the position of the arms. Undoubtedly these pillars used to support a massive wooden gate between them; the warriors' arms served as the top hinges." He referred to his map and then pointed. "And that huge hill you see just beyond the gate is no hill at all, but a man-made pyramid overgrown by the jungle: the Pyramid of the Moon."

Jay and Lila could only stare in amazement. The Pyramid of the Moon rose at least a hundred feet above the jungle floor. Stair-stepped like a huge wedding cake, its chalky, limestone surface was visible only through small gaps in the overgrowth.

"See that small, square temple at the very top?" Dr. Cooper asked, pointing. "The Egyptians built their pyramids to serve as tombs, but the Middle Americans usually built them as gigantic bases for their temples, so they could be closer to their gods."

They proceeded through the gates, walking on soil, moss, and vegetation. Sometimes they could see the flat paving stones that had once formed the main street through Toco-Rey. Jacob Cooper kept an eye on his map as he guided them along. "We go around the Pyramid of the Moon and walk due north up the Avenue of the Dead . . ."

"The Avenue of the Dead!" Tomás exclaimed.

Dr. Cooper tried to comfort him. "José de Carlon named it that, probably because it was the main thoroughfare to the Pyramid of the Sun where they practiced human sacrifice."

"Then the spirits of the dead are here!" Tomás muttered.

"There are no inhabitants here, dead or otherwise!" Dr. Basehart snapped. "Now I'll thank you to control yourselves and do your jobs!"

They circled around the Pyramid of the Moon and found the Avenue of the Dead. A flat, vine-covered expanse, it stretched straight north, about half a mile long and a hundred feet wide. Crumbling stone structures lined either side of it. Some of the buildings were tall enough to be seen above the bushes and trees; some were covered over completely so that they resembled green hedges rather than buildings. At the far end of the avenue stood another man-made mountain, a stair-stepped pyramid with another squarish temple at its peak. This one was even larger and more glorious than the Pyramid of the Moon.

"That would be the Pyramid of the Sun," said Dr. Cooper, "the religious focal point of the city."

As they walked slowly down the Avenue of the Dead, Jay and Lila imagined this street as it might have been over a thousand years ago: filled with bronze-skinned people in brightly feathered garments and jangling gold jewelry, bartering, selling, and herding among the pyramids, temples, and dwellings. They could hear the hum of the marketplace where grains and goods were sold on the stone porches and patios. They could feel the jostling, the pressing of the crowds gathering to gaze up the steep sides of the Pyramid of the Sun at another human sacrifice. These were a beautiful but ruthless people, enslaved by fear, but proud. Now they were gone forever, lost in centuries of time. Were they conquered, or did their culture simply wither away? No one knew.

They reached the base of the Pyramid of the Sun, and Dr. Cooper paused to double-check his maps and notes. "The Pyramid of the Sun stands at the center of the city and could have served as a nice decoy to lure would-be treasure hunters to the wrong place. The real location of the treasure is due east of the pyramid, toward the rising sun . . ." Dr. Cooper looked east and then pointed at one more pyramid, this one rather plain looking, heavily cloaked in green growth, and much smaller than the first two. "That pyramid over there. That's the burial temple of Kachi-Tochetin."

Armond Basehart clapped and rubbed his hands together. "Excellent!"

They walked east, following the narrow trail the Corys had hacked through the thick undergrowth. Already, the jungle had begun to move in again, and the new growth brushed against their bodies.

When they finally came to within a hundred feet of the burial temple, Jacob Cooper stopped to carefully scan the area, look at the latest Cory map, and shake his head. "Well, the first part was easy. Now is where the work begins."

It was obvious that the Corys had done a lot of exploring. A maze of trails and small clearings had been cut in all directions. But that was the problem.

"Which way do we go?" Jay wondered.

Dr. Cooper folded the map and put it in his pocket. "The map doesn't show a thing. Apparently the Corys never got a chance to write down where they found that tunnel."

Lila caught a glint of white among the greenery. "Hey look, more orchids!"

The orchids nodded in full, healthy clusters along a crumbling wall.

"Well, at least that's a confirmation that we're in the right place," said Dr. Cooper. "The Corys had some of those orchids back at their camp."

Lila found the trail the Corys had cut through to the orchids and couldn't resist giving them a sniff to see if they had a scent.

Dr. Cooper began giving out instructions. "Okay, everybody, we're going to split into two groups and work our way around the temple until we meet on the other side. Stay within earshot and keep track of each other in case there's trouble. We need to go everywhere the Corys may have been to find that tunnel into the pyramid. Lila, let's go!"

She hurried back to join them, and then the searching began. Tomás, Juan, and Carlos worked their way to the left; Dr. Basehart and the Coopers ventured off to the right, spreading out, groping, poking, and whacking their way through the undergrowth, sometimes on previously cut trails, sometimes not.

Jay was wielding a machete, widening a channel through growth higher than his head. "Man, you'd think the Corys would have left some markers or something."

Lila was about twenty feet to his right, following a well-chopped, well-traveled path through growth as thick as mattress stuffing and well over her head. "This trail might lead somewhere. It looks like they used it quite a bit. Jay, where are you?"

"I'm over here," he replied, although he wasn't entirely sure where "over here" was.

"Well, can you see the pyramid?"

Jay looked up in several directions, but all he could see were leaves, branches, and vine tendrils. "Dad?"

"Yeah," came Dr. Cooper's voice somewhere ahead of him.

"I think we're lost."

"I can see the pyramid immediately to my left, which would be to your left," his father replied. "I think you're still on course."

"And I'm a bit behind you," came Dr. Basehart's voice. "Let's just keep talking so we can keep tabs on each other."

Jay called, "You hear that, Lila?" No answer. "Lila?"

Lila had come to a wide clearing filled with chopped and fallen brush. She was probing through the debris with her machete. "Jay, I think I may have found something."

Jay stopped whacking. "What?"

Lila used her machete to brush some withering branches aside. Underneath she found a section of low, stone wall. "It's a little wall, kind of like you'd see around a well—you know, it's circular."

Dr. Cooper's voice filtered over the tops of the weeds. "It could be a well. How wide is the circle?"

She began to cut away more growth, gradually uncovering the curve of the wall as it formed a circle about ten feet across. "It's . . . uh, about ten feet across, I think . . ."

But one thing bothered her about this circle: She was standing *inside* it. "Jay?"

"Yeah."

"I think it might be a well. I can feel cold air coming up from below."

Jay heard a cracking sound, then a rustle of leaves and branches—and then a long, echoing scream.

"*LILA!*"

Dead limbs had broken, supporting sticks had snapped, and the thick, centuries-old mat of vegetation had given way under her feet. She was falling into a deep, cold place without light, sliding and bouncing over the slimy stone walls as she tried to grab something, anything.

GOOSH! She slid feet first into something soft, slick, gooey. The well must have a muddy bottom, she thought.

SHRIEKS! FLUTTERING! The stagnant air came alive with a rushing, flittering, flapping, slapping, squeaking.

She screamed and covered her head as countless

little shadows swirled around her, slick and slimy, slapping against her, against each other, against the walls.

She looked up just once and saw the opening she'd fallen through as a circle of daylight alive with hundreds of fluttering, flitting, disk-shaped shadows.

Carvies! The pit was full of them.

FOUR

"D AD!" Jay hollered.

But Dr. Cooper had heard his daughter's screams and was already on the way, crashing and thrashing in a straight line through the jungle.

Lila covered her head with her arms as the riled creatures continued to flurry about her, flapping, shrieking, flinging slime from their wingtips. She could feel the slime spattering her everywhere; it was in her hair, on her face, dripping down the back of her neck. "HELP ME!"

Jay reached the well but threw himself to the ground as two frightened, screaming carvies flew out of the pit and over his head. He scurried along the ground and peered over the wall into a black void. "Lila!"

She was screaming for help, her words lost in echoes.

"Dad! This way!" Jay yelled.

Dr. Cooper finally burst into the open. He looked into the pit only a moment before throwing off his backpack and pulling a rope from a side compartment. "Lila! Stay calm! I'm lowering a rope!"

Lila kept her hands around her head as she whimpered in fear and disgust. The stench—the slime, the mold, the carvy droppings—was almost overpowering. Carvies still fluttered and flapped around her. She could feel slime dripping off the end of her nose.

Flop! The rope dropped into the pit with a loop tied in the end. "Put your foot in the loop!" her father called.

She reached for the rope, but lost her balance and fell onto something that clattered, clinked, flipped like tiddly-winks as she landed.

Bones. Leg bones, arm bones, ribs, skulls. The carvies were living in them, crawling on them. They scattered like pigeons when she fell, flying by her face and then . . . where? She could hear them withdraw into a deep, echoing void behind her. She turned her head, still protecting her face with her arms, and could just make out the entrance to a dark passage. A tunnel? Hundreds of carvies had retreated into the cavity, clinging to its walls.

But hundreds more continued to scurry and flop like beached stingrays amid the bones around her. Others hung from the walls of the pit, their backs arched with fear, their beady little eyes locked on her.

She had to get out of there. She righted herself, put her foot in the loop and used both slime-slickened hands to cling to the rope. "Okay."

Dr. Basehart joined Dr. Cooper and Jay, and the three of them hauled in the rope hand over hand until Lila's head popped up through the tangle of weeds and broken branches. She was covered with a thin, greenish slime.

Jay reached out to take her hand, but Dr. Basehart grabbed him. "No. Don't touch her! Just keep pulling on the rope."

"Try to climb out, Lila," said her father. "Yeah, that's it."

She was gasping in fear but used her feet to kick and crawl, and she finally flopped over the wall onto the ground.

Dr. Cooper tore his shirt off. "We've got to get that slime off her! Lila, hold still!" He started wiping the slime from Lila's face with the shirt, speaking gently to her, trying to calm her. Jay took his shirt off as well and started working on one arm while Dr. Basehart used a large handkerchief to work on the other.

"We'll have to get her back to the swamp or the waterfall and wash her off," Dr. Cooper thought out loud. "We'll make a stretcher to carry her."

At that moment, Tomás, Juan, and Carlos burst upon the scene, machetes flashing, rifles ready, hollering in Spanish. At the sight of Lila and the open pit, they figured it all out.

And then they started laughing!

Jacob Cooper wanted to strangle them! "Stop laughing and help us! We've got to get her to the stream to wash her off!"

At that, Juan and Carlos looked at each other and then laughed some more.

Tomás tried to explain. "Señor Cooper, your daughter will be all right. Do not be afraid."

Neither Dr. Cooper nor Jay were ready to believe that. "Help or get out of the way!" Dr. Cooper demanded.

"The slime is green," said Tomás, pointing at Lila and the shirts used to clean her. "These are morning carvies. They are not dangerous."

Cooper upended his backpack and the contents dumped onto the ground. "Grab the rope, Jay, and secure it around the ends of the pack board. We'll make a stretcher."

Tomás kept trying. "Señor Cooper, believe me, if these were yellow evening carvies, Lila would be dead by now." He pointed to Lila once again. She was crying, frantically wiping her face and hair with clothes that had fallen from her father's backpack. "You see? She is alive, full of energy!"

Juan and Carlos added their observations in Spanish, and Tomás translated, "Juan and Carlos say her skin would be burning, and she would be paralyzed and choking to death if the slime were poison."

"We'll talk later," said Cooper, cinching up the last rope on the pack board.

SPLASH! Lila leaped into the pool beneath the waterfall and began rinsing herself off, twirling in the water. Dr. Cooper left a bar of soap, a clean shirt that could serve as a towel, and clean clothes by the pool's edge. Then he joined the others a short distance down the trail. They wanted to give her some privacy, but didn't want to get out of earshot.

"She seems to be all right," he reported, only now beginning to calm.

"What did I tell you?" said Tomás. "The carvies are only dangerous at night when they are yellow.

When they are green, they are like pets. They wouldn't hurt anybody."

"Nevertheless," said Basehart, holding up a plastic garbage bag. "I've taken the liberty of bringing back the clothing we used to wipe off the slime. I'd like to analyze it."

"I think that's an excellent idea," said Dr. Cooper. He hollered up the hill, "How's it going, Lila?"

"Okay," came her response.

Jacob Cooper allowed himself a deep sigh of relief. "Thank the Lord."

They sat down to wait.

Dr. Cooper removed his hat, wiped his brow, and asked Tomás, "Now. Would you mind explaining why the carvies are only dangerous when they are yellow?"

Tomás shrugged. "I don't know. In the morning they are green and so we know they are safe. At night, they turn yellow, which means they are deadly."

Dr. Basehart ventured a theory. "I would guess it has something to do with their feeding habits. They forage at night and hide in caves and hollows during the day, like bats. The venom could be for protection from predators while they're out in the open feeding."

Tomás waved his finger in warning. "When they are hungry, they get very mean."

Dr. Cooper wanted to be sure. "But they do go out to forage at night?"

"Sí, señor."

Dr. Cooper thought a moment and then revealed, "Lila says she saw a tunnel down there."

That got everyone's attention.

"A tunnel?" Armond Basehart was ecstatic. "Then we've found it—or rather, Lila has found it! The route to the treasure!"

"Possibly," Jacob Cooper cautioned. "It does seem to fit what the Corys said in the video."

"Yeah," said Jay. "They talked about the carvies being a problem."

"And they said something about guards that weren't helping much." Dr. Cooper smiled at the Corys' dry humor. "Lila found human bones down there. The Corys were probably joking about that."

"Well, there you are!" said Dr. Basehart. "We *have* found it!"

"So . . ." Jay could see a problem immediately. "What about the carvies?"

Just then, Lila came down the trail with wet hair and dry clothes. She was smiling a little, clean but embarrassed by all the fuss she'd caused.

Dr. Cooper put out his hand to help her down the trail. "How are you feeling?"

She was surprised, but greatly relieved. "I feel just fine. I guess Tomás is right."

Her father gave her a hug and so did Jay. Tomás grinned, jubilant.

"So what do we do now?" Jay asked.

Dr. Cooper had already been formulating a plan and announced it to everyone. "We'll come back tonight, after the carvies have gone out foraging and the tunnel is clear. If we time it right, we should finish our business before they come back."

Back at the compound, the Coopers regrouped. They cleaned their slimed clothes, restudied the maps and notes the Corys had left behind, and spent some of the afternoon catching a much-needed siesta in their trailer.

Dr. Armond Basehart said he would nap as well, but he actually spent the time in his laboratory in the third trailer, studying a sample of the green slime he'd taken from Lila. Looking at the sample through his microscope, he nodded to himself. It appeared his theory about the mysterious *caracole volante* was proving correct. Lila Cooper was a very lucky girl indeed.

And he was a very lucky biologist.

When dusk came to the jungle and the treetops looked black against the darkening sky, the Coopers led the group on their second expedition with flashlights in hand and climbing rope in their backpacks. They had extra clothes to cover themselves in case they had a run-in with yellow carvies. The men also carried their weapons again in case they had a run-in with dart-shooting Kachakas.

By the time they reached the gates of Toco-Rey, complete darkness shrouded everything beyond the reach of their flashlights. The pyramids were hidden in the night; the ruins were shrouded under the jungle's thick mantle.

Silently, they stole through the tangled brush until they reached the burial temple of Kachi-Tochetin, now a coal-black silhouette against a tapestry of stars. The birds were silent, but the insects of the jungle were chattering. The still air just above the ruins was quite busy with tiny black bats and, most important, carvies. The slugs were out foraging, just as the Coopers had hoped.

They quickly found the circular pit. Tomás, Juan, and Carlos took positions around it, keeping watch with their rifles. The others knelt in the vines and branches and quietly eased off their backpacks. Even as they prepared to go into the hole they could see a few stray carvies flutter up out of it.

"How many would you estimate were down there?" Dr. Cooper whispered to Lila. None of them wanted to talk too loudly, not knowing what enemies might be lurking in the darkness beyond their sight.

Lila gave a little shrug. "It could have been thousands. They were everywhere."

Dr. Cooper got on his belly and crawled to the wall. Lifting himself just over the top and pushing some vines aside, he clicked his light on and peered into the pit.

The walls glistened with moisture and slime, and far below, the bones Lila had encountered lay in a scattered heap like jackstraws.

"Okay," he called in a quiet voice, digging out a length of rope and tying a loop in the end. "Let's go down and check it out."

"I'll hold a position up here," said Dr. Basehart. "I hate to admit it, but I suffer terribly from claustrophobia. I would be of little use to you in a dark, cramped tunnel."

Jacob Cooper accepted that. "Okay, you and

your men can handle the rope. I'll go first. Jay and Lila, you provide the lights."

Dr. Cooper put on an extra shirt, some gloves, and a scarf to cover most of his face. Then he put his foot in the rope loop, stepped over the wall, and disappeared into the dark, clammy space below as Dr. Basehart and his men lowered him. Jay and Lila shined their flashlights after him, helping to illuminate his way.

He immediately noticed it was cooler down here. It was also dank and smelly. As he rotated on the rope, he shined his light to inspect the walls. The pit was hand dug through soil and limestone, between eight and ten feet across and about fifteen feet deep. The thick layers of dried slime on the walls indicated the carvies had lived here for quite a while. The slime was green, which brought a little comfort. It made sense: The carvies only occupied this place when they were well fed and content.

His foot scraped the wall and knocked some rubble loose. The dirt and rocks fell on the bones with hollow, clinking sounds, and a carvy—this one not so content —hissed and skittered out of the way.

"Hold up!" he called, and they stopped lowering him.

He was only four feet above the bone-covered floor. In the beam of his flashlight he could see two yellow carvies perched on a skull. They didn't like being discovered and hissed and chirped at him, their backs arched. He moved slowly, pulling a plastic spray bottle from his belt. He wished he could predict their behavior.

They bolted from the skull in a mad flutter with piercing little shrieks, moving so fast he had trouble tracking them. They came at him, flapping toward his head. Lashing out, he swatted one away with his flashlight. The other landed on his boot, and he sprayed it with the spray bottle.

The bottle contained a strong salt solution, and the carvy's hide began to melt. It flopped to the floor, squeaking and dying.

The second one came at him again, but he sprayed it in midair and it fell immediately to the floor where it flopped about like a landed fish.

"Jay," he called upward, "your spray bottle idea worked."

"All *right*," Jay called back.

"Dad, be careful!" said Lila.

He hooked the spray bottle back onto his belt and explored the floor of the pit with his flashlight. He saw no more carvies.

"Lower away."

His feet finally came down on the bones, pressing them into the thick layer of carvy droppings that covered the floor. Under his weight, they crumbled. He stepped out of the rope loop and yelled, "Okay, pull it up." Then, turning in the direction of the burial temple, he found the long, narrow tunnel Lila had talked about. Penetrating deep under the earth, it swallowed up the beam of his flashlight in limitless, black distance.

"I see the tunnel," he called. "Come on ahead. It's all clear."

Above, Dr. Basehart and his men pulled the rope back up as Jay motioned to Lila.

She saw his signal, but shook her head. "No, you go first."

It was usually Jay's custom to go last, so he could keep an eye out for his sister. But as he considered her previous encounter with this pit, he understood. "Okay. I'll wait at the bottom for you."

"It's a deal."

Jay pulled a cap down over his head and some gloves on his hands for protection, and Dr. Basehart's men lowered him. Then it was Lila's turn. She put on her drooping, billed, army surplus cap, an extra long-sleeved shirt, and some gloves, and then sat on the wall and swung her legs over the pit.

And then she froze.

"Ready?" asked Dr. Basehart.

Of course she was ready. She was just . . .

She pulled in a deep breath. *Come on, Lila,* she thought. *Get a grip. You can't get scared now, not with everybody watching.* She'd crawled into plenty of deep, dark places with her father and brother. This was nothing new.

But something about this ugly, smelly hole turned her stomach. She felt unsteady. Her hands were trembling.

"Yeah," she finally forced herself to say. "I'm ready."

Mustering just enough courage, she put her weight on the rope and went over the wall, through the tangled leaves and branches . . . and into the dark throat of the pit.

"That's it," came the voice of her father from below. "Easy does it."

She began to rotate on the rope. The walls of the

pit moved around her making her dizzy; she felt herself getting sick.

She could hear Jay and her father talking somewhere below her. "Who do you suppose these people were?" Jay asked. "Sacrificial victims, most likely," her father answered, "thrown into this pit after the ceremony on top of the Pyramid of the Sun."

She couldn't look down. "How much farther?" she called, her voice betraying her fear.

"Only six more feet, sis," answered Jay. "No sweat."

Her feet touched down on the crunching, crumbling bones and soft droppings, and she stumbled a little. Jay and Dr. Cooper reached out to steady her.

"You okay?" Dr. Cooper asked. His voice sounded far away.

No, she thought. "Of course I'm okay!" She was still having trouble standing up.

"The ground's firm a few inches down," Dr. Cooper reported.

Strange. To her, the ground seemed to be moving in waves like a water bed.

As her father led the way into the tunnel, he talked in hushed, excited tones, as he always did when he was in the midst of discovery. "I don't think this tunnel was dug by José de Carlon. The tool marks and workmanship are too much like the pit itself. And it's been here so long there are limestone formations. The Oltecas must have chiseled it out."

"Cool," said Jay, following just behind him. "Maybe this was supposed to be a secret passage into the tomb."

"Watch your head and where you step."

There was only room enough for them to squeeze through the tunnel in single file. They had very little headroom thanks to the sharp, menacing stalactites that hung from the ceiling. The floor was no better; jagged stalagmites poked up like daggers everywhere. To Lila, they looked like teeth, and she had the overwhelming impression they were walking into a monster's jaws. The flashlights of her brother and father created sharp, spooky shadows that lunged and leaped all around her head. She kept her light low and her head down. She didn't want to look.

After what seemed like an endless journey through the belly of a monster, Dr. Cooper finally announced, "Okay, there's something up ahead. You see that?"

"Wow! It's got to be the tomb!" said Jay.

Lila stopped. *Tomb.* The very word terrified her. She'd never been terrified of a tomb before, but she was now. She put her hand against the cold limestone wall to steady herself. The tunnel felt like it was pitching, rolling.

Dr. Cooper and Jay had entered a room, or was it a hallway? There was a flat wall directly in front of them, but the room seemed to stretch a great distance to either side of them.

Dr. Cooper shined his light both ways and could see that the hall turned a corner at each end. "This passage might go clear around the base of the pyramid, kind of an outer hallway around a room in the middle."

Back in the tunnel, Lila forced herself to take more

steps forward. She dared to look up and saw that her brother and father had found a room of some kind.

"Lookitthe formindiss inscriptonida walllll . . ." she heard her father say.

"Den mebbe idwazda curse dey watogginbout . . ." she thought Jay replied.

She took off her gloves and rubbed her ears. It seemed so noisy in this place. A roaring sound everywhere . . .

Dr. Cooper scanned the relief carvings on the wall. "Yes . . . pictures of the serpent god and human sacrifice. You know, human sacrifices were often dressed up in gold and finery donated by the people. Considering what a greedy scoundrel old Kachi-Tochetin was, I wonder if the priests used this passage to sneak into the pit and strip the dead."

Jay could imagine the scenario. "They kill the victim on the Pyramid of the Sun, throw the body into the pit . . ."

"As a sacred offering to some form of god . . ."

"And then sneak into the pit through this tunnel to get all the gold and jewels for themselves."

"Could be they had quite a scam going here." Dr. Cooper shined his flashlight up and down the long passage. "But if that's true, then there has to be another way in and out."

Jay could hear Lila stumbling in the tunnel behind him and looked back. "Lila?" Her flashlight beam was drooping. She seemed to be staggering. "Hey, Lila, you okay?"

"Okay your minute when it's wider, I'm a gimme . . ." she answered.

Jay reached out and grabbed his father's arm. "Dad . . ."

Dr. Cooper had also heard Lila's response. "Lila? How's it going back there?"

They could only see the beam of her flashlight coming up the tunnel. She didn't answer.

Dr. Cooper shined his light in her face.

She cowered, covering her face with her arms. "NOO! Light now, I'm over inside!"

"She's talking crazy!" Jay exclaimed.

"Something's wrong," said Dr. Cooper. They hurried back into the tunnel. "Lila, hold still, sweetheart, we're coming."

Jacob Cooper had almost reached her, was just about to touch her, when she dropped her arms and he saw her face.

Her skin had turned a pale green. Her eyes were wild, like a savage animal's. She screamed a scream that chilled his blood.

He tried to grab hold of her. "Lila—"

SWAT! She struck him across the face before he even saw it coming, her fingernails gouging him, the power of the blow enough to knock him off balance. He fell backward to the tunnel floor, a sharp stalagmite just missed his rib cage.

"Lila," Jay cried, "what are you doing?"

Her flashlight lay amid the stalagmites, still shining. Far beyond its small circle of light, Jay and Dr. Cooper could hear Lila racing back up the tunnel with incredible speed.

"Did you see her?" Dr. Cooper exclaimed, carefully getting to his feet. "Did you see her face?"

"What happened?"

His voice was desperate. "The very thing José de Carlon wrote about and warned about. Whatever it is, she has it—the curse of Toco-Rey!"

FIVE

Armond Basehart and his three men were suddenly startled by faraway, echoing screams coming out of the pit like anguished screams from hell. Tomás, Juan, and Carlos crouched, gripping their rifles, their eyes white and wide with terror in the dark of the jungle.

Even scientific-minded Dr. Basehart was unnerved by the sound. "It's—I think it's the girl."

Tomás nodded, his face etched with fear. "This is not good, señor. It's—"

The sound was getting closer, louder, wilder. They could hear running footsteps, the other Coopers shouting, the girl screaming. All the voices echoed from far below like ghosts in a deep, forbidden crypt.

Dr. Basehart leaned over the wall and shined his light into the pit. "One of you had better get down there and see what happened." He looked at his men. "It could be—AAUUGH!"

Something grabbed his arm, then the edge of his coat, then clawed and climbed over him like a wild

215

cat, knocking him to the ground. Juan and Carlos cursed in Spanish, unable to believe their eyes.

"Grab her!" Tomás yelled. "Señorita, stop!"

Juan dropped his rifle to free his hands. She was coming right at him, her eyes wild, her teeth bared, her breath huffing.

He tried to stop her, plead with her. He grabbed hold of her. "Señorita, please—"

She threw him off as if he weighed nothing, and he tumbled head over heels into the brush. Without looking back, she ran headlong into the jungle. They could hear her crashing through the thick growth into the dark night, getting farther and farther away. She screamed again.

And then they heard another scream—*the* other scream, from somewhere in the ruins. It seemed to be answering her.

"Basehart!" came Dr. Cooper's voice from below.

Dr. Basehart and his men dove at the rope and pulled Dr. Cooper from the pit.

"Where's my daughter?" Jacob Cooper demanded, scrambling over the wall.

"She . . ." Dr. Basehart fumbled to answer, still in shock.

"*Where is she?*" he yelled.

Dr. Basehart's voice trembled. "She ran into the jungle. We couldn't stop her. She was mad, out of her mind!"

"Get my son out of there!"

They quickly pulled Jay out of the pit.

Dr. Cooper was seething. "So the green slugs are harmless, eh?" He grabbed Tomás by the collar.

"You call *that* harmless? My daughter is a raving animal!"

Dr. Basehart intervened, pulling Jacob Cooper away from Tomás. "Dr. Cooper, we are just as surprised as you! We had no idea—"

They heard another scream. It was Lila.

"Come on," said Dr. Cooper, leading the way into the jungle, "we'll talk later."

Tomás cautioned, "It is dangerous! There are snakes, carvies, maybe Kachakas!"

"Come on!"

They pushed into the jungle, trying their best to follow Lila's trail. Dr. Cooper kept probing the thick growth with his flashlight, finding broken branches, trampled leaves and vines, footprints in the soft earth. Her speed and agility through this tangled mess was uncanny. Not only was she out of her mind, but a massive adrenaline rush also gave her super strength. Sometimes it seemed she had bounded over the top of everything.

"The curse of Toco-Rey," Dr. Cooper muttered bitterly, groping about, slashing with his machete. "Toxic slime! That's all José de Carlon encountered. That's all it ever was. I shouldn't have believed Tomás. I should have gotten Lila out of here right away and put her in a hospital!"

Dr. Basehart tried to defend himself. "Dr. Cooper, we can't be sure what caused—"

"Then find out!" Dr. Cooper snapped back. "You're the scientist, the biologist with the lab. Find out what the stuff is and how we can undo whatever it's doing!"

"My primary purpose here is not biological research, Doctor!" Basehart objected loudly. "I'm here to find the treasure of Kachi-Tochetin—and so are you, I might add!"

Dr. Cooper spun around, eyes blazing, clenching a fist, ready to strike. He quickly controlled himself but struck hard with his words. "Put your greed on hold, Dr. Basehart, until we find my daughter!" He turned and continued pushing through the brush.

Armond Basehart followed, clearly offended. "I beg your pardon!"

"You heard me! You and your boss can just—"

They burst into the clear.

Juan screamed. The others froze, guns in hand.

They were standing before the crumbling stone wall of what had been an Oltecan dwelling. On the ground at the base of the wall, a human-shaped mass of squirming, slimy blobs boiled, crawled, hissed, and squeaked.

For a moment, no one moved. No one could think of what to do.

Tomás came up behind Dr. Cooper and whispered in his ear. "They are turning from yellow to green," Tomás noted. "They may be more timid now."

Dr. Cooper approached cautiously, machete and spray bottle ready to take on any carvy that came near him. Some of the slimy creatures began to notice him and half-fly, half-hop away.

So suddenly that he startled the others, Jacob Cooper yelled and flashed his machete back and forth, causing a commotion that sent the carvies fluttering into the trees and ruins like a flock of frightened birds.

"Oh no . . ." said Dr. Basehart as he looked, horrified, at what remained on the ground.

Tomás took one look and then crossed himself.

Jacob Cooper approached cautiously, shining his flashlight on the remains of a person, now nothing more than a skeleton covered with green slime, propped against the wall. "It's Brad Frederick, one of the Cory party."

The others moved closer in shock and amazement, flashlights illuminating the dead, grinning skeleton before them.

"How can you tell?" Dr. Basehart asked.

"Remember the video?" Dr. Cooper responded, shining his light in the skeleton's face. "That big, white grin is unmistakable."

"No one touch it," Dr. Basehart cautioned as he knelt beside the skeleton to scrape off a sample of the green slime with a stick. "I'll take this sample back to the lab and see if I can match it with the slime we took from Lila earlier today." He carefully folded the stick in his handkerchief and placed it in a vest pocket. "But now it all makes perfect sense, doesn't it?"

"Does it?" Dr. Cooper asked.

Dr. Basehart looked up at the group. "The slug toxin. The Kachakas use it to tip their darts. We found darts at the Corys' camp, so we know the Kachakas must have attacked them. This man, Brad Frederick, must have been hit with a poison dart, and he contracted the same symptoms as your daughter: madness and extreme paranoia, followed eventually by paralysis and death. He fled the scene of the attack, wandered among these ruins, and finally succumbed here. The carvies are the jungle's housekeepers. They have, uh, cleaned up the remains in their own way." Now he directed his words to Tomás, Juan, and Carlos. "So this 'curse' you've been so afraid of is nothing more than the toxin the carvies produce in their slime. Nature itself has found a way to guard the treasure of Kachi-Tochetin: poisonous slugs."

Tomás tried to argue. "But Señor Basehart, Juan and Carlos and I have all touched the green slime before. We have handled the green slugs. We have never gone crazy. The slime does not hurt us."

Basehart thought that over. "Your ancestors have probably developed an immunity over the generations. The slime, regardless of its color, could produce a very different reaction in foreigners." He looked at the Coopers. "Which could be why Kachi-Tochetin found it so appropriate."

Jay had been pondering something for several moments, and now he finally got the chance to ask, "But Dr. Basehart, if this is Brad Frederick, then who's buried in the grave back at the Corys' camp?"

For just an instant, Dr. Basehart seemed stumped by the question. "I forgot. There were *four* in the Cory party. We buried the three we found in the camp. This one, Mr. Frederick, met his terrible fate here in the ruins." Dr. Basehart rose to his feet ceremoniously. "But now he, too, will be buried in a proper grave. We will see to that."

Jacob Cooper was quite edgy. "But first we have to find Lila, before she ends up"—he shot a glance toward the skeleton at their feet—"like this."

Jay swallowed. The thought was too horrible to imagine. "Man, let's go."

"Tomás and Juan will help you search," said Dr. Basehart, not even looking at his men to see if they approved of their assignment. "Carlos will accompany me back to the lab. I'm going to analyze this sample to see if I can isolate the toxin. We'll have to hope I can find an antidote in time."

"We'll find Lila," said Dr. Cooper with grave determination, "and we'll bring her to you."

They were startled by another long, mournful wail deep within the ruins.

"That's Lila," said Jay excitedly. "She's not too far away."

"Good luck," said Dr. Basehart, heading back toward the compound.

Dr. Cooper instructed Tomás, "You and Juan circle that way; Jay and I will go this way. We'll try to keep Lila between us until we can narrow down her location."

They split up and headed into the jungle, moving slowly, cautiously. They kept an eye open for snakes and yellow carvies while keeping an ear open for any other sounds from Lila.

After they had gone some distance, Dr. Cooper stopped and motioned for Jay to hold up. They listened a moment. There was no sound.

And then there was. Another long, mournful wail.

"Dad," Jay whispered in concern, "that wasn't Lila."

Jacob Cooper nodded, then whispered, "Which means Armond Basehart has some explaining to do."

"What do you mean?"

"He worked with the Cory party until they were killed. He had the video, he knew them by name, and now he's asking us to believe that he buried three of them and forgot about the other two."

"Two?"

"Brad Frederick . . . and now this other scream we've been hearing." Dr. Cooper listened a moment, but there was no other sound. "It's a human being in anguish, just like Lila. If you ask me, I think it's another one of the Cory party."

Jay wrinkled his nose. "So there were *five* people on the Cory team?"

"We don't know. But I'm bothered that Dr. Basehart doesn't seem to remember."

Jay asked, "If two of them went crazy like Lila, why would he try to hide that from us?"

Dr. Cooper sighed with disgust. "Greed. He's so intent on finding the treasure that he doesn't want us concerning ourselves with the Corys."

Jay thought it over, then nodded. "Yeah. If we thought the Corys were still alive, we'd be trying to help them instead of searching for the treasure."

"Exactly. I don't think a man like Armond Basehart has time for such moral considerations. And I don't think he was planning on us finding that skeleton—or hearing these screams."

"So what really happened? Were the Corys

attacked by the Kachakas or did they go crazy from contact with slug slime, or was it both, or what?"

"I think Armond Basehart knows but isn't telling. And now I'm wondering if he really has claustrophobia. It could be he's—"

A scream, then snarling and more screaming and thrashing in the brush: It was close by.

Dr. Cooper and Jay dove into the brush, shouldering their way through it, pushing, plowing, clawing ahead. It sounded like a chase out there: a victim fleeing, a predator hunting. They could envision the worst.

They broke out of the brush and into a clearing. They'd found more ruins—more gray, crumbling stone jutting up through the thick undergrowth. They shined their lights back and forth, the beams searching, searching. Someone was running, screaming, struggling on the other side of that crumbling wall. They caught sight of a droopy, billed cap.

"It's Lila!" Dr. Cooper exclaimed, running toward the ruin, his gun in his hand and Jay right alongside.

They leaped to the top of the wall. It was an old dwelling, four walls with no roof. Over in the corner, amid vines and plants, their light beams caught a young girl cowering in terror, her body curled up, her arms over her head.

"Lila!" her dad hollered, jumping down from the wall and running toward her.

Still atop the wall, Jay saw the bushes moving. Something was heading in Dr. Cooper's direction.

"Dad!"

Dr. Cooper heard the warning, felt a commotion to his left, and looked just in time to see—teeth! flashing eyes! a powerful fist!

He deflected the blow, ducked another one, then crouched down and used a judo move the third time to throw the creature into the bushes. It thrashed about, righting itself, leaping to its feet. It came at him again.

He had dropped his gun and the flashlight. No time to look for them.

The thing took a powerful leap through the air, arms outstretched, fingers like claws, a scream in its throat. Dr. Cooper ducked, deflected the weight, threw it off. Once again, it tumbled into the bushes.

No way to overpower it, Dr. Cooper thought. *I can only deflect it, but for how long?* He saw a metallic gleam amid the vines several feet away. He started to reach for it.

OOF! The blow knocked him sideways into green vines and crackling branches. He rolled onto his back and saw a face coming out of the dark. It was green, raging, other-worldly, drooling, full of murder.

The creature leaped. Jacob Cooper planted a foot in its belly and kicked it over his head and into the bushes again.

Now for that gun! He groped for it, searched for it.
BOOM!

Jay had found it and fired a round into the air.

The thing let out a cry of alarm and seemed to hesitate.

"Go on!" Jay hollered, shooting into the air again. "Get out of here!"

It turned and fled, thrashing through the brush.

Dr. Cooper got to his feet.

"Dad!" Jay screamed, "Look out!"

Dr. Cooper spun around, saw it coming, ducked.

A poison dart thunked into a branch right next to his head.

Poof! A puff of air. A second dart zipped past Jay's ear.

The Coopers dropped to the ground, scurried, crawled, then peered through the leaves and branches. Dr. Cooper found his flashlight.

The light beam fell on a small hand clutching a short length of bamboo cane, aiming it.

Poof! Another dart zinged through the leaves and branches only inches from Dr. Cooper's head.

"Don't shoot!" he called. "We're friends!"

They heard a frightened gasp. No more darts came their way.

"Hello?" Jacob Cooper called again. "Can you see us? We're friends. We won't hurt you."

They poked their heads up and waved their hands so they could be clearly seen.

A dark-skinned, native girl looked back at them, a blowgun in her hand. Her face was full of fear. But when she saw them, she seemed to relax.

Then she let out a sigh and slumped to the ground in a faint.

They rushed forward to help her, cradling her head, feeling for a pulse. Her heartbeat was strong and she was breathing okay.

"Poor thing," said Dr. Cooper. "She must have been terrified." He picked up her blowgun and slipped it into his shirt pocket, then he used his flashlight to illumine the olive-skinned face and long, jet black hair. She was young, beautiful, close to Lila's age and stature.

"She's a native," Dr. Cooper observed. "Probably a Kachaka."

Jay was dismayed. "How'd she get Lila's hat?"

"She may have found it . . . or she could have encountered Lila." He gently stroked her forehead and spoke to her. "Hello, little girl. Come on, wake up."

A glow fell upon the girl's face and the stones of the old wall. There was a sound behind them.

As they turned, they saw torches coming over the wall and the dimly lit outlines of several men—*big* men—in loose clothing, some bare-chested. Some wore straw hats. They were carrying knives, rifles, clubs. A voice jabbered at them in an unknown language. More torches appeared. The light washed over the area.

A man approached them ahead of the others, his intense, lined face clear in the light of the torches. He was a native. Wearing pants and a ragged shirt topped by a tattered straw hat, he also carried an old rifle. When he saw them with the pitiful, unconscious girl, his eyes filled with horror and then rage. He screamed at them, aiming his rifle.

They let go of the girl and raised their hands.

The man screamed orders to his men, who immediately pushed through the brush toward them, brandishing their weapons. Two grabbed Jacob Cooper, putting a knife to his throat. Two more grabbed Jay and held him, taking away his father's gun. Two others gently picked up the girl and carried her aside. One more helped himself to the Coopers' flashlights.

Dr. Cooper spoke, though he was careful not to move or give his captors any reason to use the knife. "We were trying to help her. She was being attacked."

The man seemed amused. "You like to make up stories?"

Here was a little hope. "You know English?"

The man cocked his head and smirked as if he'd heard a dumb question. "I pick up a little here and there. Yours sounds very good."

"Sir, we *rescued* your daughter. She was being attacked—"

"By *you!*" the man hollered, gesturing with the barrel of the rifle. "You cannot fool me! You are mukai-tochetin!" His eyes darted about the ruins for an instant as if looking for hidden dangers. "You are everywhere! You want to scare us and kill us. Why? We are Kachakas! We did not violate the tomb!"

Uh-oh. This could be serious. "You are Kachakas?"

"You know that. Mukai-tochetin know everything. You know I am the chief, and you know the girl is my daughter." He raised his rifle and appeared to be seriously considering pulling the trigger. "And that is why you tried to kill her, yes? To hurt *me!*"

"Sir . . . I am Dr. Jacob Cooper from America, and this is my son, Jay—"

The chief aimed the rifle directly into Dr. Cooper's face. Dr. Cooper could see right along the barrel into his eye. "No more lies! You only want to scare us, to kill us, to kill my daughter and hurt me!" He pulled back the hammer. "But I think I hurt you first!"

SIX

Another man shouted at the chief and then spoke hurriedly, as if trying to reason with him. It must have been a good argument—the chief uncocked his rifle and lowered it. The two talked a moment, throwing suggestions and counter-suggestions back and forth and pointing at the Coopers.

Finally, the chief gave in and spoke in English. "We take you to our village." He jerked his thumb toward the man who argued with him. "Manito says if you are really mukai-tochetin, it will do no good to shoot you. But he thinks you are not mukai-tochetin. He thinks maybe you are just stupid Americans. We find out."

With some not-so-gentle prodding from their well-armed captors, Jay and Dr. Cooper started walking through the ruins toward the unexplored jungle on the other side.

Jacob Cooper's anxiety was obvious as he told Jay, "We sure don't need this right now. Lila's still out there, probably dying."

"So how do we get out of it?" Jay responded.

The chief was walking just ahead of them. Dr. Cooper called to him, "Uh, Chief . . ."

"Chief Yoaxa," the chief informed him.

"Thank you. Chief Yoaxa. Listen, my daughter is lost somewhere in these ruins and in great danger. We were trying to find her when we found your daughter instead. Your daughter was being attacked by a, uh, a wild man. I don't know how else to describe it."

The chief gave Dr. Cooper a good, long look and then smiled craftily. "Oh yes. A wild man. A mukai-tochetin!"

"Mukai-tochetin." Jay was getting sick of the word. "What is that, anyway?"

The chief grinned as if being joked with. "You mukai-tochetin are very tricky. You try to test me, yes? But I know. When the great king Kachi-Tochetin was buried in his tomb, his best warriors were buried with him so their spirits would guard his treasure. You see? I know what you are." His eyes narrowed with bitter anger. "But why are you out of your tomb? Why do you bother us? We do not like to be scared and screamed at and attacked! We have never bothered your treasure! We have not even seen it! We do not deserve the curse!" He gestured with his rifle, making his message clear. "You should go back to sleep in your tomb. Leave the living world to us!"

Dr. Cooper and Jay exchanged a glance. This was the Kachaka explanation for the toxin-induced madness!

"Chief Yoaxa, listen," said Dr. Cooper. "I have

230

good news for you. These people who are wandering about in the ruins are not the warriors of Kachi-Tochetin, not at all. They are explorers from America who have . . . well, they're sick and dying. They're out of their minds because—"

"Because they are ghosts." The chief pointed his finger right in their faces. "And you are ghosts, dead warriors, just like them!"

"Chief, we are not dead warriors."

The chief was getting impatient. "You attacked my daughter!"

Dr. Cooper was also getting impatient. "We did *not* attack your daughter! We saved your daughter from—well, from one of the sick Americans. He almost killed us and your daughter shot poison darts at us . . . If anything, we deserve your thanks!"

The chief got angry when he heard that. "See? You lie! Kachaka children do not shoot poison darts. We forbid it!"

"Well, that may be true but—"

The chief held up his hand. "No more talking! When we get to the village, we find out."

They continued along a well-beaten path through the jungle. Eventually they reached a small village where at least two hundred men, women, and children waited anxiously for the return of their chief and his men. The village was an odd mixture of old and new, of civilized and savage. Grass huts stood alongside crude, wood-framed dwellings; there were campfires but also cookstoves. Both torches and oil lanterns lit the narrow corridor between the dwellings. A few folks didn't seem to mind wearing little or nothing while they worked, yet most of the people were fully dressed in white garments, some skillfully embroidered.

As for the Kachakas' choice of weapons, almost every warrior carried a blowgun on his belt, but many also carried rifles, pistols, and knives.

Some of the women in the village looked especially anxious, as if they had been dreading this moment. When they saw the limp body of the girl being carried by the two men, they threw up their hands and wailed in fear and anguish. With tears and rapid-fire babblings of concern, they gently took her from her two carriers and bore her into the nearest wooden shack where they laid her on a cot.

The chief stopped just outside the door of the crude dwelling, watching the women work to revive the girl, then turned to the Coopers. "See the pain you have brought? She has been missing since early evening, and we looked for her until it was a long time dark. We told all the children, 'Don't go into the ruins, there are mukai-tochetin there.'" The chief shook his head as he peered through the doorway at his unconscious daughter. "I think that is why she went. She has always wanted to see one." He looked at Dr. Cooper. "Well . . . now she has."

Jacob Cooper couldn't help sighing in frustration. "Chief Yoaxa—"

"Follow me," the chief said, waving his hand and leading the way.

The men holding the Coopers prodded them forward through the village, past the humble grass huts, clapboard shacks, firepits, and milling, curious people.

Jay noticed a man wearing a strange, disk-shaped charm around his neck. Then he saw another one. Then Dr. Cooper spotted two more.

The Kachakas were wearing the dried, stretched skins of *caracoles volantes* as jewelry!

"Carvies!" Jay exclaimed.

That made the chief turn his head. "You should be happy. We wear carvies to please you, but . . . I guess not today."

Jay tried to win a few points. "Oh, but we're *very* pleased."

The chief brightened. "Then you *are* mukai-tochetin!"

Jay made a sour face, mentally kicking himself.

Jacob Cooper coaxed some information. "I understand they're poisonous."

Chief Yoaxa enjoyed answering that question. "Oh, yes, they are poisonous. They will kill you just by touching you. Unless . . ."

"Unless what?"

"Unless you catch them in the morning. Then they don't hurt you. We play with them, we cook them and eat them, and there is no trouble."

Dr. Cooper nodded. "Yes. We've been told that."

They came to the end of the village and turned a corner. Directly ahead of them was what looked like a row of rabbit hutches and a large chicken pen, all made from poles and wire mesh.

The Coopers stopped short at the sight of the cages. The men behind them poked them forward.

The rabbit hutches and the chicken pen were full of carvies—yellow, angry carvies. The slugs came to life the moment the group approached. Flapping about in the cages, hissing, and chirping, they flitted from wall to wall, their little black eyes devilish and threatening.

"These carvies, they are special," said the chief. "We caught them in the morning, so it was easy, but then we kept them in these cages until night. You do that and they get dangerous. Just watch."

The chief pulled a small, sharpened dart from a quiver on his belt. Sticking it through the wire mesh, he rubbed its tip against a yellow carvy's slimy back. When he withdrew it, the tip of the dart glistened.

Dr. Cooper eyed the dart carefully. "So this is the poison dart of the Kachakas?"

The chief held it up proudly. "Yes. We make them ourselves! Now watch."

He skillfully inserted the dart into the blowgun that hung over his shoulder, then looked for a target. Some pigs were grunting and rooting in the grass nearby. He put the blowgun to his mouth, gave it a strong blast of air, and the dart shot like an arrow, sticking a pig in the flank.

The pig did more than squeal; it shrieked, twirled, grunted, scurried in a little circle, and then flopped to the ground, legs twitching. In only seconds, it was dead.

The chief grinned. "It works quick, you see? It can kill you. Unless . . ."

"Unless what?" Dr. Cooper asked.

The chief smiled jubilantly. "Unless you are dead already."

Dr. Cooper's heart sank. "Oh. Of course."

"We have a legend: The carvies belong to the mukai-tochetin. Together, they guard the treasure. If you are one of Kachi-Tochetin's warriors, the yellow carvies will not hurt you."

Dr. Cooper could see where this was leading and did not like it one bit. "But as I've been trying to tell you, we're not ghosts, or warriors, or anything else. We're living, breathing American explorers."

The chief shrugged again. "We'll find out. If you are dead already, the yellow carvies won't hurt you—so we'll take you back to Toco-Rey and bury you where you belong. If you are just stupid Americans, the carvies will kill you—and I'll admit I was wrong."

Suddenly, the chief's men had a much firmer grip on Jay and his father. They meant business.

Dr. Cooper tried to remain calm and rational, though being only a few feet from a swarm of yellow carvies made that difficult. "Chief, does it make any sense for the warriors of Kachi-Tochetin to have white skin, speak English, and dress like Americans?"

This time the chief sighed. "The warriors we have seen in the ruins have green skin, they don't dress much at all, and they don't speak English. They yell and scream."

Jay objected, "So what about us? We have white skin, we're dressed, and we speak English! I mean, *come on* . . . !"

The chief thought about that for a moment, but he was a stubborn man, and all his men were watching. "Like I say, mukai-tochetin are very tricky."

"Chief Yoaxa!" Dr. Cooper talked slowly and

deliberately, trying to spell it out. "Listen to me: Those green, screaming warriors are Americans who have come in contact with the slime from the carvies. The slime has made them crazy, and it's killing them. We've seen it. There's a dead man in the ruins right now—and my daughter is still out there, poisoned, mad, and dying. Instead of killing us, why don't you help us?"

The chief's face lit up and he pointed his finger in Jacob Cooper's face. "Ah! You see? You think you can fool me. Carvies don't make you crazy. They kill you."

"But—"

"Listen, I'm giving you a good deal. You should take it and be glad."

Dr. Cooper looked at the chief, then at Jay, then back at the chief, thinking it all over. Then, strangely, he relaxed and nodded. "All right. You've convinced me. We'll take your test."

Jay did *not* agree. "Dad! You can't let them do this!"

Dr. Cooper straightened his spine, drew a deep breath, and put a consoling hand on his son's shoulder. "Son, there comes a time when we simply have to face our destiny like real men."

"We do?" Jay looked up and read a message in his father's eyes. "Oh. Uh, yeah, you're right, Dad. Yeah. Like real men."

The carvies in the big cage were drooling and hissing at Dr. Cooper even as he looked at the men guarding him. "Gentlemen, I agree to the chief's offer. Shall we proceed?"

Dr. Cooper no longer resisted them, but stood there relaxed, willing and ready. He could tell they were impressed by that; their grip on him eased up a bit. He stepped forward to the cage door. "I only hope that once I'm dead, you'll go out and find my daughter." He looked at the chief. "And I believe your daughter will be all right. I think she only fainted." He gently raised his left arm to remove his hat. The man holding him allowed him to do so. "Let justice be done."

He turned to hand his hat to the men behind him. They were impressed by his gentle compliance; they actually released him.

The man who took his hat was the first to see a huge fist, and then stars. The other man caught Jacob Cooper's left hook a fraction of a second later, and then he saw only grass.

Jay was expecting his father's move and made some quick moves himself, first planting his foot behind the man on his right to trip him. Then he spun and planted his foot in the groin of the other man to give him something to think about.

"Run!" his father shouted, taking on three Kachakas while ten more closed in on him.

With his father holding back the Kachakas, Jay turned and ran like the wind. Out of the village and into the cover of the jungle, he had little idea of which way to go except toward the ruins. Tomás and Juan had to be out there somewhere. They had rifles and could help, if only he could find them! He could hear the struggle going on back in the village: the shouts, the blows. Then his father yelled one more time, "Run, Jay, run!" Jay tried to hold back his tears. In the dark of the jungle, he was nearly blind as it was.

By now, Dr. Cooper could see nothing but Kachaka faces, bodies, and arms. He was floating in a mob of angry, shouting natives. They held his arms, his legs, his hair. He couldn't struggle or trip or punch or even move. It was over. From somewhere he could hear the chief yell an order. The mob started moving as one man toward the cage.

Dear Lord, he prayed. *Just let Jay make it out of here. And remember Lila, wherever she is.*

He could hear someone fumbling with the cage door. The carvies were going absolutely wild.

And then the crowd fell quiet. He could hear the chief's voice now, not yelling but talking to someone. The someone was a woman.

The voice of a young girl joined them. He couldn't understand the language, but she was speaking clearly. The chief's daughter? It had to be!

The Kachakas carrying Dr. Cooper eased their grip and set him on the ground. Many of them actually let go and backed off. When enough of their bodies were out of the way, he could finally see that the chief was talking to a lovely woman, most likely his wife, and . . . oh, praise God! The chief's daughter! She was still wearing Lila's droopy, billed cap, and she pointed at Dr. Cooper, rapidly explaining something to her father. He kept objecting and trying to argue, but apparently she would not change her opinion.

Finally the chief straightened up, looked at Dr. Cooper with disappointment and embarrassment, and gave his men an order. They all let go of Dr. Cooper and gave him some space. One even returned his hat.

"My daughter says you did not attack her," the chief admitted. "She says you . . ." He really hated to say it. "She says you saved her from a mukai-tochetin."

Dr. Cooper exhaled a sigh of relief. His shoulders relaxed as he returned the girl's gaze. Her eyes were clear and beautiful. He could tell her mind and memory were intact.

She must have learned her heavily accented English from her father. "Gracias, Señor American, for saving my life."

Dr. Cooper removed his newly returned hat to show his respect and gratitude. "You're most welcome. And thank you for saving mine." He stole a quick glance at the chief to make sure he was correct in saying that.

The chief was reluctant, but finally nodded yes. "You are not mukai-tochetin. One mukai-tochetin would not fight another." He put his hand on his daughter's shoulder. "This is María. María, this is . . ."

"Dr. Jacob Cooper." He took just a few steps toward the girl, reached into his shirt pocket, and brought out her small blowgun. "I believe this belongs to you."

She took one look at it and shook her head. "Oh no," she said emphatically. "That is not mine."

Hmm. Interesting. Dr. Cooper played along.

"Oh. Well, it must belong to one of the men here."
He tossed it to the nearest Kachaka warrior, who
looked it over, shook his head, and then passed it to
the next. It began circulating among the men in
search of an owner. "But please, can you tell me if
you've seen my daughter? She's about your age and
height, with fair skin and long, blond hair. She's lost
somewhere in the ruins."

The girl's eyes betrayed some kind of knowledge,
but she was hesitant to speak.

Jacob Cooper prompted, "That is my daughter
Lila's hat. Where did you find it?"

She still hesitated until her mother bent and
spoke some quiet but firm words in her ear. Then
she admitted, "I got this hat from a mukai-
tochetin."

That brought a gasp from some of the women
standing nearby and alarmed looks from all of the
men, including her father.

"Tell him the rest," her father ordered. "Tell *us!*"

"She was a girl, like me. Her face . . ." She
touched her cheek as she spoke it. "Her face was
green, like a lizard."

The Kachakas muttered to each other, exchanging looks of alarm.

"Did she attack you?" the chief asked with a suspicious, sideways glance at Dr. Cooper.

The girl hesitated, then answered timidly. "Sí. She
. . . she jumped out of the bushes and screamed at
me. She was like a crazy person. . . ."

"*She* was a mukai-tochetin!" the chief proclaimed
as if trying to regain his pride. "What did you do?"

240

"I ran."

"You ran away?"

"Sí."

The chief patted her shoulder. "Ah. That was good."

Dr. Cooper asked, "Then . . . how did you get her hat?"

The girl thought a moment, then replied. "I found her later. She was lying on the ground. And I took her hat."

Dr. Cooper leaned forward. "Lying on the ground? Why? Was something wrong with her?"

The girl looked from Dr. Cooper to the Kachaka men and women to her father and mother, and then at Dr. Cooper again. "She is dead."

SEVEN

J acob Cooper could not give up hope. "Can you take me to her? Can you show me where she is?"

She looked to her father. He nodded that it would be okay. "Sí, señor."

"We need to go," said Dr. Cooper. "Right now. Jay's out there somewhere, too."

Chief Yoaxa chose four of his toughest men to go with them. Then quickly, to get it over with, he handed Dr. Cooper his gun and two flashlights. "You will want these in the ruins."

María headed through the village while Dr. Cooper, her father, and four burly Kachakas followed. They took the main trail into the jungle, carrying torches and lanterns, guns and knives, as well as Kachaka blowguns with plenty of darts.

Jay thought he knew where he was when he came to an old stone wall, but it was so covered with jungle growth that he totally lost his bearings as he tried to explore around it. Finally, breaking out from under the thick jungle canopy, he saw stars overhead and determined which direction was north. He'd gotten turned around, all right. Doing a complete about-face, he headed the other direction, south, hoping to encounter the Pyramid of the Sun or any other familiar landmark. He had to get back to the compound and find help.

He was thinking of his father and sister, and how little time there was. Hope was hard to hang onto, but he tried.

Lila Cooper was not dead. She was dazed, half-conscious, half-dreaming, lying amid vines and rubble at the base of a lone, basalt pillar that had held up a roof centuries ago. She was still dressed in the extra clothes she'd put on to protect herself from slug slime, and she was feeling hot, sweaty, tired, and achy.

But she didn't want to wake up. Somehow she knew there was a very spooky world beyond her closed eyelids. It was better to hide inside her dazed mind where the world was all laughing, dancing colors; the ground was still moving like a carnival ride; and no bogeymen could get her.

"Señorita?" came a voice from somewhere.

Who was that, the bogeyman? Go away. I don't believe in you.

"Señorita?" came the voice again, and then it started talking in hushed tones with another voice. It was all Spanish; she couldn't understand much of it.

She could sense a light shining on her eyelids. It made her squint.

"Aha!" said the voice. "Está viva!"

She raised her hand to her face and then opened her eyes just a crack. There were lights out there, shining in her face.

"Señorita Cooper, it is us, Juan and Tomás. Are you all right?"

Tomás. It took her a moment to remember who he was. She opened her eyes completely and could make out two men kneeling beside her with their flashlights.

"Tomás?" she heard herself saying.

"Sí, señorita. It is a good thing we found you. How are you feeling?"

"Hot."

She sat up and removed her gloves and extra shirt. When she raised her hand to wipe the hair from her eyes, she saw something peculiar. She looked at her hand again, then leaned forward to view it in the beam of Tomás's flashlight. "What happened?"

"We think it was the carvy slime, señorita. It made you loco . . . crazy . . . and it made you look a little green." Tomás chuckled, and so did Juan.

"A little . . . ," Her hand looked *very* green to her.

Juan shined his flashlight on her hands and face and made some comments.

Tomás agreed and told Lila, "It was much worse, but you seem to be getting better now. Can you stand up? We will take you back to the compound."

She tried to get her feet under her. With Tomás's strong arms to help, she finally stood up. "Ouch!" Her hand went to her leg. "My leg hurts."

"Would you like me to carry you?"

She tried to walk. After a few shaky steps, it came a little more easily. "Where are my father and brother?"

"They are out looking for you. We'll get you safely back, and then we'll find them, don't worry."

María knew the ruins well, even in the dark. She led her father, the Kachaka warriors, and Dr. Cooper directly through the jungle to an old basalt pillar that had once supported a roof.

There María was disturbed to find Lila gone. "She . . . was lying right here! I saw her! I took her hat!"

Chief Yoaxa puffed up his chest and crossed his arms. "Ha! She is a mukai-tochetin! She cannot die. She will haunt these ruins forever!"

Dr. Cooper looked at the area carefully. It was matted down as if someone had been lying there. "María . . . how long ago was that?"

"It was before the mukai-tochetin chased me."

"The wild, green man?"

"Yes. He came from over there." She pointed toward a spooky looking, pillared temple just barely visible in the dark.

"He chased me, but you came to help me—"

"Yes, he came to help you, like the great hero!" Chief Yoaxa cut in, tired of hearing that story. He glared at Dr. Cooper. "Manito thinks you are okay, and María thinks you are okay, but I think you are a mukai-tochetin, like your daughter. You have bewitched María to lie!"

Dr. Cooper had no time to argue further. "Lila's still out here somewhere, and we have to find her—"

The scream. It came from *out there* somewhere, out in the limitless dark jungle.

Chief Yoaxa and his men were clearly frightened. "We must get back to our village now."

"No, wait," Dr. Cooper objected. "I need your help."

The Chief gathered his daughter close to him. "You do not need *our* help, Dr. Cooper!" He looked into the dead ruins and ink-black jungle. "You have the mukai-tochetin! They are your friends, yes? Your daughter is one of them. I think you are too. Maybe this is all a trap!"

Chief Yoaxa's men started to buy into his argument. They began to edge away.

"Wait!" said Dr. Cooper. "You know these ruins. You can help me search!"

The scream echoed through the ruins again, and they all turned tail and ran, leaving Jacob Cooper alone amid the aging stones, the bottomless shadows, the eerie sounds.

Dr. Armond Basehart held the syringe up to the light. It was full of red blood, a good sample. He was satisfied.

Lila had shed the extra clothes she'd worn into the pit and sat comfortably on a couch in his lab, pressing a cotton ball to the puncture in her arm. "What about my father and brother?"

"Tomás, Juan, and Carlos are out searching for them right now," he answered, preparing to distribute her blood into several small test tubes. "They'll be all right. But we have to do all we can to find out what happened to you before the symptoms are totally gone."

She looked at her arms. They still had a greenish cast but were steadily returning to their natural pink. "It's going away pretty fast."

He leaned over her with a cotton swab. "Lean back."

She looked up. "Huh?"

He forced her head back with his hand on her forehead, a touch she did not appreciate, and took a smear sample from her nostrils.

"What's that for?" she asked, wrinkling her nose to relieve the tickle of the swab.

Instead of answering her question, he asked, "Did you see or touch anything unusual before you fell into the pit the first time?"

She thought it over and then shook her head. "All I remember is falling into all those slugs and getting slime all over me."

"Anything afterward?"

"The pit," she answered. "The pit was weird."

"Mm-hm."

Dr. Basehart rolled the cotton swab along a microscope slide. Then he put the slide under his microscope and slowly turned the focus knob.

From the look on his face, Lila could see he'd found something interesting. "What do you see?"

He ignored her question.

She didn't mind asking again. "What's . . . uh, what are you looking at?"

He gave an exasperated sigh like he didn't want

to answer her question, but then he turned and smiled at her. The smile looked a little phony. "Oh, pollen, dust . . . even a tiny bug!"

In her *nose*? "Oh, yuk!"

He just laughed.

"Can I see?"

He waved her off. "No, not now. I have too many things to process here."

His tone actually sounded a little harsh. She didn't argue with him. She was too tired and she didn't want to aggravate him. Besides, a burning itch on her lower leg was screaming for attention. She pulled her sock down to scratch it and found a welt. "Hey, Dr. Basehart. The green's going away faster around this insect bite. Does that mean anything?"

He didn't seem to mind that question. He came over immediately to take a closer look. The welt seemed to fascinate him for a moment, but then he just shook his head. "Mm, no, I think that's coincidental."

"Sure hurts," she complained.

"Well, the insects around here can bite pretty hard!" He patted her on the shoulder. "I think I'm all through with you for now. Why don't you go to your trailer and see if you can sleep?"

He went back to the counter and started arranging various samples in a neat row. Lila recognized some of them: the slime he'd wiped from her after she fell in the pit; the blood he'd drawn from her arm; the smear he'd just taken from her nose. He wouldn't say anything, but he had figured something out, she could tell.

And he was excited about whatever it was.

At last! Jay came to the huge pillars that formed the gate to the city. A spare flashlight would have helped immensely, but he had no time for a side trip to the burial temple to get his backpack. Running through the gates, he prayed the Lord would help him find the safe route through the treacherous swamp. He couldn't wait to get back to the compound.

Jay didn't know that his father was only a mile or so behind him, rushing desperately to catch up. Dr. Cooper could not call out for his son for fear he'd attract the mad man again. All he could do was hurry along, picking his way through the jungle. He located the Pyramid of the Sun, the Avenue of the Dead, and the Pyramid of the Moon. He'd been putting pieces together in his mind and was certain there were no friends waiting for Jay at the compound— only a cunning enemy.

Lila decided she'd follow Dr. Basehart's suggestion and go back to the guest trailer to get some sleep. Soon she would see her father and brother again. After they all rested up, they could get back to finding the treasure with no more interruptions.

I've caused everyone enough trouble, she thought.

But she had another reason for wanting to get out of Armond Basehart's lab trailer, and that was Dr. Basehart. Something about him gave her the creeps, and she didn't need any more needle pokes in her arm or cotton swabs up her nose—not from him, anyway.

She stepped outside, closed the door behind her, and paused to listen to the jungle sounds on the still night air. When would this long night be over, anyway? She wasn't sure what time it was, but it had to be getting close to morning by now.

Hmm. Was that another vehicle parked just behind the rig the Coopers had brought? Had someone new come to the compound? As far as she knew, Dr. Basehart was the only person in the lab trailer. The lights were on in his living trailer, but she couldn't see anyone through the windows.

Well, she could find out in the morning. All she wanted to do right now was wash up as best she could and go to bed. She headed for the guest trailer, stretching her arms and bending out the kinks she still felt from her ordeal.

What was that? The sound wasn't much more than a low thud, but the jungle was spooky. Her nerves were raw enough for the sound to make her jump. It came from behind the lab trailer—from a small, windowless shack she'd never noticed before.

There. Another thumping noise. She could feel her skin tingling with fear.

But now she was curious—and suspicious. Dr. Basehart had a strange way of not answering her questions and keeping information to himself. Just what was he not telling? And what might that little shack be hiding?

She stood on her tiptoes and craned her neck to see through the window of Dr. Basehart's lab trailer. He was still in there, busily at work on the samples.

Ducking down so she wouldn't be seen and moving silently, she slipped into the shadows behind the trailer. There she got a clear look at the thrown-together shack that stood in a clear area all by itself. Fresh soil lay on the ground all around it. It could have been an outhouse with a pit dug under it, but it sure seemed big for an outhouse.

Besides, the narrow door was locked shut with not only a padlock but also two hefty slide bolts—all on the outside. Outhouses had little slide bolts on the inside to keep people from bursting in unexpectedly; this one was well secured from the outside to . . . well, to keep someone or something from getting out.

And one other thing: It didn't smell like an outhouse. This shed had a strange, musty smell, like mold or mildew. She wrinkled her nose. Not a good smell.

But it seemed strangely familiar. Where had she smelled it before? She stepped closer, sniffing curiously.

A shriek! Flapping wings, flying feathers! Lila almost jumped out of her skin as a huge macaw fluttered from the roof of the shack, disturbed by her intrusion.

She tried to remain motionless while she found her breath again, her eyes on the rear window of Dr. Basehart's lab trailer. That silly bird must have been making that thumping noise she'd heard, and now it made such a racket she feared she would be discovered.

She could see Dr. Basehart through the window. Apparently he was used to jungle noises. He didn't seem bothered, but just continued cleaning off his work counter. It looked like he might be closing things up for the night. He'd opened a folding partition and was putting some small jars away on a shelf behind it.

Wait a minute. What's that in the room behind the partition? She only caught a glimpse of it before he closed the partition again, but it looked like . . .

CREAK! She flinched, shaking. It was the door to Dr. Basehart's trailer. He was stepping outside. She froze, her mind racing. *What if he sees me back here?*

Click. Dr. Basehart turned out the lights of the lab trailer and closed the trailer door behind him. Maybe he was turning in for the night. Yes, she could hear his footsteps crossing the open space between the three trailers, and then the door to his living trailer squeaked open.

The door slammed shut, and everything went quiet again.

Her heart was still racing—but beginning to slow down. He was gone. She was alone now, hiding in the close, shadowy confines behind his lab.

And she was thinking—not that she *wanted* to think it; it just occurred to her—that if she wanted to, she could take a look inside that trailer. She might be able to figure out what he was working on.

She could also take a peek behind that partition. If nothing else, she could have a look at the bug he'd found in her nose, *if* there really was one. She even remembered that Dr. Basehart kept a flashlight by the door.

Stepping carefully and silently, she peeked around the corner of the lab trailer to be sure he was really gone for the night. She could see one light still on in his living trailer, but then it winked out. Armond Basehart had to be calling it a night.

The thought of taking a look inside the lab trailer became more than a thought; it became a plan.

She built up her courage, drew a deep breath, and then moved like a cat around the lab trailer to its door. It creaked a bit when she opened it, but she got inside without drawing anyone's attention.

Dr. Basehart's emergency flashlight was on a little holder next to the door. She clicked it on, keeping the beam low so it wouldn't be seen, and went to the counter where Dr. Basehart had been working so intently.

The samples were still there, all very orderly: slime from the pit; some other slime she had not seen before; the smear from her nose, still under the microscope; her blood, now distributed into several small vials for testing; and . . .

What is this? She hadn't noticed the glass jar before. Sealed with a lid, it contained a piece of cloth. Somehow it looked familiar. She gave the jar a few turns so she could view it from every side—gray cloth, with a green, chalky dust on it.

Then she remembered. The rag from the Corys'

video! She recalled the images of John Cory using this rag to wipe the golden artifacts from Kachi-Tochetin's tomb. Why would Dr. Basehart want to keep it in a jar?

Oh, wait a minute. She remembered the very first carvy she and her father and brother had seen; it had been hiding in the Corys' tent under a rag just like this one. Maybe that was the connection; Dr. Basehart seemed to want a sample of anything a carvy might touch.

The microscope had its own lamp to illuminate the slide. She found the little switch and clicked it on. Then she peered through the eyepiece and slowly turned the focus wheel.

What in the world? This was no bug. Maybe it was dust, like Dr. Basehart had said. But it was the weirdest looking dust she'd ever seen: thousands of little fuzzy balls—they looked like cockle burrs, or chestnut husks, or sea urchins—with sharp quills sticking out all over them. They looked absolutely wicked.

These were in her *nose*? She shuddered at the thought and clicked off the microscope. She had to know more.

With the flashlight beam low, she moved silently to the partition that divided the trailer in half. Maybe there was nothing important back there after all, but just the fact that Dr. Basehart kept it closed all the time was reason enough for her to want to open it.

She placed her hand on the small plastic handle and slowly drew the partition to the side.

Something glimmered in the beam of her flashlight.

She gasped, her hand over her mouth, frozen in terror and disbelief as a horrible revelation streamed into her mind.

What to do? Where to go?

She had to get out of there. She had to find her father and brother.

She clicked off the flashlight, slipped it back into its little holder, and stole out the trailer door. *Dad, Jay, where are you?*

Dr. Basehart's trailer was still dark. There was no visible activity. She hurried toward her trailer, constantly looking over her shoulder. If she could just get back there and try to act normal—

BUMP! She leaped with a start. The gasp she drew in could have inflated a blimp. She tried not to scream but a small squeak escaped her throat. She'd bumped into someone or some . . . *thing.* It hollered, just as startled as she was, and started stumbling in the dark, trying to recover.

"Shhh!!!" she shushed it.

The wide and startled eyes of her brother gawked back at her. "Lila! What are you doing here?"

She waved her hands to shush him and hissed, "Will you be quiet? You'll wake everybody up!"

"You're all right?" he whispered back, touching her to be sure she was real. "You're still green."

"I'm okay," she answered. Then she started tugging him toward Dr. Basehart's lab. "Come on! I've got to show you something!"

"But Dad's in trouble! The Kachakas have him!"

"We're *all* in trouble!"

They stole quickly into the lab trailer. Lila got the flashlight and then drew back the partition.

Jay took one look into the room beyond and then moaned. "You're right. We're all in trouble."

On two wide shelves against the rear wall were the golden vase, cups, jewelry, figurines—everything—from the Corys' video.

"What are we going to do?" Lila wondered.

CLICK! The sound of the light switch and the sudden flood of light made them gasp and jump and spin around.

There in the doorway, with one hand on the light switch and a gun in the other, was Dr. Armond Basehart. "I thought I heard some noise over here. Looks like I've found two little mice sticking their noses where they don't belong." He got a cunning gleam in his eye. "You've asked a very astute question, Miss Cooper. Now that you know our little secret, just what *are* we going to do?"

EIGHT

D r. Basehart stepped into the trailer and then beckoned to someone outside. Immediately, Tomás climbed through the door, eyeing the kids grimly, ready to do his boss's bidding.

"So I guess you've figured it out by now," Dr. Basehart said resignedly. "There never was a raid on the Corys' camp. I may as well tell you, the Kachakas can give quite a show of strength and they are excellent hunters, but when it comes to violent raids and murder . . ." He just shook his head.

"So what really happened to the Corys?" Lila asked.

"The same thing that happened to you. The 'Curse of Toco-Rey.' They went crazy, tore up their own camp, and then ran into the jungle like animals. As your brother can tell you, one of them is dead, his bones picked clean by the carvies."

"But what about those graves?" Jay asked.

"Fake, just like the poison darts you found." Dr. Basehart chuckled. "Well, *one* grave is genuine, as was the blood you found in the tent. Another worker of mine, Chico Valles, was killed by a crazed Cory.

257

We buried him, then created two mock graves so we could tell our little story about a Kachaka attack."

"But why?" Lila wondered.

Dr. Basehart's eyes narrowed. "To settle the whole matter before anyone like you came along and started to ask questions. You and your family were brought here to find the treasure room of Kachi-Tochetin. What happened to the Corys was to be none of your concern."

"But . . ." Lila couldn't fathom Dr. Basehart's callousness. "But these are people, human beings, in trouble! We can't just let them die!"

Dr. Basehart brushed her off. "A few human lives are a small price to pay for what we've discovered."

She became indignant. "No! Listen. If you've found a cure for the curse, then you've got to use it to save them!"

"They are beyond saving, my dear."

"*I* got better!" Then she added, "And I think you know how!"

He weighed that for a moment. "I might. One more experiment would resolve a few problems, though." He shot a glance at Tomás. "Bring the explosives. We'll do this quickly."

Dr. Cooper knew he could not hurry through the swamp if he wanted to get through it at all. So despite the agony of not knowing the fate of his children for a few additional moments, he carefully retraced the Corys' trail markers and picked his way through. Once on solid ground again, he barreled down the trail through the entangling jungle, his arms protecting his face. His legs grabbed distance in long, powerful strides.

When he reached the Corys' devastated campsite he raced right past it, barely giving it a glance. He had to get to the compound. He had to find his kids.

Hidden behind the Corys' sagging tent, Armond Basehart held Jay while Tomás held Lila, their hands over the kids' mouths so they could not cry out. Once he was sure Dr. Cooper was far past, Dr. Basehart prodded the kids with his gun—"Okay, let's go"—and they headed up the same trail their father had come down.

Dr. Cooper pulled his gun as he reached the compound, his eyes alert for trouble. Dawn was approaching. The compound was quiet. There was a light on in Basehart's lab trailer.

Taking cautious, silent steps and pointing his gun skyward, he approached the door of the trailer. Through a window he could see a man bent over the work counter, tinkering with samples and looking through the microscope. Dr. Cooper put his hand on the door handle, then jerked the door open suddenly, aiming his gun inside. "Don't move!"

The man complied and became very still.

"Put your hands on the counter where I can see them."

The man placed both of his hands on the counter, then said pleasantly, "Dr. Cooper. I've been expecting you."

Dr. Cooper stepped through the door, still aiming the gun. "I've been expecting you too, Mr. Stern."

"May I turn around and face you?"

"Hands in the air, please."

The man raised his hands and turned around. It was Mr. Stern from the museum, all right, dressed in jungle fatigues instead of a fancy suit but still the dapper, gray-haired gentleman. "So it seems you've figured out our little ruse."

"I've learned that the Kachakas know nothing of any raid on the Cory camp. They think the Corys are ghosts from the tomb. They've never even seen the treasure and the poison darts they use are quite different from the fake ones your people planted at the Corys' camp—better, actually."

Mr. Stern was impressed. "Very observant. But here's something else for you to note." He nodded toward the clothing Lila had left on the couch. "As you can see, we have your children, so I have plenty of advantage. That gun won't do you much good. You're a reasonable man. Perhaps you'd like to have a discussion instead of a shoot-out?"

Dr. Cooper kept the gun in his hand. "Fine. Let's discuss my children."

Mr. Stern liked that response. "Certainly. Armond Basehart has them. You'll be glad to know that they are both alive and well, and Lila *is* recovering from her illness. Tomás and Juan found her in the ruins and brought her here where Basehart had a chance to run some tests. Thanks to your daughter, we've made some exciting discoveries."

Dr. Cooper tightened his grip on the gun he was aiming at Mr. Stern. "Where are they?"

Mr. Stern smiled, amused. "Now doctor, you know I can't give up my advantage. We haven't had our discussion yet." He looked at his raised hands. "And may I put down my hands?"

Jacob Cooper considered, then replied, "Cross your arms in front of you—and start explaining what you're really up to."

Mr. Stern crossed his arms and relaxed against the counter. "All right. First of all, my name isn't Stern, and second, I don't work for the Langley Art Museum. I have a few friends there who helped me set up our meeting in the museum's work room, but that was purely for the sake of appearances. My real name is—" He stopped himself and smiled. "Well, let me just tell you the name I use in my profession. In all your visits to the Middle East, you've no doubt heard the name Manasseh."

Dr. Cooper had heard the name. "The international weapons dealer?"

The man known as Manasseh nodded. "A supplier of weapons of all kinds to terrorists, revolutionaries, or anyone who wants to start a war. If you have the right kind of money, I don't care whose side you're on."

Dr. Cooper knew he was facing a man with no trace of conscience. "So what do you want with me and my children?"

"Oh, exactly what I hired you for: to pick up

where the Corys left off and find the treasure room of Kachi-Tochetin."

Dr. Cooper was puzzled. "What would a weapons dealer want with ancient artifacts?"

Manasseh laughed. "Not the artifacts, doctor! The *curse* guarding them!"

"*What?*"

Manasseh's eyes sparkled with devious delight. "Imagine entire armies stricken with madness—turning into raving animals, turning and attacking each other instead of the enemy, generals going out of their minds! Whoever possessed such a wonderful biological weapon could win a war without firing a shot!"

Dr. Cooper quickly scanned the work counter behind Manasseh. "So that's what Armond Basehart was working on all this time?"

"Exactly. He acquired the journals of José de Carlon and developed the theory that the curse of Toco-Rey might be due to a rare toxin the Oltecas planted in the tomb. He came to me with his idea. I bought into it, and, well, here we are."

"And you hired Ben Cory and his crew to find the tomb for you."

"And to unwittingly serve as guinea pigs. They entered the tomb, encountered the toxin, and later went berserk, proving our theory. You can imagine our elation! We had discovered a toxin that had remained dormant for a thousand years but still came to life upon contact with human beings. It is the ideal weapon! It can be stored for years—sealed in shell casings, kept in jars, whatever—and still work when we want it to. But our archaeological team was reduced to raging animals, and we still didn't know exactly where the tomb was. Besides, neither Basehart nor I had any intention of going into the tomb ourselves. So . . ."

"You hired me."

Manasseh nodded. "And staged the raid on the Cory camp so you wouldn't know our real intentions."

Dr. Cooper was appalled. "You're a mad man."

That only amused Manasseh further. "No, just a businessman. Thanks to the Corys, we were able to discover a perfect weapon that could devastate an army, a city, or a nation." He pointed to a jar on the counter containing a preserved dead carvy. "And thanks to your daughter, who was affected by the toxin and then recovered, we were able to discover the cure. So we now have a product we can sell to the right people for millions. In a way, there's treasure in the burial tomb of Kachi-Tochetin worth far more than the gold."

Dr. Cooper wasn't entirely impressed. "So what do you intend to do, start a carvy farm?"

Manasseh burst out laughing as if he'd heard a terrific joke. "That's good, doctor! Very good! But let's get to the real discussion here. You want your children, I want your cooperation. Let's cut a deal."

Jacob Cooper said nothing. He just listened.

Manasseh made his pitch. "We need your expertise in further explorations of the tomb and any other sites that might contain the toxin. We'll harvest the toxin, and any treasure you find, you can keep for yourself. You'll be a millionaire, doctor, overnight— *if* you join us, and *if* you keep our little secret."

"Assist you in profiting from the deaths of millions of people? You're talking to the wrong man."

Manasseh only smiled wickedly. "I've heard about your deep moral convictions, Doctor. But I'm willing to wager that your Christian morality can only govern you up to a point. Beyond that, well, as they say, every man has his price."

"I got my Christian morality from God, and He's a far greater treasure than you could ever offer me. I'm afraid I'll have to decline." Dr. Cooper raised the gun threateningly. "Now where are my kids?"

Manasseh eyed him a moment, then tested him. "We can throw in an immediate bonus, a little incentive: How about two million dollars—today?"

Dr. Cooper pulled the hammer back. "Where are they?"

"Two *more* million once you've found the tomb and made it accessible."

Dr. Cooper spoke slowly and clearly. "I strongly suggest you take me to my children."

Lila and Jay stared into the pit near the burial tomb of Kachi-Tochetin, closely guarded by Armond Basehart and Tomás. The morning sunlight was piercing through the trees and the carvies had returned from their night foraging. There were so many of them that their restful muttering and shuffling echoed out of the pit like the hum of a beehive.

"You gotta be kidding!" said Jay.

"Make no sudden moves or noises, and green carvies can be quite indifferent to your presence," said Basehart. "Tomás, the ladder."

Tomás seemed very nervous but obeyed, opening a bundle and removing a long rope ladder.

"Hook it over the wall and lower it down very slowly. Let's not upset our little friends down there."

Tomás anchored the top end of the ladder to the wall, then let the ladder out one rung at a time, lowering it into the pit. The hum of the carvies stayed steady. So far, so good.

"Why do we have to go down there?" Lila asked.

"Oh, indulge me," said Dr. Basehart. "One final little experiment. Tomás here insists that green carvies are harmless. We're going to find out if he's right."

Manasseh seemed to weaken. He'd tried several tempting offers to buy Jacob Cooper's loyalty, but the Christian was unshakable.

"You certainly are a man of conviction."

"Some things are more important than money," Dr. Cooper said simply. "Now we can spend the rest of the day in a deadlock or we can bring everything to a conclusion. It's up to you."

Manasseh thought it over, then nodded. "All right."

"Where is Dr. Basehart?"

"Actually, he and Tomás went into the ruins at first light to gather some more samples. I have your children. They're locked up in a shed in back."

Dr. Cooper gestured toward the door with his gun. "Let's go."

Manasseh made his way out under Dr. Cooper's watchful eye. Then he led him around to the back of the trailer where the shed stood, still locked up with a padlock and two slide bolts. "This was rather hurriedly built, I'm afraid. We weren't expecting to house prisoners."

"Open it up."

Manasseh took a key from his pocket and unlocked the padlock. The two bolts slid easily aside, but the door wouldn't budge when he tugged on the handle. He turned to Dr. Cooper, looking apologetic. "As I said, we put this together rather in a hurry."

Dr. Cooper stepped closer and grabbed the door handle. With both of them tugging, the door finally jerked open. It was dark inside. He could tell immediately his kids were not—

OOF! Something hit him from behind with tremendous force, hurling him through the door. The shed had no floor and he fell, tumbling head over heels through empty space until he landed with a soft thud. The dust rose up in a cloud around him, choking him, blinding him. He could feel it grating between his teeth, burning in his nose.

Struggling to his feet in the dim light, he blinked his eyes clear and discovered he'd fallen into a pit about eight feet deep. He could hear the voices of Juan and Carlos above, laughing and chattering. "Very good job," Manasseh told them. "Muy, muy bueno!"

The door slammed shut and the pit went dark except for thin ribbons of light that came through cracks between the boards.

Manasseh had a quick conversation with Juan and Carlos, and then Dr. Cooper could hear the two men walking away. "Sorry to slam the door on you, Dr. Cooper," Manasseh called from outside. "But we can't let any of that fine green dust escape. The stuff is lethal."

Jacob Cooper looked around as his eyes adapted to the dim light. The shed was sealed up with clear plastic and the air inside was murky with green dust. It covered the walls of the pit and lay several inches thick on the pit floor. He was covered with it. He could taste it.

And he wasn't alone. A dead man sat in a corner of the pit, his eyes gone, his jaw hanging open, barely recognizable under a thick layer of green mold that covered his entire body.

"Dr. Cooper," Manasseh called, "may I introduce you to John Cory, the only one of the Cory party we were able to recover and contain. We were lucky enough to find him in the jungle just after he died but before the carvies had a chance to pick his bones clean. And now that Juan and Carlos are gone and we can talk privately, may I also introduce you to the deadly curse of Toco-Rey, that lovely green dust."

Jacob Cooper looked at himself. He looked as if he'd fallen into green chalk.

"I had to laugh at your question about starting a carvy farm," said the ruthless weapons dealer.

"Carvies aren't worth the trouble. Their poison doesn't drive you crazy, it just kills you. But *this* stuff . . . ! Remember the video of the Corys admiring the artifacts they'd brought back? Remember how John Cory wiped them down with a rag, wiping off all the green dust? It's more than dust, Dr. Cooper. It happens to be a spore that can sit dormant for centuries until it infests the respiratory system of a human being. Once you inhale it, it germinates, giving off a toxin that turns you into a raving animal until . . . well, you saw what finally became of Brad Frederick and now John Cory: The spores grow into a deadly fungus that eats you alive. Kachi-Tochetin must have covered his treasure with the stuff, forever guarding it from outsiders. He was a clever old brute, wouldn't you say?"

"Manasseh . . ." Dr. Cooper could hardly talk because of the spores in his throat. "What have you done with my children?"

"You're still worried about *them?* What about yourself?"

"Manasseh!"

He laughed. "Basehart is taking them to the tomb to seal them inside. As you can see, this pit isn't big enough for all of you. The 'deadly curse' of Toco-Rey is too important a secret for kids to know about. They must not leave the jungle to tell the world."

Horror and anger coursed through Dr. Cooper's veins. "NO! Manasseh, go ahead, take me, do what you want, but let them go!"

Manasseh scolded him. "Dr. Cooper, I'm already doing what I want with you. You see, we were hoping we could salvage some spores from the artifacts the Corys brought out, but unfortunately, the carvies found them and licked them clean. Then we thought maybe we could harvest spores from Brad Frederick's body, but the carvies ate all of those too. So, since you won't help us access the tomb to gather more spores, I guess you'll just have to serve as a human incubator right here in this shed! As you can see, John Cory has provided us with a healthy crop of fungus already, and it won't take long before you do the same.

Dr. Cooper could observe John Cory's body being processed from flesh to fungus before his very eyes. "*How* long?"

"Oh, the speed of the infection depends on how much of the spores a person ingests. The Corys wore dust masks in the tomb, but received a light exposure from handling the dusty artifacts back at their camp. Their infection took awhile. Your daughter Lila got only a small dose, so her infection took some time as well. But Dr. Cooper . . ." Manasseh made a *tsk-tsk* sound. "With the heavy dose of spores you've inhaled, I would say you'll be a raving maniac within an hour. As for the kids . . . well, it may be a few more centuries before anyone ever finds out what happened to them." He laughed again, amused by his own cleverness. "Too bad for you it's morning."

"What? What was that?"

"Never mind. You should have taken the deal I

offered you, doctor. You could have looked forward to being alive and rich. Good-bye."

Jay and Lila stood very still on the soft, gooey floor of the pit, afraid to make any sudden moves. All around them, the walls were alive with an unbroken, living layer of green carvies. They were humming and twitching, slithering and sliming over each other's bodies and occasionally flitting from wall to wall.

Tomás stood beside them with a gun in his hand, trying to act like a tough guy but obviously as scared as they were. Dr. Armond Basehart, suddenly cured of his claustrophobia, was just coming to the bottom of the ladder.

"Ah, yes . . ." said Dr. Basehart, shining his flashlight around the walls of the pit. "They just thrive down here, don't they?" He shined his light sideways and found the tunnel. "And that would be the route into the tomb, correct?"

"Yes, sir," said Jay, also pointing his flashlight that direction. "But this time it's full of carvies."

"No matter. A little green slime won't hurt you."

Lila couldn't figure that. "But I thought . . ."

"Trust me. I've learned a lot from your blood tests, young lady—and from your nose. Go ahead." He handed Jay an extra flashlight and then prodded them with the barrel of his gun. They started stepping slowly over the bones and through the carvies toward the tunnel. "Tomás."

Tomás answered, "Sí, señor," but he didn't take a

step or take his eyes off the thousands of little black eyes that looked back at him.

Dr. Basehart opened a bag he carried over his shoulder and brought out a hand-sized explosive charge with an electronic detonator. He put it in Tomás's hand and whispered, "It's preset for five minutes after you activate it. Get them inside, and then . . ." Tomás hesitated. Armond Basehart gave him a nudge. "Go on!"

Tomás pocketed the explosive, clicked on his flashlight, and followed the kids down the tunnel.

Jay and Lila kept moving, crouching down to stay clear of the carvies that clung to the stalactites above, and stepping gingerly on the slime-slickened tunnel floor.

They could see a light shining on the floor ahead of them. It was Lila's flashlight, still lying where she had dropped it. When they reached it, Jay picked it up and handed it to her. "You feeling okay, sis?"

"I'm not sick or crazy, if that's what you mean," she answered. "But we're not doing okay, not at all."

Jay looked back at Tomás. "Why are we down here?"

Tomás waved the gun at him. "Just keep moving." Then Tomás looked back.

Dr. Basehart stood in the pit, still watching them go. "Farther, Tomás."

Unhappily, Tomás waved his gun at the Cooper children. "Farther. Into the tomb."

"Why do you listen to him, anyway?" Jay asked.

Tomás smiled weakly. "Mucho dinero, muchacho. Much money."

They came to the hallway that circled the inner chamber of the pyramid. This was as far as Jay and Dr. Cooper had gotten last time. Jay examined the intricate carvings in the wall—the ones they had guessed might be a warning not to proceed farther.

"How you doing, sis?" Jay asked again.

"I'm all right, don't worry," she insisted.

"Go on, get back farther," said Tomás.

The kids walked down the narrow stone hallway, still stepping around and crouching under resting carvies.

"I think Dad was right," said Jay, exploring the passage with the beam of his flashlight. "This hallway must go clear around the pyramid with an inner chamber in the middle."

"So maybe there's a door somewhere to get inside."

Tomás watched the kids recede down the hallway, then called back up the tunnel, "They are inside!"

Dr. Basehart, waiting at the bottom of the pit, answered back, "Very good, Tomás. You may proceed."

Tomás started fumbling with his gun, his flashlight, and whatever he had in his pocket while trying to keep an eye on the kids.

Dr. Basehart quickly reached into his bag, brought out another explosive charge, and looked around for a bare surface of stone on which to place it.

Suddenly, he heard a whisper from above. "Basehart! Basehart, can you hear me?"

Armond Basehart scurried to the center of the pit

and looked up. It was Manasseh! "Have you taken care of Cooper?"

Manasseh made an "okay" sign with his fingers. "Tucked neatly away in the shed. Where are the children?"

Basehart smiled wickedly. "Inside the pyramid." He held up his explosive charge and grinned. "It's going perfectly."

Manasseh smiled, very pleased. "Then let's be rid of them."

Basehart hurried to the tunnel entrance, anchored the charge, and set the detonator. "Tomás, you are far too trusting," he whispered to himself.

On the ground above, Manasseh held a small radio transmitter in his hand. "I hate to share, Dr. Basehart."

He pressed a button.

Dr. Basehart suddenly saw a red light on the detonator.

The ground shook with a mighty explosion. Smoke, dust, pulverized rock and liquefied carvies shot out of the pit like a geyser.

The sound of the explosion rang through the stone hallway like a bell. Tomás was knocked off his feet and across the stony floor, his own unarmed explosive still in his hand. Jay and Lila dropped to the floor with their arms over their heads as the earth shook beneath their feet.

Standing in the jungle above, the man called Manasseh watched the dust and debris settle and smiled pleasantly, satisfied that the secret of the world's most hideous biological weapon was now safe with him alone. He slipped the little transmitter into his pocket and started hiking back through the ruins.

Dr. Cooper had tested the walls of the pit for handholds, any way to climb out. He'd tried jumping a few times in an effort to grab the ledge above, but the soft ground broke away in his hand and he fell back, kicking up more of the green dust.

Next to him, the body of John Cory had all but disappeared under the rapidly growing fungus. Every time Dr. Cooper moved, more green fungus puffed around him.

His nose and throat burned. He could imagine the spores burrowing into his nasal membranes and throat lining. He was getting dizzy. Disoriented. Scared.

Jay and Lila ran back to help Tomás to his feet, and then they all raced up the tunnel, stepping around dead and stunned carvies, shining their light beams through the dust and smoke. When they reached the end of the tunnel, their worst fear was confirmed: the tunnel was blasted shut.

They were trapped.

NINE

The kids. The tomb. The curse.
The cure.

Come on, Cooper. Think! Think! You've got to find a way out of here. You've got to save your kids.

He felt like the ground was moving beneath his feet. He planted his hand against the dusty, dirty wall of the pit to steady himself.

A raving maniac within an hour? He could feel his mind start to spin even now. Millions of little spores were busy.

The cure. There was a cure. Manasseh said so. But what?

"Too bad for you it's morning," he had said, but what did he mean?

"Thanks to your daughter . . . we were able to discover the cure."

Dr. Cooper's mind wandered. He began to stare at the green, chalky walls and the rapidly vanishing remains of John Cory. Fear began to course through him. *I'm finished. I'm going to die!*

NO! He shook his head and forced himself to think.

Too bad for you it's morning. A carvy in a jar. Carvy poison doesn't make you crazy, it only kills you.

Too bad for you it's morning. What happens in the morning? What *can't* happen in the morning?

Wait. Wait. Morning slugs. The slugs are green in the morning, green and docile. They've been eating all night.

Green?

What did Manasseh say about the artifacts? The carvies licked them clean.

And what did he say about Brad Frederick's dead body? The carvies had eaten all the spores on it.

They'd found a carvy underneath a rag in the Cory tent. The Corys had used those rags to wipe the green dust off the artifacts. The carvy could have been attracted by the dust on the rags.

Jacob Cooper prayed, *Dear Lord, keep my mind steady. Help me to think!*

Yes! It had to be: The spores must be like candy to the carvies.

So what does that mean?

Why don't the spores kill the carvies?

The carvies must be immune to them. They get happy and docile and turn green, but they don't go crazy and die.

Lila helped Dr. Basehart and Manasseh find the cure.

Too bad for you it's morning.

The yellow slugs must carry the *antitoxin*. But how did Lila get a dose of it?

He had a hunch. There were pieces missing. But it could be the answer. It had to be the answer, there was so little time.

Dr. Cooper's breath was coming in deep chugs through his clenched teeth. His fingers were curled like claws.

No, this pit isn't going to hold me! I'm going to get out of here! WITH GOD'S HELP I'M GOING TO—

Without thinking, with a loud cry and a huge, semicrazed leap, he shot out of the pit and clamped two iron-strong hands onto the frame around the shed door. With a growl, several kicks, and a violent wrenching, he tore the door loose, snapping off the slide bolts and sending the padlock spinning into the weeds. He was free. He moved out in front of the trailers, groping about in the dark, trying to think, trying to plan.

Uh-oh. He could see Juan and Carlos bursting out of their little hut with rifles in their hands. They must have heard all the racket.

No problem. They took one look at him, screamed, and ran, first in frightened circles, and then to their Land Rover.

"Hey!" he called.

They didn't even look back, but cranked up the old machine and roared down the rutted road toward civilization.

He didn't know what had scared them, and he didn't have time to think about it. Only one thought kept pounding in his hazy mind. Get to the Kachaka village!

With the speed of a gazelle, he bounded up the trail toward the ruins.

The man who called himself Manasseh walked along the Avenue of the Dead briskly, humming a happy little tune and thinking up his next move. He figured he could hire Juan and Carlos to harvest the spores from the shed—after the two incubators were fully used up, of course. He would have to devise airtight containers in which to store the spores as well as a way to measure them out and weigh them for marketing.

Then he would have to figure out a neat and clean way to dispose of Juan and Carlos. Perhaps they, too, should become incubators. As always, the secret had to be protected.

He stopped. He thought he saw movement in the bushes near an immense stone head, a likeness of a past king, no doubt. He drew his pistol from a holster at his side. He didn't like having an animal sneaking around that close, especially when he didn't know what kind of animal it was.

But nothing moved. He relaxed, put away the pistol, and quickened his step. He did not like this place. Too many things could go wrong, there were too many unknowns.

A scream! A pouncing figure struck him from behind before he had time to react. He was on the flat pavement stones, staring up at a green face, flaming eyes, bared teeth.

His screams echoed across the dead ruins for a quick, terrible moment, and then fell silent.

"We are going to die!" Tomás wailed, no longer the tough guy. He'd stuffed the explosive charge back in his coat pocket without thinking.

"Hey, come on," said Jay. "Get a grip! We haven't even weighed our options!"

They were huddled in the dark hallway under the pyramid, acutely aware that a man-made mountain of limestone lay between them and freedom.

"The tunnel we came through can't be the only way out of here," Jay insisted. "The priests got in another way. Dad and I were theorizing about that."

Lila was already exploring down the hallway. "Let's have a look."

They headed down the hallway, and Tomás followed timidly behind. As their lights swept over the cold stone walls, the sounds of their footsteps and breathing resonated up and down the long, narrow passage. The hallway, only six feet wide and just high enough to walk in, was laid out in a big square, tracing the shape of the pyramid but providing no way to reach whatever rooms might be inside. They explored it carefully as they worked their way around, finding a few primitive stone tools, some items of jewelry but no other passageways.

Then, when they rounded the third corner, they found a massive pile of rocks that appeared to have fallen in from above.

"What is this?" Tomás asked. "A cave-in?"

Lila studied the wall. "Look here, Jay. Slots in the wall, just like a ladder."

Jay used his light to follow the ladder slots up to the ceiling. "Yeah, and look where they go: That used to be a way out."

Lila's heart sank. "But it's full of rocks."

Jay was not happy about his conclusion. "After they buried the king, they must have filled in the entrance to this level of the pyramid."

"We will run out of air!" Tomás whined. "We will starve to death!"

Jay and Lila paid him no attention but conferred again.

"The Corys found the treasure room," Jay mused.

"And we haven't," Lila added. "Which means they got in and out of here a totally different way. Remember what Dad said? He thought the tunnel we used was dug out by the Oltecas. The Corys thought the tunnel they found was dug out by José de Carlon. There *has* to be another tunnel somewhere!"

"And it has to lead into the treasure room."

"So if we find the treasure room we're bound to find a way out through the other tunnel."

Jay pointed his flashlight at the wall. "Is there any soft mortar along that wall? Tomás, help us look!"

They backtracked through the hallway, searching the inside wall with their lights.

"We're looking for old mortar, for cracks. . . ."

Jay instructed their captor-turned-helper. "Somewhere there has to be an entrance to the tomb that was sealed up after the king was buried. After a thousand years the mortar should be soft."

They moved along quickly, tapping and poking at the wall as they went. *Tick, tick, tap.* The wall produced a solid, stony sound as they struck it. They kept moving, kept tapping.

THUNK. About halfway down the hall, Lila's flashlight hit something soft, and she made a slight dent in the decaying, powdery surface. "Hey."

"This could be it," said Jay. He picked up one of the old tools they'd found and used it to chip at the soft spot in the wall. The material broke away freely, falling to the floor in dusty, jagged chunks.

"Hurry," said Tomás. "Please hurry!"

Lila got into it, chipping and gouging with a sharp rock. Tomás found another rock and started bashing away, driven by fear.

The leaves and branches of the jungle raced by his face in a blur; the whole world kept tilting, first one way, then the other. Dr. Cooper felt he was running on the deck of a ship in a storm.

Dear Lord, keep me steady. Help me get to the Kachaka village.

The Pyramid of the Sun was right in front of him, so he must have passed through the gates of Toco-Rey, though he had no memory of it. The mind of an animal kept forcing its way into his head. He felt like a panther, running with the wind, hungry for blood, superpowered by a rage that made everything around him an enemy to be destroyed. His breath came in deep, guttural chugs. He had to force himself to think, to remember who he was and what he was doing. Though he felt amazingly strong, part of him knew he was getting very, very sick.

He had a hunch. Sometimes he forgot what it was, but he kept running for the Kachaka village anyway, trusting God would bring the memory back.

"You are Dr. Jacob Cooper," he kept telling himself. "Run to the village. Run to the village."

He raced up the Avenue of the Dead. In his desperate struggle to hold on to his mind he didn't notice the blood or the remains of what had been the world's most ruthless weapons dealer. He ran right by without slowing down.

Jay struck another blow against the wall, and this time the mortar and stones crumbled, falling into a cavity on the other side. "All right! We're through!" He poked his flashlight into the hole and peered through. "Yeah. There's a chamber in there."

"Can you see anything?" Lila asked.

Jay swept his light back and forth, probing the darkness. "Whoa . . . oh wow . . ."

"What is it?" Tomás demanded.

Jay turned to them, jubilant. "It's the treasure room! We've found it!"

They bashed and chipped and pounded with even greater determination, enlarging the hole, pushing the old stones and gray mortar into the chamber beyond. As soon as the hole was big enough to squeeze through, Jay did just that, crouching down, going one leg first, then his body, then the other leg.

He found himself in a large, square chamber with carved pillars at each corner. The ceiling was at least fifteen feet above him. A huge, stone coffin took up the center. "Okay. Come on in."

Lila hopped through the hole. Tomás poked his head in first, made doubly sure it was safe, and then squeezed through the hole with a little more difficulty.

All three were astounded. The walls around them held intricately carved figures of warriors, kings, and fierce, toothy gods. The four pillars had huge faces, all looking inward toward the coffin; they probably represented Kachi-Tochetin and his family.

The coffin in the center of the room was a huge box of limestone on a stone pedestal. It, too, was intricately carved with faces, suns, moons, gods, and plants that swirled in a continuous pattern all around its four sides. Carved into the lid was the stern face of Kachi-Tochetin, superimposed over the sun so that the sun's rays seemed to emanate from the king himself.

But the real eye-catcher was the *treasure*. All around the room, stacked up high against the walls and taking up much of the floor, was the wealth of Kachi-Tochetin. Masks of gold and turquoise, necklaces and breastplates, piles and piles of coins and beads, golden cups, plates, vases, idols.

On a ledge around the room were more small golden images of Oltecan gods the Corys had referred to, positioned to stand guard over the treasure and the remains of the king.

Then came a gruesome discovery: In each corner, at the base of each carved pillar, was a length of chain. And on the floor, in a dismal, helter-skelter pile, were bones. Tomás let out a gasp of fear. Jay and Lila went to take a closer look.

"The guards the Corys talked about," said Jay. "They must have been chained to the pillars to guard the king."

"Buried alive!" said Lila.

Now Jay understood. "These must be the mukai-tochetin that the Kachaka chief talked about. They really were buried with the king!"

Tomás picked up a golden vase. He immediately put it down in disgust when he saw the green dust it left on his hands. "Eughh!" He slapped his hands against his pantlegs, stirring up a green cloud.

Now the kids noticed too. It was very dusty in here. A thick layer of green dust was all over everything. They'd left footprints in it. Everything they touched left a handprint—and left green dust on their hands.

"Wow," said Jay, slapping the top of the king's coffin and raising another cloud of dust. "Weird stuff."

"The Corys talked about this dust too," Lila remembered. "They were wiping it off the artifacts in that video—" She stopped. The smell in this place was oddly familiar. She tried to remember where she'd smelled it before. Thoughts came to her; memories. "Jay . . ."

She looked at her brother. He'd scratched his nose and left a green smudge. Just then, Tomás sneezed and wiped his face with his hand. That only drove more dust up his nose and he sneezed again, stomping his foot and raising even more dust.

"Jay!"

He was wiping off an artifact with his shirt sleeve. She could see the tiny particles dancing around in the beam of his flashlight.

"Jay, stop!"

He stopped. "Huh? What's the matter?" Then he made a little face, rolling his eyes and teetering slightly. "Whoa! Did we just have an earthquake?"

The Kachaka village! Jacob Cooper burst out of the jungle and recognized the small huts of grass and sticks, the ramshackle, plank structures, the busy people. . . .

He stumbled and fell in the grass, his head reeling. *WhydidIcomeherewhatfor . . .*

He heard excited shouts and people approaching.

Come on Coop gedup you godda meg sense to these peeble . . .

With great strength he leaped to his feet again. "Where da chief? Lemme talk gotta get him or here!"

The women and children took one look at him, screamed, and ran away, wailing, waving their arms, sounding an alarm.

Fierce anger coursed through him. *Whatza matter widese peeble? I'll kill them! Kill them all!* He ran after them, hands like claws, teeth bared. "Stop you iddits! Whatzamatta wi'yu?"

He stopped. What in the world was he doing? *Oh man, Lord, I'm losing it! Help me!* He dropped to his knees in the grass, trying to think, trying to clear his head. *Calm down. Control, control! You have to get . . . you have to get . . . what do I have to get?*

Then he heard a familiar, angry voice. "Doctor Jacob Cooper, the stupid American!"

He looked up. It was the chief, whose angry expression turned to one of fear the moment Dr. Cooper raised his head. The chief muttered, gawked at him, started backing away.

Dr. Cooper tried to speak clearly. "Chief Yoaxa . . ."

Yoaxa looked at the others who cowered behind him, staring at the weird animal that had burst into their village. He started hollering an explanation to them. Dr. Cooper couldn't understand it, but he easily heard the word *mukai-tochetin* used over and over again.

Jacob Cooper struggled to his feet. "Please . . ." His voice came out like a growl. "I need . . . I need . . ."

"Go away!" the chief hollered. "You are mukai-tochetin! I knew it all along!"

Some warriors came running with rifles, spears, and blowguns, ready to use them all.

That brought a new fit of rage Jacob Cooper could hardly control. "You fools! Can't I make you

286

understand!" he growled. He was clenching his fists, shaking them at these stupid people—

He stopped, horrified, at the sight of his hands. They were lizard green.

TEN

Lila's voice trembled with fear. "Jay . . . I think it's the dust!"

He looked at her dully. "Huh?"

She ran over and grabbed his arm. "Listen to me! Remember what Dr. Basehart said? He said he learned a lot from my blood samples—and from my *nose!* You remember that?"

Jay had trouble remembering. "Your nose?"

"Jay, I've smelled this stuff before! I smelled it coming from a shack behind Dr. Basehart's lab, and—are you listening to me?—I smelled it on an orchid near where we found the pit. This dust was on that orchid! I snorted it right up my nose, do you understand?"

He looked at her with impatience. "What are you trying to do, scare me?"

She gripped his arm tighter. "You feel afraid?"

He jerked his arm away. "NO! There's nuddin wrong wid me!"

"Jay! It wasn't the slime from the carvies that made me green and crazy! It was this dust! Dr. Basehart had samples of it in his lab. He had that rag the Corys used to wipe off the artifacts! He had a

288

sample from my nose—Jay, you should have seen it under the microscope! It was like hundreds of little spiky monsters, that's what this dust is!"

He looked directly at her now. She seemed to be getting through. "It's the dust?"

She looked at him carefully, noticing the glazed look in his eyes and the way he tottered as if drugged. "Jay, it's happening to you! The same thing that happened to me is happening to *you!*"

He got defensive. "You look okay."

She tried to keep from crying, but fear still brought tears to her eyes. "I got better somehow, Jay. I don't know how it works. Maybe you only get it once, like the measles."

Jay tried to listen to his sister. Her words were so garbled and there was such a rushing noise in his ears. The floor still seemed to be moving. "Lila . . . Maybe we bedder ged ouda here."

She looked all around. "Jay, we can't. There isn't any way out. I mean, I can't see it, I can't find it."

"We havetuh fine it."

She grabbed his arm to steady him. "Jay—"

He jerked away with a growl. "Leggo! You don't touch me!"

He's losing it, she thought. He's going to do something really crazy if I don't—

"Lila!"

"What?"

Jay stared at a corner of the room. She followed his gaze and saw a pile of bones and the black, rusty chain that had once held the doomed guard.

"You better chain me up," Jay said. "Chain me up before I really go nuts."

The thought was unbearable. "Jay . . ."

"Do it!" he growled. "Before I can't think straight anymore!"

He stumbled over to the pillar and flopped against it, his breath raspy, his eyes getting wild. She grabbed the chain and looped it around his body, his arms, his legs.

He began to struggle against her. "What are you doing?"

"It's okay, Jay. Don't worry!"

"Quit it! Let me go!" he growled at her. Then he tried to grab her. She ducked sideways, barely avoiding his flailing arms and clawlike fingers. He was dazed, disoriented. She jumped in close to finish looping and twisting the chain into a knot behind his back.

For just a moment his mind returned. "Get out of here, sis."

She looked all around the room. "I don't see the way out."

"FIND IT!" he screamed at her, his eyes ablaze with animal anger. He tried to lunge at her but the chain held him fast. He fell back against the pillar as the chain rattled against the stone.

Lila hurried around the room, looking everywhere. How? How did the Corys do it? How did they get in and out? She could see their footprints in the dust all over the floor, but there were so many she couldn't tell which direction they'd come from or where they were going. She checked in one corner, then another, then she climbed over some of the treasure to check against a wall.

Nothing.

She ran to the next corner. Maybe there was a movable panel, or a scrape mark on the floor showing where the exit was, or—

TOMÁS! He suddenly leaped to his feet from behind a large chest, a golden vase in his hands. His face and hands were covered with green dust, and his eyes looked absolutely wild! She jumped backward, horrified. She'd forgotten about him in her panic about Jay.

He leaned toward her, teetering a little, his shoulders hunched, his mouth stretched into a toothy sneer. "Come here, señorita. Come here!"

Her eyes shot to the hole in the wall, the only way in or out of this room that she knew of.

Unfortunately, he was standing right next to it.

Dr. Cooper took a step forward and all the Kachakas took a step backward. His mind kept flipping back and forth, and he couldn't stop it: *Kill them.* No, they're people. *Kill them.* No, help them, make them understand. *KILL THEM!*

"NO, DEAR GOD, NO!" he finally cried in anguish. "Help me, Lord! Help me to think—"

The Lord answered his prayer. His mind cleared, if only for a moment. He looked at Chief Yoaxa, who had several armed warriors at his side. "Chief . . . where's your daughter María?"

Instantly, every rifle, blowgun, ax, and spear was aimed at him.

He raised his hands, pleading with them. "Don't!

Don't shoot me!" He just couldn't keep his voice from sounding growly. "I needa ask María a question . . . jus' one question."

The chief thought for less than a moment and wagged his finger at him. "Oh, no. No, you cannot fool me! María is not yours! You cannot have her!"

ANGER. Dr. Cooper gritted his teeth and prayed. He knew he would tear Chief Yoaxa limb from limb if he didn't control himself. He strained to say it clearly. "Just one question."

Now the chief took a rifle himself. "I don't care if you are mukai-tochetin, I shoot you anyway!"

Slowly, one difficult word at a time, Cooper asked, "Did María shoot my daughter Lila with a poison dart?"

That got a reaction. The chief lowered his rifle and looked at his men. It seemed they knew something.

"Chief . . ." Jacob Cooper knew the man was almost impossible to reason with, but he had to try. "Your daughter María had a blowgun when we found her. She shot . . ." His mind fluttered. He struggled to find it again. "She shot at my son and me. If she shot at us, maybe she shot at Lila." The chief and his men looked at each other. They knew something, Dr. Cooper could see it! His next words sounded like the roar of a lion. "TELL ME!"

"Yes!" came the answer, but not from any of the warriors. The voice came from beyond them.

It was the voice of María. She pushed her way forward until her mother and brothers grabbed her and held her back, but she could see Dr. Cooper, and he could see her. "Dr. Cooper, yes, I shot your daughter with a dart. I thought she was going to kill me!"

Jacob Cooper shot a glance at Chief Yoaxa, who looked a bit cornered. "She . . ."

"WHAT?" came the lion's voice again. "TELL ME!"

"She did have a blowgun," Chief Yoaxa continued. "The one you found didn't belong to any of us. We learned it was hers."

With a roar so loud it startled the men and brought terrified screams from the women, Dr. Cooper charged forward, waving his arms for people to get out of his way. They got out of his way, all right. They didn't want to be anywhere near him.

"Wait!" the chief hollered, following after him. "Where are you going?"

Dr. Cooper didn't answer. He just kept running past the huts and shacks until he came to the end of the village. He rounded a corner and there was the cage full of carvies, as yellow and fierce and poisonous as ever.

Lila backed away, her hands out in front of her. "Now . . . now Tomás, listen to me . . ."

He just growled back at her and threw the golden vase aside with a crash and a clang. He was going to come after her, that was easy to see. She backed away some more. Her only hope was to lead him away from that hole.

With an animal roar he leaped over the treasure

and came after her, growling with every breath. She ran around the big stone coffin and he chased her, scuffing and slipping in the green dust, sending up clouds of the stuff. She ran for the hole in the wall—at least she'd lured Tomás away from it—and dove through headfirst, tumbling and rolling out the other side into the hallway. She got to her feet and ran. It would take him a moment or two to squeeze through behind her, which would buy her some time . . . to do what?

She ran first. She'd think of something later.

The carvies flitted from side to side in their cage, slapping against the wire mesh, chirping, hissing, arching their backs. They were bright yellow, angry, and throwing slime every time they fluttered their fins. A whole night had passed and they hadn't eaten a thing.

Jacob Cooper had already made up his mind. He was going to die anyway and go stark raving mad before that. He had nothing to lose.

He found a small empty cage about the size of a suitcase. It would work perfectly. He grabbed it, then went to the carvies' cage and started to untwist the crinkly old wire that held it shut.

The chief and his men came running around the corner, but stopped dead in their tracks the moment they saw what he was up to. "He is crazy for sure!" the chief exclaimed.

"They won't hurt him," said Manito. "Will they?"

"They will hurt *us!*" the chief reminded him.

They scurried backward, still watching, spell-bound. They'd never seen this done before.

Dr. Cooper got the wire undone. He opened the little door on the cage he was carrying, then yanked the door of the big cage open, took a breath . . .

And jumped inside.

Slap! Splat! Flop! The carvies descended on him like angry hornets, sliming him, slapping against him, slithering over his back, his arms, his head. Their shrieks sounded like all the rats in the world getting stepped on, their slime burned like fire on his hands, his neck, his face, and he couldn't help but scream and gasp from the pain. One clamped onto his ear like a sticky pancake and started biting him. He thought he would pass out. He reached up, yanked it loose—it felt like a sticky, slimy, flattened water balloon in his hand—and threw it into the small cage. It flopped and fluttered around, trying to get out. Then he grabbed another from his arm and another from his side and both went into the cage. He stayed hunched over, one hand holding the cage, the other arm around his head to protect his eyes. He needed more of these critters, many more.

His world was reeling. All he could see was cage wire and carvies moving in waves past his eyes. The sight made him dizzy. He stretched out the hand holding the cage and three more carvies slapped against his arm like wet pancakes fired from a sling-shot. He peeled them off with his other hand and threw them into the little cage, slamming the door shut.

That should do it. That should be plenty. He got

295

the big cage door open and, with carvies still crawling on his back, shoulders, legs, and head, he took off running.

The Kachaka village looked strangely deserted. Every last person must be hiding.

And with good reason. It was a bizarre sight, this wild green man running through the village with hissing, chirping, yellow slugs stuck all over him. At least a hundred more fluttered above and behind him, chasing him like angry hornets.

Lila ducked around the first corner in the hallway, spotted a piece of stone, and grabbed it to use as a weapon. Then she pressed herself tightly against the wall, clicking off her flashlight. Hiding in the dark, she could hear Tomás squeeze through the hole and flop into the hall. She saw no beam from a flashlight. He must be too crazy to think of using one. His footsteps started coming her way. What to do? What to do?

"Señorita!" he hollered like a drunken man, his voice like gravel. "Señorita, come here! I'm going to get you, muchachita!"

She waited. He got closer, his feet shuffling, dragging along in the dark. His voice sounded like it was inside a huge bell. "I'll get you . . . and I'll . . . I'll . . ."

She didn't care to hear his plans. The instant his stubbly, sweating, disheveled head appeared around the corner, she smacked it hard with the stone. He fell sideways. She slipped around him and ran back toward the treasure room. Maybe there was time to find the way out. Maybe.

The carvies in the cage were shrieking and bashing against the sides, trying to get out. The carvies overhead were swooping down and slapping at him. The carvies on his body were hanging on, looking for some bare skin so they could bite him. Dr. Cooper just kept running with powerful strides through the ruins until he spotted the Pyramid of the Sun in the center of Toco-Rey. From there, a left turn would take him to the burial tomb of Kachi-Tochetin.

He wasn't dead. That thought did occur to him. As a matter of fact, he was feeling better. The slime wasn't burning quite as much, and best of all, his mind was clear. He knew who he was, where he was going, and why. Praise God, his hunch was correct: the poisonous slime of the *caracole volante* and the toxin from the spores canceled each other out. Lila had recovered because María had shot her with a poison dart, just a big enough dose to neutralize the spore toxin.

Which made Dr. Cooper wonder, how much of this slime is enough, and how much is too much? Right now he was getting an abundant dose of slug slime. Would the load of spores he carried in his body be enough to counteract it?

All he could do was hope and keep running.

Lila clambered through the wall into the treasure room and got a terrible scare when Jay—at least it used to be Jay—growled and snapped at her, pulling against the chain with the ferocity of a junkyard dog. If that chain should break loose . . .

She was trapped in this place with two mad animals. There had to be a way out! She climbed over the treasure, searching the walls, looking for cracks, for chinks, for a hidden door, for a hatchway, *anything*. How did the Corys do it? How did they get in here?

A howl echoed up the hallway outside, and then galloping footsteps. Tomás was out there hunting for her. It was only a matter of time before he found her here.

And then it would be too late.

As Dr. Cooper ran toward the burial temple, he was glad to see that the carvies chasing him had finally vented their anger or had gotten tired. They'd given up the chase, and even the ones still clinging to him were losing interest. Two let go of his back and fluttered into the bushes.

Well, he thought. Of course. They were crabby because they were hungry, so let them get something to eat.

He dashed through the jungle, made some quick turns along the trail near the burial temple, and finally reached the pit.

He stopped. His heart sank. The pit was still smoking from the blast that had caved it in. Looking over the wall, he saw nothing but rubble and shreds of dead carvies. Apparently Armond Basehart had succeeded in sealing the tomb.

But Jacob Cooper had been expecting this and was already working on another hunch, another theory. The question was, How did Lila come in contact with the spores in the first place? What did she do? Where did she go that no one else did?

He dashed back the way he'd come. He was pretty sure he knew the answer.

Lila rested her elbows on the stone coffin and clenched her hands together as she prayed, "Oh Lord, what am I missing? How do I get out of here? How do I save Jay? How did I get better?"

Her leg felt cold, as if in a draft. She reached down near the floor with her hand and felt cold air coming from somewhere.

Somewhere under the coffin? She probed around the stone pedestal the coffin was sitting on. Yes! There was definitely cold air coming into the room through a crack between the coffin and the pedestal. A very tight crack. Maybe the pedestal was hollow. Maybe there was a passageway under the coffin!

She put her hands on the coffin's edge and pushed against it sideways. It wiggled only about a sixteenth of an inch. She moaned. The coffin was carved from solid stone! She couldn't push it sideways, and she knew she would never be able to lift it!

The orchids! Where were they?

Dr. Cooper doubled back on the trail and finally found the spot where Lila had left the main trail to smell orchids on their first trip here. He knew it was a desperate guess, but it seemed reasonable: The Corys had orchids in a vase in their camp. Lila had found the same sort of orchids growing in the ruins and gone off the trail to sniff them. If she got spores in her nose from those orchids, it could be because the Corys had already passed by that spot and had unknowingly spread the spores from their clothing, their hands, or the artifacts. If there was another way into the tomb, it could be near those orchids.

There they were, over by that old, crumbling wall! Dr. Cooper made a quick dash through the thick growth. This was the place, all right. Now. Was there any sign of a tunnel, a passageway? He started moving along the wall. He thought he saw the signs of a trail the Corys might have cut.

He was hit from the side! He tumbled through the branches and tangles as the cage of carvies flew from his hand. Growling! Snapping! Not again! Ben Cory, wild as a tiger, green as a gator, teeth bared, went for his throat. Dr. Cooper fought back, twisting, and kicking.

Lila tried to rock the coffin. It didn't move. She tried to lift it and discovered that was out of the question. She tried to push it sideways again, and it wiggled just a little. Maybe that was it: sideways. Maybe it rolled or pivoted or—

She heard a growl and spun to see Tomás squeezing through the hole, his mouth drooling, his skin turning green, his eyes full of menace.

ELEVEN

B en Cory had pinned Dr. Cooper and was trying
to bite him, claw him, choke him. Cory was
amazingly strong, but Jacob Cooper was still just as
green as his opponent and still supercharged with
enough toxin-induced strength to throw the wild
man off and roll free.

The tunnel! He was stunned. He was on his belly
in the brush in the middle of a fight, but he'd found
it, dark, deep, and round like a gopher hole.

Ben Cory came at him again, staggering, growling,
drooling!

Time to end this. The cage of carvies was close by.
Dr. Cooper lunged through the brush, grabbed it,
and leaped to his feet. He turned just as Ben Cory
came at him—and he smashed the cage down over
Ben Cory's head. Cory's head broke through the
mesh and into the cage and the carvies pounced. The
wild man screamed, spinning around, pushing and
banging against the cage, trying to get free while the
venomous slugs clamped onto his head.

Dr. Cooper had no time to waste. He tackled Ben
Cory, flipped the cage door open, and plucked a

carvy from Cory's head with each hand. "Come on, guys, I need you below!" They didn't want to go and shrieked and fluttered to get away as they hung from his fists by their tails. He held them firmly and they went with him as he scurried down the tunnel.

He had no light with him and just pushed ahead through the dark, his arm out in front to feel his way along. José de Carlon's men did a good job. The walls of the tunnel were smooth and consistent, and there were no hazardous bumps or dips. They could have dug a little more headroom, though. Dr. Cooper had to crouch to get through.

Lila was careful to keep her distance from Jay, who seemed ready to chomp a piece out of her if she got close enough. On the other side of the room, Tomás squeezed through the hole in the wall and tumbled to the floor.

She grabbed a tall gold vase from a stone ledge and cradled it in her hands, ready to hit a homer with Tomás's head if she had to. "Tomás, you come near me and I'll knock your block off!"

"Get her, Tomás!" Jay hollered. "Get her!"

Tomás got to his feet but hesitated when he saw the vase in Lila's hands. Then cunning began to show through those crazed eyes, and he smiled a crooked, wicked smile. "Oh, you godda use a weapon? Know me, I godda weapon too, know that?" He reached into his coat pocket and brought out the explosive charge with the detonator attached. "Dr. Basehart give me—to kill you!"

Oh no. Could a mad man be reasoned with? "Tomás . . . Don't do anything stupid. Give me that bomb."

He laughed a deep growly laugh and pressed a little button on the detonator. A red display flashed on: *5:00, 4:59, 4:58, 4:57* . . . "You get away? No you don't!"

He lunged for Lila. She ran around the coffin, slipping in the dust and almost getting grabbed by her brother who was still trying to work himself loose from the chain. *Don't lose it, Lila! Don't panic!* Tomás came the other way around the coffin to head her off. She scrambled over the top of it, dropping the vase on the floor. Tomás leaped over the coffin to grab her but she ran around to the other side again, squeezing past her brother who nearly reached her. "Lord God . . . if you've got a way out of this, I'd be glad to hear it!"

"Lila!" came a voice from nowhere. "Lila, are you all right?"

She knew that voice. "DADDY!"

"Lila! Where are you?"

Tomás heard the voice, too, and stiffened with anger. "Where? *Where?*"

"Where are you?" Lila called.

Dr. Cooper had no idea. All he knew was he'd come up through the tunnel to a flat stone surface that seemed like it might move, but didn't. With one hand hanging onto the hissing, flapping carvies, he only had one hand with which to explore or push. "I'm under a slab of stone. Can you see where it is?"

Lila looked at the pedestal under the coffin. Her father's voice seemed to be coming from there.

In the moment she looked away, Tomás lunged for her.

He didn't see the vase lying on the floor in front of him. He tripped on it, sailed through the air, and slammed into the coffin at full speed. It pivoted with a stony rumble as he rolled into a stack of gold cups and utensils. The bomb flew from his flailing hand and skittered across the floor; the display still blinked the shrinking time.

The pedestal was hollow. With the coffin spun cockeyed and leaving a gap, Dr. Cooper was able to poke his head into the middle of all-out chaos.

"Daddy, it's a bomb!" Lila screamed, pointing at the device.

He jumped out of the tunnel to run to her.

Jay screamed at him, rattling the chain. Dr. Cooper hurled one of the carvies. It sailed through the air, spinning like a Frisbee, and hit Jay's forehead with a loud splat. Now Jay really had something to scream about as the venom went to work.

"Look out!" Lila screamed.

Tomás came leaping over the coffin and landed on Jacob Cooper like a ton of bricks, knocking him to the floor. They rolled and grappled and tumbled into gilded battle shields and war masks, which crashed down around them like a chorus of gongs and dinner bells. Tomás was grabbing and clawing and looking for something to bite; Dr. Cooper was just trying to get out from under him.

Lila got into it, grabbing up a candlestick to hit

Tomás on the head. WHAM! He swatted her away with his arm, and she fell against the coffin, hitting her head.

Dr. Cooper saw her sink to the floor, out cold. Then he saw Tomás take a swing at him and blocked it. With a quick twist and a good wrestling hold, he flipped them both over so he was finally on top.

Not for long. Tomás was young, strong, and supercharged with toxin. He threw Dr. Cooper off with one powerful shove, and he went sliding through a pile of gold trinkets.

The air was filling with green dust. Through the green haze Jacob Cooper could see little red numbers blinking across the room: 2:38, 2:37, 2:36.

"Lila!"

She didn't answer. She didn't move.

Tomás came after him again. He used a judo move to trip the man and sent him careening into another stack of gold dishes.

In the excitement, he had let go of the other carvy. Where was it? If he could just get the venom on Tomás . . .

Oh no. He spotted it on the corner of the coffin, happy as a clam, gobbling down the spores and already shifting color from yellow to green. Jay was close to that corner. Maybe he could reach it.

"Jay!"

Jay didn't hear him. He was too disoriented, trying but unable to peel the carvy off his head.

Dr. Cooper dove for the bomb. Tomás dove for Dr. Cooper. They collided before Dr. Cooper could reach the bomb, and they went at it again. Dr.

Cooper threw him off and reached for the bomb. Tomás grabbed him again and threw him over the coffin and into more crashing, tinkling treasure.

1:32, 1:31, 1:30 . . .

Jacob Cooper struggled to his feet, looked everywhere trying to get his bearings, coughed in the green dust, and then spotted the red numbers: *1:20, 1:19, 1:18.* Tomás was coming after him again.

Another head popped up out of the tunnel under the pedestal! Ben Cory!

Oh no. Two of them?

Dr. Cooper shot out his left hand, grabbed the remaining carvy off the corner of the coffin, and prepared to throw it. It didn't resist him. It didn't hiss, or bite, or chirp angrily.

It purred. It was a beautiful, deep green.

I'm sunk, Jacob Cooper thought.

Tomás was half laughing, half growling, slinking like a big cat around the cockeyed coffin.

0:44, 0:43, 0:42 . . .

Ben Cory jumped up out of the tunnel and grabbed Tomás from behind. They fought, they growled. Tomás kicked. Cory hung on. They were busy, occupied with each other.

Dr. Cooper scurried the other way around the coffin and finally grabbed the bomb. *0:30, 0:29, 0:28 . . .*

How do you stop this thing? Dr. Cooper tried pressing some of the buttons on the key pad. He tried cancel, he tried pound and star, he tried 000, he even tried reset. The thing just kept counting down, *0:15, 0:14, 0:13 . . .*

Ben Cory finally got the upper hand, landing a punch to Tomás's jaw that sent him tumbling over the coffin and to the floor, out cold.

Oh great! I'm next! thought Jacob Cooper.

No time left. Dr. Cooper ran for the hole in the wall. Maybe they would survive if the bomb exploded in the hallway.

Ben Cory jumped in his path!

Dr. Cooper braced himself. *You or me, buddy, but this bomb's going through that hole!*

Ben Cory didn't throw a punch. He held out his hand, palm up, gesturing, Let's have it.

Dr. Cooper hesitated, not sure.

0:05, 0:04, 0:03 . . .

Ben Cory grabbed the bomb from his hand, and with amazing skill and dexterity tapped out the correct cancel code.

The display froze at *0:01.*

There was a sudden, eerie stillness. Was it all over?

Ben Cory sighed, then tossed and caught the bomb playfully in his hand. "It's one of mine. I know the cancel code."

Dr. Cooper could just barely feel some relief setting in. "Ben Cory?"

Ben Cory looked at him curiously, cocking his head. "Jake Cooper? What are you doing here?"

"Oh . . . nothing special."

"You look kind of green."

Jacob Cooper chuckled, looking at his green hands. "You ought to see yourself."

Just then, Lila moaned and stirred, rubbing her

head. Dr. Cooper went to her. "Easy now. Don't get up too fast."

"Ooo . . ." she moaned. "What happened? Are we still alive?"

"Dad . . ." It was Jay! "Hey, is that you?"

Dr. Cooper couldn't help smiling as he looked at his son. "Yeah. Is that *you?*"

Jay had finally gotten the carvy off his head and tossed it onto the coffin to join its buddy. "Oh yeah. It's me."

They were alive in the spooky, dusty treasure room of Kachi-Tochetin.

On the plane returning home from Central America, Dr. Cooper tapped out a journal entry on his laptop:

We had to confine Tomás until Ben Cory and I could convince Chief Yoaxa to give us a few more yellow carvies for antitoxin. Upon seeing me, Ben Cory, and then Tomás recover fully, the Kachakas began to realize they were not dealing with spooky mukai-tochetin but with a sickness, and they became helpful friends.

With great solemnity, we helped Ben Cory dig real graves, and the remains of John Cory and Brad Frederick were laid to rest in a peaceful setting near the waterfall.

As for Tomás, Juan, and Carlos, the laws in that part of the world were rather vague about what to do with men who have been duped by

*foreigners and doped by dust, so I doubt they
will see much jail time, if any.*

*The Kachakas found the remains of the man
called Manasseh and buried him under the thick,
entangling vines of Toco-Rey to be forgotten.
We can only conclude that Dr. Armond Basehart
perished in the bomb blast that sealed the first
tunnel. We never found his remains at all.*

*As for the deadly curse of Toco-Rey, we con-
sulted a mycologist from Mexico City, who
studied the fungus and its spores and discovered
it was a whole new species never before identi-
fied. The Latin American Mycological Society
wanted to name the new species after him, but
he chose to give it the name Kachi-Tochetin,
after the ruthless king who used it to curse his
treasure. He theorizes that the Oltecas knew the
carvies carried the cure for the spore toxin and
so were able to survive. The Oltecas probably
used foreign slaves who had never encountered
the spores or the carvies to act as incubators in
the tomb, chaining them to the four pillars
until the fungus consumed them and filled the
treasure room with spores.*

*The fungus is still there in Toco-Rey and it is
still deadly, but the strange flying slugs are also
there, keeping nature in balance as they have
for centuries.*

*Happily, the secret of the deadly curse of
Toco-Rey is no longer a secret. An international
team of toxicologists have begun studying the
slugs and extracting their antitoxin, meaning*

*the spores will no longer be of any use to ruth-
less weapons dealers.*

*The treasure we found has been granted to
the Langley Memorial Art Museum in recogni-
tion of their past work in preserving the history
and artifacts of ancient civilizations around the
world. The Langley Museum never really hired
us, but I understand they have a bonus waiting
for me as a token of gratitude. Nice people.*

*To conclude, I'll make one observation
about all this treasure hunting . . .*

Dr. Cooper looked up from his laptop and across
the aisle where Jay and Lila sat reclined in their
seats, peacefully catching up on some much-needed
sleep. Their skin was normal again, and except for
some bumps and bruises, they were all right.

Dr. Cooper smiled as he typed,

*Having found a fabulous treasure beneath
the ground while in the act of saving my two
children, I have affirmed one truth I will carry
with me for all time: Apart from the dear Lord
Himself, my children and my integrity are my
greatest treasure, and having them safe with me
now, I am the richest man in the world.*

The Cooper Kids Adventure Series®
By Frank Peretti

N ow that you've read *The Secret of the Desert Stone* and *The Deadly Curse of Toco-Rey*, you won't want to miss any of the exciting books in this fiction series by master storyteller Frank E. Peretti. Each volume tells a story about the challenges faced by biblical archaeologist Dr. Jacob Cooper and his children, Jay and Lila, as they travel the world together.

Books 1–4 in the Cooper Kids Adventure Series® are available from Crossway Books. Books 5–8 are available from Tommy Nelson®, a Division of Thomas Nelson, Inc.

Turn the page for a sneak-peek at some other adventures that await you in The Cooper Kids Adventure Series®!

An Excerpt from
The Legend of Annie Murphy
Book Seven in The Cooper Kids Adventure Series®

L ila put her finger to her lips. Jay could read the fear in her eyes and froze, silent. They listened.

From somewhere amid the ruins of the ghost town, they heard an eerie sound. A coyote? No. It was human. A woman's voice. For a moment they could hear it, and then it faded.

They waited, stone still and silent. Their eyes scanned the barren, moonlit landscape. They could see the old chimney some distance away and, nearby, some jagged boards sticking up through the sagebrush. But nothing was moving out there.

The breeze shifted slightly. They could feel it in their hair.

The voice came to them again, carried on the breeze. A woman crying . . . no, more like wailing, her voice full of fear. The voice was faint as if far away, and yet they could tell it was coming from somewhere close, somewhere in the ruins.

Jay had to make up his mind not to be afraid. Right now, panicking would be very easy. "You okay?" he whispered.

Lila's eyes were wide, continually scanning in the direction of the sound. Her throat was so dry she couldn't speak, so she nodded to her brother.

Jay reached into the camera bag and pulled out his father's night camera, flipping off the lens cap.

Now they could hear the woman's voice clearly.

She seemed to be crying out in fear, pleading with someone, but they couldn't make out the words.

"Don't move," Jay cautioned Lila. "We don't want to scare it."

Lila's head snapped around and she gave him a look that carried a clear message: *We* don't want to scare *it*?

Then she saw Jay's eyes and knew he'd spotted something. She turned to look in the same direction, not wanting to, but wanting to.

It looked like a blue puff of smoke coming up the road toward them, floating, wavering, the edges unclear. A moment later they could tell it was someone running. As it came closer, they could see a face.

It was a woman in a long blue dress, with long hair waving in the wind behind her as she ran. Her face was contorted with fear. Her faint, faraway voice came in agonized gasps. She was transparent; they could see right through her.

"The ghost!" Lila whispered. "The ghost of Annie Murphy!"

An Excerpt from
Mayday at Two Thousand Five Hundred
Book Eight in The Cooper Kids Adventure Series®

C huck flew closer and kept calling over the radio, "Rex! Rex! Please answer, can you hear me? Rex, you've got to pull up or you'll rotate into the ground! Rex, you hear me?" Then he silently prayed, Dear Lord, please wake him up, nudge him, get him on those controls!

Aboard the Skyland, Jay was asleep, dreaming about riding a merry-go-round and hearing somebody yelling for his Uncle Rex. Whoever it was just kept yelling and yelling and Jay started wondering, *Why doesn't Rex answer?*

Then he became aware of noises: the rush of wind, a loud engine revving and shaking, metallic vibrations and rattles getting louder and louder.

Jay felt sick, like he'd been on the merry-go-round too long.

"Rex!" There was that voice again. "Rex, please answer me!"

"Uncle Rex," Jay muttered, "somebody wants you. . . ."

"Rex!" came the voice through his headphones.

Jay's hand went to his ear and bumped into the large ear protector of his headset. It finally registered in his mind: *It's the radio! Somebody's calling us!*

"Level the wings, Rex! Get that nose up! Come on now!

Jay's mind cleared enough to think, *Oh man. Something isn't right here. We're in trouble. What's happened?*

Fear stung him through the heart. The dream was over and he'd awakened to a nightmare. He groped for the control yoke, found it, and pulled back.

Oof! His body was pressed into the seat as if he weighed a ton. G-forces. Like in tight turns. The kind that make you want to barf.

"*Level the wings? What was wrong with the wings?* He pressed his radio talk button and asked, "Uh, which way?"

"You're spiraling to the left, Rex! Roll out to the right!"

Jay cranked the yoke to the right.

Oof! G-forces again. *I'm going to barf, I just know it!*

Chuck saw the Skylane snap out of the turn and then swoop skyward like a barn swallow, climbing, slowing, climbing, slowing more, hanging from the propeller.

"Get the nose down, Rex! You're going to stall!" Jay shoved the yoke forward. *Ooooohh,* he felt like his stomach was in his throat.

The plane went over the top of the climb and nosed down, going into the same sickening left spiral. Sweat was trickling down Chuck's face. He felt he was watching the death of Rex Kramer being played out before his very eyes. "Level the wings, Rex, you're spiraling!"

"Which way?" came a voice through Chuck's headphones.

Suddenly Chuck realized it wasn't Rex Kramer's voice. It must be Rex's nephew! "Level the wings, get the plane level!"

"Which way?" the nephew asked again.

"Right. Bank to the right-NOT TOO MUCH!"

The Skylane teetered to the right and swooped upward again the moment the wings were level.

"Full throttle! Ease the yoke forward, get the nose down!"

The Skylane went in to a dive again. *No, no, no! Can't this kid see what he's doing?*